WITCH BITCH

NOTES OF 5 NECROSOPH

AL K. LINE

Copyright © 2022 Al K. Line

Didn't Go Well

"But why can't we turn the lights on?" whined Jen. "It won't hurt to let me play a movie. Hey," she said optimistically, "we could all watch something. How about that boxing movie?"

"Rocky?"

"Yeah. You've been saying we should check it out ever since he moved in."

"Nice try," I chuckled, "but another time. Come on, Jen, it won't kill you to be without electricity for one day a week."

"Stupid Dark Wednesday," she moaned, pouting as she stared longingly at the blank TV.

"It's one day a week," laughed Phage, raising her eyebrows at me.

This wasn't the first time we'd had a similar conversation. In fact, we'd had it for as many days as we'd had the weekly blackout. Plus some extra nagging and whining on the weekend just to sour everyone's mood.

"Yes, but it's been going on for almost a year now. It's stupid. We've got solar and wind, we have crappy batteries that still store some of the energy, so why can't we use it? I can't find anything in the dark."

"Oh, please, spare me," I groaned, putting my hands to my head in mock despair. Although, all this complaining was getting seriously irritating. "It's summer. It doesn't get bloody dark until bedtime, anyway. We have more than enough candles from our quota, and what, you think in the past nobody could ever find anything because they didn't have electric light? I think it's cool. It's mysterious and romantic." I winked at Phage. She licked her lips. I gulped.

"So unfair."

"Time for an early night?" I ventured.

"Soph," laughed Phage, "it's the middle of the afternoon!"

"Yeah Dad, it's... Oh, wait, I can't tell you the time because I can't see my watch!" she shouted.

"Drama much?" I asked, unable to keep a straight face.

"Come on, just a single light? I'll make tea," she offered hopefully.

"Nope. No kettle."

"Aha, we can use the stove. I'll light it and even get wood. Or the gas camping cooker. We could use that."

"No gas," Phage told her. "We get oil for heating, but you can't find gas bottles for love nor money anymore."

"Stupid rules. Stupid restrictions."

"Hey, it's the job of you kids to get behind this," I told her. Again. "You should be proud that your generation is living in a world where natural resources aren't as exploited. Aren't you happy you saved the bees, and the earth is cooling? That the air is clean and people aren't dying of starvation or thirst in the numbers they used to?" My words felt hollow. I was towing the party line but, same as most other people, it just didn't ring true any longer.

"Well, duh. Yeah, obviously. But watching a movie won't make any difference to that. And I don't see why we can't use the car."

"Because there is no fuel allowance at all any more. You know that," I told her. "Since the kill switch thing, they changed so much. No more driving, period. No power on Wednesdays, stricter electricity quotas, more sunscreen, next to zero imports now, and well, you know the rest." There was much she didn't know, too. But I got the feeling she'd find out soon enough.

"It's dumb. Why can't we use the power we have?"

"Honey, we've explained this. It's because we don't want to stand out," Phage told her. Again. "How do you think it would make others feel if we had the lights on and were watching movies when nearly everyone else in the country is making do without? Think how annoyed you'd be."

"We live in the countryside. There's nobody here apart from the neighbors."

"That's not the point, and you know it. Someone might see, and we don't need the hassle. Plus, there are bloody drones everywhere. New ones, clever ones, and they are checking everyone follows the rules. Yes, strictly speaking, we can use power we generate, but do you really want an official knocking at the door to check on us and what we're doing? I bloody don't. And besides, I think it's good for us. All of us. You know I had that problem with the Necronet, and you're getting too obsessed with gaming and TV. Not to mention it gives us a break from that bloody stupid dwarf in the basement. God, you should hear him complain about it. Every single day he asks if the blackout is over. He's utterly addicted to Neighbours."

"See, so we should let him watch it."

"Bloody hell, talk about desperate. So, you'd rather watch a rerun of Neighbours than spend time talking to your family or playing board games? How about cards?"

"Fine," she huffed. "But no cheating," warned Jen.

"Me? I don't cheat."

"You do," said Phage.

"The worst," agreed Jen.

"Do not," I grumbled. I did, but they weren't supposed to know that. "Go get the cards then."

"I would, but I can't see, can I? Stupid Dark Wednesday."

"It saves an unbelievable amount of resources by having a day off from the grid," I told her. Again. I glanced out the window into the garden. It was another beautiful, clear blue sky. Even our often gloomy living room was bright and cheery. Any brighter and we'd be seen from space.

"Whatever." Jen waved a hand over her shoulder, then screamed when she cracked her shin on a low table.

"Careful," I told her.

"Gee, thanks, Dad. It's super helpful to be told to look out for something after you've probably disfigured your legs for life."

Phage and I rolled our eyes at each other. Yes, that most terrible of times had finally arrived. The one every parent dreads. When you truly fear your children and the wrath they can unleash.

Jen had just turned thirteen and been taken over by a strange alien creature that looked like her, sometimes even sounded like her, but was mean, argumentative, grumpy, slept an ungodly amount, and had her stomach replaced with an infinite hole that could not be filled.

The alien invasion had begun slowly, a stealth attack. At first, our "daughter" still seemed like her old self, just a touch more moody and quiet. But over the last six months the takeover had become hostile, until now our adorable princess of old was gone, replaced with a monster that liked to wear too much make-up and follow the textbook rules when it came to being a teenager.

And she liked to share her misery as far and wide as possible. All the bloody time.

I loved her for it. My baby was growing up. But she was still my little girl and always would be. I just kept quiet about telling her that, as last time I did she gave me such a glare I worried her gifts were emerging and I was about to be genuinely set on fire, or my head would pop. Such is the focus of a young girl's evil eye.

Happy times. I wouldn't have it any other way.

"Don't forget to change out of your school uniform," I called to Jen as she stormed off. "You know the water's metered now and the prices are extortionate, and we seem to get to our quota way too fast, so you need to wear your old clothes if you're going out with Tyr later."

Jen poked her head back around the door and rolled her eyes. "Duh, I'm not stupid. I was just about to do it."

"Were you?" I asked, doing my best to look serious.

"Yes. God." Jen banged up the stairs, trying to see if she could break them. Phage and I smiled at each other.

"So sweet at this age," I laughed.

"Soph, it isn't funny. She's driving me nuts."

"It's just a phase. She's changing into a woman. She's grown so much this last year. You know what they're like at this age."

"No, I don't. It's alright for you, you have experience. I don't."

My mood darkened instantly, even though I knew she didn't mean anything by it. But unbidden memories always surfaced when such topics were raised. "Yeah, maybe."

"Sorry, I'm so sorry. You know I just meant... Damn, I don't know what I meant. Just that you're better at coping with Jen than I am. You have experience. I didn't mean it in a bad way. I know you miss them." Phage came over and straddled me in my recliner. She cupped my face and stared into my eyes. She kissed me. Coffee and biscuits. A rare taste nowadays, but it was my birthday and she'd gone all out with the goodies.

Not only had we enjoyed our annual epic bedroom antics while Jen was in school, but Phage had somehow managed to acquire proper coffee. From abroad! The smell was incredible. The taste divine. The teenage terror had even helped brew it this morning before she stomped off to school.

"It's fine. Just made me think of the other kids, that's all. Not your fault. And listen, you are doing a great job. Perfect. Just keep reminding yourself that she loves us and is having a hard time. It's difficult for them at this age. All those hormones raging around. All the growing. I mean, she's a proper young woman now, and that has to be tough. And those lady things going on," I said uncomfortably.

"You are such a fossil at times. Lady things? You mean she's growing breasts and has her period and fancies boys?" Phage's eyes sparkled with mirth as she kissed me again, then hopped nimbly off my lap.

"Boys are for when she's old enough to get married. Not before," I warned, only half joking. Although I'd have preferred it to be the case.

"Good luck with that. She's a stunner already. You wait until she fills out a little."

Silence fell as we pondered a future where there were boys putting their grubby, trembling, eager hands on our daughter. Bastards.

I heard the catflap bang open and my heart skipped a beat then stuttered. I was close to having a panic attack. I knew, I just knew, that this was it. However many times it happened, I never got used to it.

Every fucking year the same shit, the same dread. The same bouts of sickness and diarrhea. Stuck on the toilet, my guts churning, my stress levels high. But I had to hide it, be brave for my family. Never let them know how stressed out it made me. Phage knew, she experienced the same damn thing, the dread hanging over you all year only for it to be made a reality on a day that should be for celebration.

But Jen never knew until recently that the Necronotes existed, and now it was more important than ever that she didn't see the anguish it caused us.

So I wasn't surprised when Mr. Wonderful sauntered into the living room with a soggy piece of paper in his mouth.

The immortal cat that deigned to live with us and let us feed him, even have the honor of him sitting on our lap when he felt like it, and shitting in our slippers whether we liked it or not (which we did not), kept up an inner monologue I could hear clear as the bastard day. He often thought he kept his thoughts to himself, when in reality he was broadcasting to the world. He wasn't as smart as he thought he was. Although I would never say that to him, as my slippers had been clean for quite a while now.

"I own this carpet. That rug's mine. I own that smelly chair, but the man can use it because I let him. That woman's mine. I own that stupid dog. This paper isn't mine, though."

"What you got there, Mr. Wonderful?" I asked, playing along. I don't know why, as we'd decided not to play this game of let's-pretend-we-don't-know-what-this-note-is a few years back once we realized it was stupid, but for some reason we were back at it now.

Mr. Wonderful dropped the soggy paper onto the murder rug, scene of countless crimes against the much-reduced population of anything smaller than the cat, then considered me with disdain and said, "How should I know? It's a note, I suppose. For you."

"How'd you know it's for me?"

"Got your name on it?"

"But you can't read. So how do you know?" I asked, getting into the swing of this now, my guts easing a little as the familiar scene unfolded.

"Because I'm a cat. And very smart." Mr. Wonderful licked at his perfectly clean paw, then rubbed it over his head several times. When he was done, he bothered to meet my gaze, then shrugged.

"What does it say inside?"

"Ugh, really, are we doing this?"

"Hey, I thought you wanted to? You brought the note in."

"Only because it was in my way. Can I go now?"

"Is Mr. Wonderful playing with a new toy?" asked Jen as she breezed into the room, smiling, seemingly on a temporary hiatus from grumpy land.

She skipped over to the murder rug and bent and grabbed the soggy mess of a Necronote as Phage and I screamed, "No!"

But it was too late.

As Jen stood with the ball of paper in her hand, shocked by our outburst, the truth suddenly dawned. Her eyes went wild, beads of sweat popped to the surface on her forehead, and then all hell broke loose.

Her now long, dark hair that usually framed her angelic, pale face shot up like she'd been electrified. The air crackled as the Necronote flipped up from her palm, shook itself out, then flattened to a crisp, sharply folded piece of paper. It slapped into her still-open palm, tearing at her flesh angrily.

Blood dripped to the murder rug as the apple of my eye screamed in terror.

Woofer barked manically as he ran around the room searching for intruders. I shot out of my chair and grabbed for the note, but it had other ideas, and as Phage wrapped Jen in her arms to try to protect her, the fucking Necronote slashed across Jen's palm again, opening up a deep wound.

Jen cried in agony as I lunged for the note again. This time I got it, and ignored the pain as it sliced my hand repeatedly while I gripped it tight. I joined Phage in cocooning Jen, then we shuffled to my tatty recliner and piled onto it with Jen protected at the bottom.

I jumped back and dashed towards the door, checking over my shoulder that Jen and Phage were okay.

Mr. Wonderful decided now was a good time to make a dash for it, and as I turned back to the doorway I caught his tail. He meowed loudly, swiped out with a sharp claw and ripped at my heel, and I stumbled, arms waving wildly as I careened headfirst through the open doorway.

Or I would have, if my momentum wasn't halted by something very solid. My neck clicked loudly and I feared I'd snapped my spine, but as I bounced back and landed flat on my arse then looked up, I knew I'd survive. At least for a second or two.

Thick, otherworldly smoke filled the room as first one, then two more bright red, impossibly muscled, naked daemons filed through the doorway then stood in a line and glowered down at me.

"Who are they?" screamed Jen.

"The postmen," I sighed as I rubbed at my head and got rapidly to my feet.

The Necronote squirmed in my hand, but it seemed to settle at the presence of the daemons.

"Notes are private," growled the middle daemon.

"So is my fucking home," I growled back at the bastard. "Fuck off."

"Dad, who are they? What are they?"

"Ssh, let him handle this," I heard Phage say, soothing Jen. Their voices sounded a long way off as the bloodlust took me over and I reached for Bone Slicer.

The warm elven wood of the handle gave an instant sense of power. A calm washed over me. I was the storm. I was the whirlwind. The tsunami. A force of nature. I was death. Lost to the thrill of battle before it had even begun. I would not let them near my family.

"No Necro but the recipient may touch the note. These are the rules. There must be punishment," said the same daemon, as if reading from a script when he really wanted something less boring to be doing.

"It was an accident. Get out of my house," I hissed.

The daemon on the right shifted a leg and I sprang into action. Bone Slicer was out of the holster and my arm punched out low at the bastard's leg. The blade slid through like the thick muscle wasn't even there. So satisfying.

The red fool backhanded me casually. My teeth rattled as I grunted, but I felt nothing, merely focused on my next series of moves, already planned out but fluid enough to change without conscious thought.

As if of his own free will, Bone Slicer slashed across the middle of the next daemon, opening up his stomach. Steaming guts plopped to the floor with a satisfying squelch.

I sidestepped and swung high and hard at the last intruder, taking an arm off before he had chance to do anything but turn his head towards me. As the thick limb thudded to the floor, I was already sweeping behind them and slashing furiously. Bone Slicer cut deep and true, the elven runes gleaming.

Chunks of flesh hung from ruined skin, revealing wormlike trails of pulsing veins. Muscles spasmed oddly as I cut nerves that felt no pain and never had. The blood sliding from the damascus steel left the blade as clean as the day it was handed to its first owner ten thousand years ago in an utterly foreign land.

I skirted around the daemons and stood in front of them, guarding my family. I was sweating and panting, but ready for them.

They regrouped, stood immobile in the room like they were queuing for something unexciting. They looked at me, then the bits and pieces on the floor, and the speaker said once more, "Notes are private."

The entrails, the limb, the blood, the chunks of meat, steamed then turned to smoke and filled the room as the three stooges slowly became ethereal. Then they too were gone, leaving nothing but a warm stench behind.

"Good boy, Woofer, well done."

"Woofer very brave. Would have bit them if came near Jen or Phage." He wagged his tail and looked to me for confirmation.

"I know you would. Thank you for guarding them." I patted his head, then secured my knife as I moved to a shocked Jen and a very tearful Phage.

"You both okay?"

Phage nodded.

"They were... monsters." Jen burst into tears.

I felt about as rotten as a father could. This was on me. Nobody else to blame but myself. Over three centuries, and I'd let myself become too lax with the notes. Never again.

"I'm sorry, so sorry. They were daemons. They work for those behind the notes, or anyone else that knows how to call and control them. Just dumb messengers. Creatures that enjoy pain and suffering. You can't hurt them or kill them, I'm not even sure they're actually real beings in their own right, but yeah, bit of a shock. Sorry."

Jen flung herself forward and clung to me as she sobbed. My baby had just grown up in ways none of us wanted.

The Necronote writhed in my rear pocket.

I ignored it.

My daughter was more important.

Meltdown

Jen calmed down quicker than I'd expected. In under a minute, she was drying her eyes and squirming with discomfort as she realized how tightly she'd been holding on to me.

"You'll never be too big for a cuddle, remember that," I told her softly.

"Dad! And anyway, it was you cuddling me. I was just trying to hide in case any other daemons, and I can't believe I'm saying that, came back."

"Yeah, not good. Sorry about that. It was a lesson for all of us. I should have kept you away until after I'd dealt with the note. Usually I never get assaulted in company."

"That wasn't normal," said Phage. She was dancing from foot to foot, clearly dying to comfort Jen, unsure if it was the right thing to do or not. She worried about being rebuked by our willful teenage daughter.

"Mum, it's okay, you can have a hug," laughed Jen.

"Oh, thank god." Not needing to be asked twice, Phage wrapped Jen in her love and buried her face in her hair. They were nearly the same height now. Jen was going to be a looker, and tall. Not that either of us were ever going to be mistaken for basketball superstars.

"Jen, I want this to be your very first lesson when it comes to receiving the notes. You do not touch another person's note. You don't ask what it says, you don't discuss the details, you never, ever tell anyone, not even us, what happened when you confront the person you are directed to, and you need to learn how to be cool with the freaks that sometimes come to screw with you when your Necronote arrives."

"Okay, I won't. You already told me most of that. But not about daemons or just touching someone else's note. That was terrifying. Aren't you scared? I'm still shaking. Look at my hands!" Jen held out her hands palms down; they were calm as you like.

"I think she's fine," I told Phage.

"Hmm. Maybe."

Someone, or something, pounded on the front door like they were using a battering ram.

"Hell, what now?" I groaned. "You two wait here. I'll deal with it."

Mother and daughter huddled close, Woofer stood in front of them, bless him, and I nodded to all three then went to rescue the front door from death by hammer blow.

As I stormed down the hall, in no mood for this crap, the door was banged hard again. Daemons didn't knock, but there were plenty of other unsavory things that did. I unfastened the popper on the strap keeping my knife in place, then yanked the door open with my best "don't fuck with me" face in place. It hardly needed any adjustment at all.

"Are you Jen's father?" asked a red-faced bull of a man wearing a football kit, expensive trainers, a wide sun hat, and a very pissed-off expression.

He had his arm on a young lad's shoulder. The boy was shaking and had clearly been crying. His face was a mess of bruises. He had two black eyes, a lump on his forehead the size of a golf ball, a clearly broken nose, and two missing front teeth.

"I am," I said calmly as I tried to soften my features. It wasn't easy, they were kind of set in a scowl after so many years of having plenty to get angry at.

The overweight guy tugged at his red shirt, pulling it down over his paunch, and squared his shoulders as he assessed me. He took a slight step back but shoved out his head and spat, "Look what your fucking kid did to my boy. A girl!" he hissed, glaring first at me, then his son. The kid squirmed from under his father's hand but remained motionless, his head hanging lower by the second.

"Sorry, I think there might be some mistake. Jen's here, with her mother and I. She's been in school all day."

"I know she's been in bloody school! So has my son. And then on the way home, she kicked the absolute shit out of him. A girl!" He clenched his fist and sneered at his son. The boy practically melted under the intensity, his face purple, and not just from the bruises.

"Sorry, can we all calm down a minute so I can understand this properly?"

"Don't tell me to calm down, mate! Who the fuck do you think you are?"

"Whoa there! Take it easy," I told him. "Don't come here shouting at me and acting threatening. If there's a problem, we'll sort it. Okay? Just tell me what happened?"

"Go on then, tell him," the man ordered his son.

"I told you," the lad mumbled. "We got into a fight and she went nuts. I couldn't get her off me. She wouldn't stop hitting me."

"See? See? Your girl beat the living crap out of my boy. What you gonna do about it, eh?"

"What I will do very much depends on why she beat him so bad."

"You fucking what, mate?"

"Don't call me mate. I don't know you, and I doubt we'll ever be friends. Lighten your tone, and drop the attitude. You're on my property. If you can't act respectful, you can leave. Now." I stared at him hard, but I didn't act threatening, just remained cool and kept my hand well away from my knife.

"Ah, I get it. Like father, like daughter."

"I've been nothing but respectful, and I'm sorry about your son. But you need to tell me what happened. What's your name?" I asked the squirming kid.

"Pike," he mumbled.

"Oh, right. The one who calls my daughter names and tried to take her money for a school trip that one time? That you?"

He said nothing. His father turned to Pike and asked, "You did what? You picked on a girl?" He slapped the boy around the back of the head. Pike winced, but kept his head down. It clearly wasn't the first time.

"So, why did you both fight today?" I asked, trying to keep my anger with Jen in check but beginning to fume inside.

"Dunno." Pike shrugged.

"Tell us!" yelled his father.

"I was just messin'. I ran past and pushed her, just a bit, and she fell over. She went crazy. Proper wild thing."

"So you pushed my daughter over and she stood up for herself?" I asked.

"Dunno. Maybe."

He got another, much harder, slap for his shrug.

I turned back to the incensed father. "Look, I'm sorry about your lad, and Jen will certainly be in for a world of trouble over this. But he's a bully, and maybe this is a lesson to him."

"Don't you call my son a bully. He stands up for himself, that's all." The guy stepped forward, fists clenched, and got right up to me, his feet touching the front of the step.

"No, you're wrong. He tried to intimidate Jen in the past. He tried to bully her. And now he tells me he shoved her to the ground. He got a beating because he picked on her. You just don't like it that he got beaten by a girl."

"I'm sorry," mumbled Pike.

"Don't you apologize," his father shouted.

I ignored the idiot and turned my attention to Pike. "Look, I know you hate that you got beat-up by a schoolgirl, but let this be a lesson. Nobody likes a bully, and there's always someone bigger, stronger, or smarter than you are. Instead of picking on people, make friends with them. That's how you get the girls." I winked at him, then straightened and turned back to the fuming football fan.

"You got something to say?" I asked him.

"I... You... Fucking joke of a father." He didn't know what to do, how to act.

"He got beat. Yes, she went too far, and she's in serious trouble because of it, but she was defending herself, like she's been taught. Maybe teach your boy to be respectful. Oh, and if you ever talk to me like this again, we will have a serious problem. Understand?"

He glowered, then faced his kid, slapped him over the head again, then said, "Let's go."

"Have a nice day. Oh, and can you close the gate behind you, please?"

They left it open as they marched down the lane.

I sighed, then stepped out into the afternoon heat and closed the gate gently.

"Get whatever you need for a night away. You have five minutes," I told Jen as I walked into the living room. Her and Phage were standing by the front window, having clearly listened to every word.

"What? Where are we going?"

"I'm going to show you how to make it past your teenage years," I snapped.

Jen turned to Phage and gave her a look. Phage shook her head.

"Dad, I'm sorry, okay? He pushed me, and he's always giving me grief. I fought back, that's all."

"Spare me the excuses. We all know that you lost your cool. You beat the absolute crap out of that kid and didn't stop when you knew you should have. We didn't raise you to be worse than a bully. We have taught you things, shown you things, and guided you so you act responsibly and never overstep. Well, you overstepped big time, so now you pay the price. Four minutes left, then we go. Get to it!" I roared.

Jen jumped, frightened. I never, ever raised my voice to my family. Ever. It shocked us all.

Jen ran crying from the room.

"You okay with this?" I asked Phage, trying to calm down.

Phage nodded sadly. "She needs a wakeup call. I know what you're thinking. Are you sure it's a good idea?"

"We got her into this mess, into this world, now we need to show her what we, and others, went through. How other Necro kids are treated. She needs to understand that you can't use an unfair advantage to act like that when people don't deserve it."

"He was a bully," said Phage.

"I know, and he deserved a bit of shaming. To be put in his place. But she could have killed him. I saw the signs on him. Jen lost the plot and went wild. She had no restraint. Now she needs a shock to get her to accept that's not how you do things. Not with regular people."

"But she's my baby." Phage broke down and I took her offered hands and pulled her in tight.

"She's a great kid. She just needs to understand how to handle things. It's my fault, so I'll sort it."

"What about your note?"

"The note can wait a day or two. Jen's more important. Just go with this, please? We have to be tough for now, but we'll be back tomorrow afternoon, okay?"

"Sure."

Jen edged back into the room, face red, looking utterly terrified. "Dad, I'm so sorry. Please, where are we going? You aren't sending me away, are you?" Jen wiped at her eyes with her sleeve and dropped her backpack onto the floor.

"You'll find out. But no, we would never send you away. Ever. But there are some things you need to understand. To learn." I turned to Woofer who was hiding behind the recliner. "Come out, Woofer. Sorry for shouting, but Jen's been naughty. I didn't mean to scare you."

"Soph never gets angry. Scared Woofer."

"I know, and I apologize. Be good for Phage and we'll see you soon."

"Woofer always good." He lay down and rolled over. I went over and tickled his tummy, then smiled at him.

With a nod to Phage, I asked Jen, "Ready?"

"Not really."

"Tough." Without really thinking about if I could even do this, I stepped up to Jen, scooped up her pack, took her suddenly very childlike seeming hand in mine, but noticed the bruising on her knuckles, and gripped tight.

"Don't let go," I warned.

And with that, we vanished.

Lessons Learned

My nerves screamed. Every organ felt ready to burst from my skin. Synapses fired, my head pounded, my fingers had locked solid, and my eyeballs were just about ready to pop.

And yet the morph left me elated. Not that I'd let my daughter know that. I bent over, gasping, then straightened as soon as I could to check on Jen, who would surely be in a world of pain.

She stood there with her head cocked quizzically, cool as a cucumber.

"You okay?" she asked, gnawing at her bottom lip.

"Fine. Just a long morph. How about you?"

"Alright. It tingles, but I'm good. I didn't know you could do that. Bring someone along, I mean. I know Tyr can, but I didn't think people could."

"Special circumstances," I told her, amazed and rather proud I'd done this and it had worked. Another surprise from the Necroverse.

What was more shocking was her reaction. But she wasn't your average Necro, and had spent the last year morphing almost daily with Tyr. Yet as far as I knew, she was unable to morph on her own. But still, we'd come a long way—she should have been on the ground screaming. Not that I wanted her to, mind you, and this was a last resort kind of thing, but it was damn impressive.

"Dad, I'm so sorry about Pike. I lost it, okay? You know I did. And it was wrong. He shoved me over and I went mental. I got taken over, like how you said the bloodlust makes you. I just knew I could beat him, and kind of zoned out."

"I get it, kiddo, I really do. But you're a thirteen-year-old girl and a very gifted one. You are meant to blend in, not kick the shit out of lads almost twice your size and not have a mark on you."

"Yeah, I guess."

"You guess? Not good enough. You cannot act like that. You have all these gifts, and they'll blossom just like you are, so this is part of your training."

"But I thought I was being punished."

"You are. Think about what you've done, how badly you could have hurt him. You broke his nose. He lost two teeth. How would you feel if you'd disfigured him for life? Or worse?"

"I didn't think about that," she mumbled.

"No, because you're young. But people are soft and easy to kill or permanently maim. All it takes is a good punch to the throat and you've killed someone."

"Really? Can you teach me that?" I raised my eyebrows. "Okay, bad timing. Maybe not. So, um, what's my punishment?"

"You'll find out. First, we need to set up camp for the night."

"But we don't have anything. How can we camp?"

"We make do with what we have."

"And what's that?"

"Our wits. And the things you brought with you. What did you bring?"

Jen looked away, abashed, then retrieved her backpack and pulled out the contents.

I couldn't help but laugh. "A pair of leggings, some make-up, a t-shirt, and Mr. Snuggles. Well, guess we'll be fine then."

"Hey, don't laugh. I didn't know we were staying overnight. You gave me five minutes to get my things! I didn't know what to bring."

"Then let this be a lesson. When a Necro has to go away suddenly, or when you're older and you're out there in the world, you always have a basic bag packed. Always. You have a weapon, emergency food, matches in a watertight container, or better yet, flint and steel, and something to boil water in."

"That it?"

"Depends on the time of year. Best to have two bags always packed. One summer, one winter. Just in case the weather turns weird. But regardless of season, you want spare underwear, clothes, and a lightweight waterproof coat. And wine. Always wine."

"Sweet." Jen held up a hand for a high-five. For once, I got to leave someone hanging instead of being the one left with my hand up.

"This isn't a game," I told her. "So, you made a start bringing clothes, but now you know for next time. Jen, this is serious. This kind of thing was going to happen way into the future, but you forced my hand, so here we are. Come on, let's go."

"Hey, wait a minute. Where's your pack? Where's your gear? You haven't got anything."

"No?" I grinned as I held out my hands and my pack fell straight into them. I winked at Jen.

"What!? How? Where?" she spluttered.

"Come on, we need to get set up." I walked off into the woods, hiding my smile. She and Tyr may have been best friends, but even she couldn't tell he was close when he was invisible.

I sent out a silent thank you to the proud dragon.

"Soph look after best friend in world," he insisted.

"I will. You can count on it. This is it, Tyr. The beginning of her real lessons. Don't worry. I would never let any harm come to her."

Tyr was silent, brooding, as he returned to Sanctuary.

"Dad, where are we?" Jen ran to catch up, then matched my long strides as I took us deeper into the woods.

"A long way from home," I snapped, still acting gruff even though all I wanted to do was cuddle her tight and promise all would be well.

"Yeah, but where?"

"All in good time. So, where's a good spot?" I asked.

Jen stopped next to me and spun around as she inspected the forest. After frowning, and chewing her lip for a while, she said, "I guess it depends if we're trying to hide or not."

"Let's just say that we aren't exactly hiding, but we don't want to make it super obvious."

"Okay, then let's keep walking." Jen ventured further into the forest, then paused in a natural clearing. "Here. This is good."

"Why?" I asked, already impressed.

"There's mossy ground so it'll be comfortable. It's surrounded by trees, so it's sheltered. And that thick coppiced area is a perfect screen if anyone comes the way we just did. Plus, there's that large dead tree just over there," she pointed, "so we have dry firewood close at hand." Jen put her hands on her hips and beamed at me.

I nodded. "Good job. Right, let's set up camp."

Jen dropped her pack, then without being asked wandered off to begin gathering firewood. I collected wood from the base of the dead tree, then when she wandered deeper into the forest I morphed beside her, hid the hurt best I could, and wagged a finger at her.

"First big mistake, kiddo."

"What? I didn't do anything. And ugh, you made me jump."

"Where's camp?"

"Back there," she said, frowning as she pointed.

"And where's your pack?"

"At camp."

"If you can't reach your gear in a couple of strides, you take it with you. Someone could come and take it."

"Okay. Makes sense." Jen bent to gather firewood.

"Well?"

"Well, what?" I waited until she got it. "Oh, you mean go get it?"

"Yes, that's exactly what I mean."

Jen was about to give me some backchat but clearly thought better of it, so hurried back to camp with her arms full of kindling.

Sure, it was a lesson I still failed to heed myself—I was always stumbling off into the woods for a pee when I was pissed, leaving my gear unattended. Most recently when Shiun had found me and the unfortunate shifter had eaten my food and messed up my camp. But better to break the rules than not know them in the first place.

Once we'd gathered the firewood, I showed her again how to use the flint and steel, how to set the fire for minimal smoke, always thinking of the wind direction, and endless other small snippets of information I'd performed without conscious thought for so long it surprised me how much actually went into it.

Thankfully, I always kept a modest emergency stash of tobacco and a spare pipe in my pack, so I leaned back against a tree and smoked the stale leaves while Jen laid a few short branches on the fire.

"So, what's for dinner? I'm starving."

"There's no food. Not unless you brought some."

Jen's eyes went wide; she loved her food same as we all did. Then she smiled. "Good one! You said always have emergency rations in your pack. So what have you got?"

"There's none in there," I lied. "I haven't had chance to replace the last of it. So let that be a warning. Do as I say, not as I do."

"What then? We'll starve!"

"Jen, it's one night. We won't starve. We'll just be a little hungry. But hey, we can hunt if you want food."

"Cool. Let's do that then."

I explained how to set traps, the best way to track the small creatures of the forest, and gave tips on reaching out for the innocent minds of rabbits. My wayward little girl was accomplished at sensing other creatures when she focused; I was impressed. Finally, I showed her where they were most likely to gather at dusk to feed and drink.

Jen surprised me with how easily she picked it all up, but this type of training had been going on for years and years now, just in a much less direct fashion.

It wasn't long before we had a rabbit and a selection of fresh greens we'd foraged, so I went over how to skin and gut the creature, finishing with how to cook it using the fat beneath the skin to stop it sticking to the small pan.

It was nice. We'd never spent time alone like this. We were always at home, where it was comfortable and easy, and she'd been shown things in a much more sanitized environment. This was the real world, where real things happened, although our home wasn't exactly quiet and without its drama.

Still, this was different. You had to put the effort in, consider every action. Much as it pained me to admit it, I understood that Jen needed these lessons if she was to eventually master the future that lay before her.

But I didn't press it, never talked about the reason for all this. It was there, that understanding. That why I knew such things was because every year I stepped out into the madness and had learned over the years how best to cope with it all.

One thing I could never prepare her for, though, was killing another human being. That would be all on her. Every day I raged inside for being unable to take that from her and leave her pure, innocent, uncorrupted by the Necroverse.

"They're so beautiful," whispered Jen, eyes dancing with excitement as she turned from the sprites dancing in the air above the fire and smiled at me.

"They sure are. This is a rare treat. They never normally come to those so young. You're special, and they know it." I pulled her closer, and me and my little girl cuddled up and watched the sprites dance late into the night.

It was one of the most perfect evenings of my life.

The morning was a different matter entirely.

Kids!

"But why can't we go hunting?"

"Are you serious!? No toothbrush?"

"I need to do my make-up!"

"Dad, you are so out of touch."

"You did what!?"

"Ugh, I'm not peeing in the woods. So gross."

"Why can't you morph and get fresh water?"

"No, I am not being grumpy."

"Of course I want to spend time with you. But I need my breakfast, and I need a comb. I'll just *die* otherwise."

"What do you mean it's your phone and I can't touch it?"

"Dad, Dad, Dad."

And all that was within the first five minutes of waking up.

Jen was not a morning person, so she told me repeatedly. I reminded her that mere months ago she would rise early and be super chatty. Always full of beans while she helped her mother in the kitchen. That she'd then go about her morning chores without complaining. She'd conveniently forgotten all that now.

I was, and I smiled even as I shuddered, marooned on an island of teenage angst, with no Phage to save me from my rising blood pressure.

With shaking fingers, I heated stale coffee and frantically puffed on rancid tobacco. Only once the caffeine and nicotine hit did I relax, mainly because Jen had wandered off to do, what she called, "Unspeakable things in the woods."

I chortled as I pictured her wandering around looking for a suitable tree to hide behind whilst muttering about lack of proper toilet roll and her empty belly.

The laugh turned to a cough as I got a lungful of foul smoke, so I swilled my mouth with lukewarm coffee that was way out-of-date and hadn't been much nicer when first purchased, then set about breaking camp in the lovely peace and quiet.

Birds sang, the sun forced its way between the dense canopy, and as I started clearing things away, I decided how best to go about the day. To teach Jen the lesson she so sorely needed, and the reason I'd actually brought her here.

Forcing Jen here felt low and mean, and it was absolutely a rash decision. Part of me was disgusted with my behavior. Shouting and acting all "mean Dad" with her didn't sit well with me. I never got angry or forced my views on my family; it was anathema to me. We weren't that kind of family. We were patient and understanding with each other, not hot-headed and impulsive.

This was the side of me kept in reserve for when confronted with the bad things in the world, not my most cherished ones. Was this right? Should I have acted this way? It was certainly a shock to Jen. Phage too. And I'd surprised myself.

Was this justified? She'd kicked the shit out of a bully. He seemed to deserve a good beating, but deep down I knew that he didn't. His father was the real bully. The kid was acting out because he wasn't happy at home, that was as clear as his father's fat belly and dubious taste in long banned public football matches.

But here was the age-old question. How do you deal with a bully? You can't reason with them. They won't admit they're unhappy and seeking attention, because life isn't that simple. Sometimes a short, sharp shock is what's needed. I had my doubts about Jen's actions putting Pike on the straight and narrow, because his father was more pissed he got beaten by a girl then that his son was picking on those presumed weak and vulnerable, so what should she have done?

Stand up for herself, but not push it too far. That's what she needed to learn. How to control herself and not get caught up in the bloodlust.

What frustrated, saddened, and scared me the most was that I had no right to give this advice, force her to confront what she did and offer her a better solution. I might have known what was right, but I'd killed plenty of bullies. I'd murdered men for actions that by rights should have been dealt with by the authorities. I'd maimed, killed, split heads, got Tyr to spew acid on men not much older than my daughter when they tried to take what was mine.

Mind you, it was always justified in my eyes, at least at the time. I tried to do what was right, but often I'd failed miserably. That guy with the peaches, he was a bully, and I'd almost left him alone, but my pride, my anger, my bloodymindedness had got the better of me and I'd destroyed him. Utterly.

Who was I to give advice?

Did I have the right?

As I looked back on my life, on the killings I could recall, I came to a surprising realization. Maybe I wasn't as bad as I'd believed. The men I'd killed deserved it. Drunk drivers showing no remorse, young Necros who would murder me for my belongings, insane twats who'd ram you off the road over a few pieces of fruit, even old men who'd tried to kill me over a few bottles of wine, and those who'd threatened my family.

Each and every killing was justified, right? Until it came to those on the yearly Necronote. They weren't always deserving of their fate. I could never justify so many murders. That would be as wrong as the deaths themselves. It was self-preservation and nothing more. Me playing along with this sick game because I valued my own life above that of strangers.

When I searched deep inside myself, I think I finally, truly understood for the first time that I was wild at heart, would always choose to survive rather than let another live, and above all I'd do whatever it took to protect my own.

I was not a good man, but I wasn't pure evil either. Would never kill or hurt for pleasure, as it gave me none. These acts were despicable and I realized that, so maybe that was something, at least. An acceptance, and maybe not a forgiveness or even a justification, but merely an admission that I would do these things, and continue to do so, because I felt my family was worth fighting for.

Jen was still gonna get the shock of her life, though. My girl would understand that she couldn't mete out unjustified beatings when she could have stopped sooner and the outcome would have been better for all concerned.

I smiled as she came stomping back into camp, face like thunder.

"What's up?"

"Stupid woods. Stupid rubbish toilet roll. Stupid nettles."

"You got stung on the bum, didn't you?" Jen glowered at me and rubbed her backside. I chuckled. "Come on, time to get this show on the road."

"Dad, I am sorry. Truly. I don't know what came over me. I knew I should have stopped, but it was only a small part of me that was saying that. Most of me was kinda gone, lost to the fight. I just kept on hitting him, even though I knew he was beaten and would never pick on me again. I didn't even feel bad until after. And then I couldn't tell you and Mum because I knew it was wrong and I felt so guilty. What's wrong with me?" She tried to fight it, but a steady stream of tears gushed down her cheeks and dripped to the cleared ground.

"It's okay, just let it out. You did the wrong thing, but now you know what you're capable of." I took my girl into my clumsy arms and squeezed tight like I could protect her from all the bad. Her body shook, frail and delicate against my much larger frame, and more than anything I longed to keep her safe like this for eternity.

"Am I a terrible person?"

"Oh, of course not. You're stronger than others your age, know how to fight, and have this drive, same as I do. Once you set your mind to something, nothing will stop you. Mostly, that's a good thing, but you have to learn when to admit you're wrong, when to back down, when to offer mercy. Mercy is a fine thing, and you must understand that winning at all costs isn't always the best course of action. Sometimes, running away is the bravest thing. There's no shame in it. There's pride in knowing you did the right thing, even if in other people's eyes you acted like a coward. What's important is being confident enough in yourself that you always know what you did was right. If that means sometimes you take a beating, or sometimes you look foolish, then so what? It won't kill you, only make you stronger."

Jen lifted her tear-streaked face and asked a very profound question. "Do you ever run away? Have you ever run away?"

"No, my sweet child, I don't think I ever have. And let that be one of the most important lessons. Don't become what I have."

"Dad, how can you say that?" My daughter lifted her head again, locked her eyes on mine, and spoke words that truly broke my heart because they were so full of innocence and the naivety of youth. "You're perfect. Such a great person."

What cut the deepest was that one day, and not too far into the future, she'd discover, just like all children did, that her father was far from perfect. Just struggling through, same as everyone else.

As she battled her way down the centuries, she'd come to learn that it doesn't matter how many years you have under your belt, all that happens is the older you get, the more stupid crap you somehow manage to do.

I was very old, so had done an insurmountable amount of idiotic stuff. Had made a veritable mountain of bad decisions.

But I could still live with myself.

Just.

I wasn't a bully. And no child of mine would be, either.

"Come on. I've got something to show you."

Blast From the Past

"What is this place?" Jen shielded her eyes and stared at the massive pile of misery sitting smugly at the summit of untold acres.

"It's my childhood. This is where I grew up, got my schooling." I swallowed, my throat dry and raspy.

"Where you learned about the Necroverse?"

"Yeah, amongst other things. My parents weren't good people, Jen. They taught me about being a Necro from a very young age. More like punished me for it. I wasn't like you, always asking. I was told before I even had chance to form the questions. From as far back as I can remember, I knew at least a little about what awaited me. My abilities emerged quite young, same as yours. Looking back on it, I can see that my folks were genuinely scared of me. They couldn't handle it, so bundled me off here."

"That's terrible. Like boarding school?"

"Kind of. But for Necros. Those stories you used to read, about the kid going off to magical school and having all these cool adventures? It wasn't like that. It was fucking miserable."

"Dad!"

"Sorry, excuse the language. Day after day, year after year, nothing but misery. Of course, life was very different then, with archaic values. There were no second warnings, no nice teachers, no kindness or hugs. Us kids didn't have adults to talk to about our problems, worries, or insecurities. They basically just beat the crap out of everyone and got us ready for when we were twenty-one. That was their one goal. Teach us how to survive at all costs, consequences be damned."

"That sounds absolutely awful. Dad, I'm so sorry. Mum had it bad too, didn't she? With Grandma?"

"She did. Pethach is a hard woman to understand, and she did her best, but again, she is from a very different age, much older than me, so her values were pretty twisted. Still are to some extent. She's coming around slowly, and you're helping her see what life could have been like with Phage, but it's also too late and the damage has been done. But yes, this was worse. Not just for me, but for all us kids."

"And it's still running now?"

"Sure is. Probably always will in one form or another. Full of children whose parents either can't handle the gifts of their children, or simply don't understand what goes on here. Or plain don't care and are glad to be rid of what they see as damaged goods. And make no mistake, we are tainted, Jen. I don't mean that in a cruel way, but with our Necro life comes a terrible burden. Nobody gets out of that without it causing pain and inflicting terrible scars on your mental health."

"You seem alright to me," she said, squeezing my hand and smiling.

"I could have been worse," I admitted. "Some of the children that left here were close to basket cases. A lot of them went off the rails then got wiped out by other Necros. I even had to... Anyway, that's all in the past. The reason I brought you here is so you could watch. Come on, let's go say hi to the bastards. And trust me, they are bastards."

"I'm going to start implementing a swear jar," complained Jen.

"You can't," I chuckled.

"Why not?"

"Because we don't have any cash, remember?"

"Okay, a forfeit jar, then. You write down a load of things you don't want to do, and every time you swear one gets added to the jar. Then you have to do it within a week. Deal?"

"Um, only if everyone plays," I conceded reluctantly. "You and Mum have to have forfeits too, and if you miss your chores, or Phage... Um, what does your mother do that isn't just perfect?"

"Hmm, not sure. Oh, I know! She sometimes forgets to take the recycling out."

"That's my job," I said glumly.

"Oh."

Silence settled while we both tried to think of Phage's faults.

●

"Let's just give your mum a free pass and admit she's damn perfect."

"Forfeit!" Jen laughed and pointed a finger at me.

"What? No way! I think we need to agree what's a swear word and what isn't, and then decide the forfeits before we do this. And look, can it wait until we get home? This is gonna be a bastard of a morning."

"Dad!"

"Sorry." I grinned at my soon-to-be-less-innocent daughter and, hand in hand, we clambered up the wall of the *ha-ha*, a design feature of many grand estates that stopped cattle chewing on the posh lawns, then onward towards the throng of children. They were training under close supervision on the yellowing grass outside a large stately home that had certainly seen better days. I wished it had been razed to the ground centuries ago.

Jen didn't question how we'd made it back through the woods, along a path, and then out into the open without being stopped. Did she know the reason, or had she not considered it? A lesson for another day.

Eyes were upon us, though, and the magic was stronger here than anywhere but at a witches' camp. Some would say stronger. But not the witches themselves.

We stopped well away from the group of youngsters being "tutored" by formidable looking men and women in matching black, loose-fitting training attire. All the kids wore white, something I remembered only too well that seemingly hadn't changed.

It was just one of the little sadistic traditions amongst too many to count. You had to keep your outfit pristine, or there would be severe consequences. Any dirt, stains, or streaks were met with swift punishment, which is why half the kids were training naked and covered in bruises.

The coaches scowled at us but didn't engage, and the kids daren't pause their training, having to make do with furtive glances that still got them severe reprimands.

Most continued their wrestling or various forms of sparring in the small groups of five to ten. I led Jen past them all, keeping a close eye on her.

"Looks good, right? Learning how to fight in all these different ways?"

"I guess," she said, confused by the whole thing, not knowing what the point of me bringing her here was.

"They will be tough, and can certainly look after themselves already. That's no bad thing, but look over there." I pointed to a small group away from the others. I guided Jen over; she gasped as we got close.

Two adults were holding a girl of about Jen's age under the arms while a boy of about seventeen, a hulk of a lad, punched her repeatedly in the face. She was a mess. Broken nose, eyes so swollen she couldn't see, split lip, smashed teeth, her naked, pre-pubescent body blue from bruises.

"Dad, stop them."

"I can't. This isn't my fight. Or yours. This *school* is run by some of the most powerful Necros in the land, and they don't screw about. If anyone, and I mean anyone, even every witch under your grandmother's command, came here and tried to interfere, they'd be wiped out within the hour. There's too much power here, too many bodies, and too much single-mindedness to stop."

"But they're going to kill her!" Jen's fist went to her mouth and she gnawed her knuckles as she watched, unable to tear her eyes away from the grunting lad and the pulverized face of a girl that should be at home complaining about make-up and the lack of movie selection.

"You mean like the others?" I asked, turning her so she could see the seven kids sprawled out in the dirt, half-dead from their beating. All were soaked in sweat and panting. Many were crying and groaning quietly.

"They beat them too?"

"Sure. Each kid beats on another, then gets beaten themselves. They have to do it. It happens every week. Every single week that you're here. For years, Jen. Year after sickening year. And then the teachers fix you right up after you've suffered for a few hours. Unless it's an emergency and then they attend immediately."

"That's sick! What's the point?"

"Toughens you up. Makes you unafraid of a fight. Shows you that being beaten so bad you can't see or even think isn't the worst thing in the world. And it teaches you how to kick the living shit out of another without an ounce of remorse. I mean, you get beat, they get beat. That's fair, right?"

"No, that's the opposite of fair."

I grunted. "Tell that to the lad almost killing that girl. Look, she can't even stand on her own."

"I want to go home. This is sick. It's twisted. Please? I want to leave."

"No. Sorry, but no. My dear daughter, who I love more than life itself, understand that this is what happens when you forget what is right and wrong. What other people feel. You must always have empathy, consider the feelings of others. Otherwise you end up like those adults, holding up a poor wreck of a girl while you force her friends to half kill her."

"She's going to die!"

"No, she won't. Not yet, anyway. Do you understand me now? You don't beat on people because you want to. You don't hurt others because you're made to. You do it to survive, nothing more. And yes, before you say anything, I'm well aware of the utter contradiction as all Necros go and kill because they're told to. That's the one choice we make for ourselves. We decide to do it or not. Nobody can actually force you. But these kids, they're young, malleable, and made to half-destroy their comrades or face a much more severe punishment than a weekly beating by their mates."

"How could you live here? How did you cope?"

"I had nowhere to go and couldn't escape. As to coping, yeah, I don't think I did. Come on, plenty more to see."

As we wandered around the decrepit monstrosity of a mansion, similar scenes of brutality played out in various forms. There were also sweet scenes of young children sat cross-legged beneath the shade of ancient sweeping willows, staring, rapt, at chilled teachers giving them instructions or reading from textbooks. It was all about the Necroverse, never anything concerning the regular world. No guidance on how to cope, maybe even thrive, in a world they were utterly unprepared for.

Seems like the curriculum had changed little in over three centuries, and I didn't doubt, same as back then, that most of these kids would end up in the gutter not long after they were unceremoniously booted out. Banished from the only environment they'd ever known and thrust into a cold, uncaring, unforgiving world they knew nowhere near enough about.

Once we'd completed the circuit of the grounds, I guided Jen towards the sweeping front steps that led up to a large portico and the ancient, double oak doors of the school itself.

Still nobody tried to stop us, or even came to cast an inquisitive eye. We just shuffled right on in like we belonged.

I did. Jen most certainly didn't.

She clung to my arm as we entered the expansive foyer. Two sets of stairs, complete with polished oak handrails and decorative newel posts of demonic faces, black with time and the hands of endless children, led up to the dormitories for the kids, and the apartments of the teachers. Nobody went home of an evening or on the weekends, and most teachers remained even during the occasional weeks they had the nerve to class as holidays.

Being here brought back more memories than I would ever care to face, let alone dredge up. They surfaced, unbidden, haunting me still after so many years out of the clutches of the sadistic bastards that ruled this prison with iron fists and cold, hard, closed minds.

Magic practically crackled and hissed. Hints of whispers slithering and sliding in the shadows. Words imbued with meaning and power that seeped into the unconscious mind and led all who remained here down torturous paths.

The worst thing about this place and the things they did to impressionable children? That those in charge believed with all their hearts that they were doing the right thing. The only approach they could take to ensure the survival of Necros in a world that neither knew nor cared about them.

They were wrong. So very wrong. They broke more than they saved. I knew for a fucking fact that those who grew up in places like this were five times as likely to be dead before they hit thirty. Necros who grew up without such training, and instead lived in caring homes where love and nurture prevailed, rather than death and brutality, were much more likely to have a future.

"Come on, I'll show you the dorms." I softened my features because I knew I was gritting my teeth and growling, about as tense and uncomfortable as I could ever recall, and smiled best I could at Jen.

"It's okay, Dad, I'm here with you. Nothing bad is going to happen." Jen smiled sweetly and squeezed my hand.

I could have picked her up and cuddled her, gushed a lifetime of sorrow into her sweet head, but I couldn't, and I didn't, so I just said, "Thanks, that means a lot. Truly it does," then led her up the stairs.

"Here's the boys' dorm," I told her as I pushed the door open.

"It's freezing in here." Jen shivered as we stepped into the musty room.

"They never heat it, never open the curtains. Damn, I think they're the same ones." The ancient, heavy red drapes, now faded to pale pink, kept the room constantly gloomy. Electricity had been installed at some point throughout the building, but apparently they'd reverted to candles like back in the day.

It was as soulless and barren as it had always been.

"Where's everyone's stuff?" asked Jen as she took in the room.

"In the trunk at the base of your bed. Not that you're allowed anything personal. Just your uniform, nothing else. Nothing. Understand? Nothing."

"Okay, I got it."

I led her out and then into the girls' dorm. It was identical to the boys.

"Um, where's the showers and the toilets and things?"

"Let's go take a look."

I led Jen down the corridor. Buckled oak floorboards creaked as we went. Thick dust billowed in our wake. The bare walls were smeared dark where thousands of children had trailed their often bloodied hands along the walls as they staggered to the huge bathroom block.

"God, it's gross!"

"Same as in my time," I told her. "It gets so bloody every day, then cleaned last thing at night. It was always filthy during the day time."

"Where's the girls' bathroom?"

"Jen, don't you get it? This is for boys and girls. Everyone comes in together."

Jen looked at me in horror. "But there are no doors on the toilet cubicles, and all the showers are open. It's like a prison shower room."

"Yes. Imagine what it's like for girls just beginning to mature. Having a load of sneering boys in here with them. Picture what a load of hormonal eighteen, nineteen, and into their twenties young men are like when confronted with this. Girls at all levels of development will be naked in the showers with nobody to protect them and nobody who cares. These kids are raised to be brutal."

"No, they don't let that happen? Seriously?"

I nodded my head. "Come on, we're leaving."

"This is barbaric. Unspeakable." Jen searched my eyes as if waiting for me to explain things, to help her understand how this was possible, that it couldn't be as bad as it seemed. That maybe I was joking.

I shook my head. There was nothing I could say to excuse or even explain this life. Nothing.

We retraced our steps past the open dorm doors and I paused at the boys' with Jen beside me.

"I try never to think of this place. And now you know at least partly why. But just this once, and only this once, I'm going to tell you some of what went on here. It may seem cruel, it's certainly a harsh lesson I'm giving you, but you need to understand what happens to many of the children you will meet over the years and maybe cut them some slack. Does that make sense?"

"I... I think so."

"So here it is. Boys and girls were in separate groups, and it was brutal. One thing the twisted overlords of this hellhole never gave a shit about was what went on behind the closed, and locked, dormitory doors once it was lights out. Just another part of the training."

"They locked you in?"

"Yes. Every night. Alliances were made or broken once the key was turned. Kids banded together for safety or to terrorize the weak. I remained alone, only ever got close to a few kids, but never formed a gang or did more than look out for each other when the need arose."

"That must have been so lonely."

"Maybe," I shrugged. "That was in the early days when everyone had been tested by the other kids. There were always new children appearing, so they were put through the wringer by the older, more experienced children to see how far they could be pushed. See what their breaking point was. That way, their position in the hierarchy was marked."

"Dad, I'm so sorry. I had no idea."

"It is what it is. And your dad's tough. From day one, I made it abundantly clear that I took shit from nobody. I got my arse kicked for almost a year on a nightly basis because I refused to back down, acknowledge the older kids as my betters, or ever cry. I fought back every time, and after a year, once my training here had left its indelible mark, I won my first fight and never lost another."

"You fought the older kids alone? But some were in their twenties! How'd you win?"

"I never gave in and would never call it quits. Soon, I got the reputation as the guy you left alone, didn't fuck with. I was then, as I am now, confident beyond compare when it came to my deep-seated conviction, my belief, my faith in my own abilities, and that no fucker could ever kill me."

"You're doing a lot of swearing. But it's okay, we won't do forfeits today," she said, trying to lift my mood as it was clear I was lower than she'd ever seen me.

"Thanks kiddo. Be good after today."

"Yeah, right!"

"I never became a leader, though. I wasn't interested. Hated the place and most within its sprawling walls. Kids and teachers alike. Many had been turned into monsters. Some came here already damaged, then were pushed and pushed until they broke. Reformed into something even more terrifying and damaged than before."

"You don't have to tell me," said Jen softly, her tears tumbling down her perfect cheeks.

"I have to. For you, and for me. The worst was the muffled cries of the young boys and girls as they were assaulted in ways no child should ever experience. A rite of passage for most that passed through here. Ignored by the teachers, reveled in by the more psychotic adolescents who knew no other way to take out their frustration than to abuse unwilling victims."

"You too?" she gasped, almost too afraid to ask.

I shook my head. "Not me. Never. It was why I took a year of beatings before they left me alone. I refused to be sodomized. They tried, over and over, but I never let them get me."

"You fought them off," nodded Jen. "I knew you would."

"So many were abused, it became almost tradition. We probably inflicted more mental anguish on each other than our teachers ever did. But they were complicit, knew exactly what went on, and never heeded our screams or our pleas for mercy. All part of toughening you up so you could venture forth, unshakable in the belief that so much bad had already been done to you and you'd survived that when it came time for your yearly Necronote, you knew that you could kick serious ass and never experience anything half as brutal as what you'd already gone through. And that's it. That's what it's like for these Necro kids. It's why we help you out at home, teach you things as you grow, but try to make it fun, Jen. We don't want this life for you. You will never have this life. Your mother has her own horror stories, but they aren't like this."

"Grandma would never go this far, would she?"

"No. She wouldn't. But listen to me. Don't become like so many did. Be kind, compassionate, know when you have won, know when to lose, and never, ever hurt people just because you can. Do you understand why I brought you here now?"

Jen was shaking with rage, her face locked in a rictus of disbelief verging on terror. Sympathy too. For me, for all the kids. She nodded. "I... I will never be like this. I'm a good girl, aren't I, Daddy?" She flung herself at me and sobbed into my chest.

"You're the best. More than I deserve. The best thing that ever happened to me. My pride and joy. I will never do anything to hurt you. Except this. I'm sorry I had to show it to you, to tell you these things. But the world is dark, and can be cruel. You will see many terrible things over your long life, but you must remain true to yourself. There is a difference between good and bad, and it's hard to always know which is which, but look deep down inside yourself and you will know. You know what's right and wrong."

"But we have to do wrong. We have to kill."

"And there lies the contradiction of life, Jen. But do good in the world to atone for what is undoubtedly a terrible sin. Damn, this is so hard to talk about with you. You're so young. But you don't use more violence than is necessary. You do not become a bully, and you never, ever use your Necro gifts to take advantage of your peers. Understand?"

"I do. I do," she sobbed.

I turned at the sound of a familiar set of footsteps coming along the hallway. I locked eyes with a man whose face I would never forget. He held my gaze as he stopped, then bowed his head in recognition.

With Jen still wrapped in my arms, I turned my back on him and morphed us out of there and back to camp. The pain I felt was nothing compared to the hurt the headmaster had inflicted on me and all the others for so many centuries. I could not talk to that man, could not bear to be in his presence. It was like I was a child again.

But no, I was a man, and he didn't scare me any more. I just despised him. Pitied him. If our paths ever crossed when not in the presence of my daughter, I would obliterate him. And God help me, I'd enjoy it.

"Time to go home," I told my daughter sweetly.

"Dad, I'm sorry."

"So am I. So am I."

Goodbye Francis

We collapsed in a tangle of limbs onto the gravel just inside the oak gate to our property. Mainly because I had bent double and got Jen all caught up in my pain.

But the pain was nothing compared to the memories. Even they faded as, for once, I welcomed the searing heat on the baking stones and the ferocious light stinging my eyes and drying my tears.

We untangled ourselves then sat there, staring at each other as the strong scent of rose, lavender, and chamomile drifted on a lazy breeze and grounded us. We exchanged a silent sense of joy at being home. Back to safety, warmth, love, and hope.

Jen smiled at me and it was too much to bear.

I broke down completely. I tried to stop it, to push it all away, but in all my years, this was the hardest thing I'd ever done. All because I wanted to teach my girl a lesson I no longer even understood the meaning of.

My words caught in my throat, my whole body shook, and the tears came and I simply couldn't stop them.

I was racked with shame and guilt. For what I'd done, what I would do, and for believing taking my innocent daughter to such a place was a good idea. A short, sharp shock to make her understand how lucky she was, how unlucky others were, and that she must never become like them and let herself be coerced.

But what was my point, really? I couldn't think straight, was unable to grasp the concepts. Left confused and so fucking sad and depressed I wanted to tear my chest open and rip out the blackened, shriveled lump of meat that was my corrupted heart and throw it away, be done with it for good.

"Dad, Dad. Oh Dad, please don't cry. It's okay, we're home now. I'll be good, I promise I will. I promise. Don't cry."

"I... I..." It was no use, I had no words. Only tears. For all of us. But most of all for my daughter. Please don't let her become like me. Even her mother. But especially not like all those poor children who never had a chance. No childhood, no fun, no games. No love.

Jen cradled me as you would an infant as I bawled like her babe in arms.

At some point Woofer came and helped by laying his head on my lap. Phage was there too, holding us both, saying nothing, knowing the depths that place had sunk to. Understanding what I'd endured, what we all had. What Jen never would.

Slowly, the tears dried as they always did, and eventually I sank back onto my haunches and smiled at the concerned faces of my wife and daughter.

"Sorry. Didn't mean to break down like that. You shouldn't have to see me that way. It's done now, over with. Jen, do you understand?"

"I do."

"What do you understand?" I asked her.

"Don't let the bastards grind you down!" she raised a hand to her mouth, eyes shocked at the use of bad language.

"Forfeit!" I laughed.

Phage stared at us both, confused, then shook her head as she smiled when Jen and I burst out laughing.

"What exactly have you two been up to? Apart from the obvious," she said hurriedly.

"Jen decided I swear too much. And judging by her foul language, I'm clearly a bad influence. So we're implementing a forfeit thing. Swearing gets you a forfeit. Or if Jen forgets her chores, she gets one."

"And what about me?"

"Mum," laughed Jen, "don't you know that you're already perfect?"

"She's right," I agreed. "We couldn't think of a single thing you do that deserved a forfeit. Unless, maybe we should make her have one for being so damn perfect."

"Forfeit!" shouted Phage and Jen with glee.

"Hey, no way. That's not swearing. I think we need to sort out the rules before I end up having to do everything around here while you two ladies swan around in tiaras, insisting on cups of tea and slices of cake while I'm on my hands and knees scrubbing the floors."

"Yeah, like that'll ever happen," complained Phage.

"I've scrubbed the floors."

"When?"

"Um, you know, that time when... Fine, I never have. Shit."

"Forfeit!"

And just like that, the past faded and all that remained was joy.

A happiness so deep I often had to pinch my arm and tell myself that yes, this was real, and yes, I did deserve it.

But sometimes I wondered if I did.

More often, I got a knot in the pit of my stomach, dreading the day it would all come crashing down.

But it wouldn't. I wouldn't let it.

Nothing would come between us.

Ever.

"What the hell is that?" Phage shouted above a rumbling, grating, screeching, high-pitched wail that seemed to be coming from the other side of the hedge.

I hugged my family, nodded my thanks, then brushed myself down, wiped my face, not that the tears were visible because of the sweat, and we went to investigate the godawful sound.

We got to the end of the lane and there on the road, almost touching the hedges either side, was a behemoth of a vehicle. As high as a house, a huge, misshapen truck of sorts with a massive steel container on the back. On our side was a ladder leading to a small cab attached to a crane arm that looked like it could reach to the stars.

"Damn, I forgot all about this."

"Is it today?" asked Phage. I just raised an eyebrow. "Um, yes, it's today."

"What's today?" asked Jen. "I don't want anything else to happen today."

"No, neither do I," I lamented, wishing we could go inside and hide.

We watched a man in dark overalls climb down from his cab then check a tablet before coming over to us, a jaunty spring in his step and a whistle on his cracked lips.

"Hey folks. Nice day for it," he said cheerily. His jowls wobbled as he laughed at what I could only assume he believed was a joke.

"You got the old girl ready?" he asked.

"What old girl?" asked Jen suspiciously. "What's happening?"

"Hey little missy. Do you want a lollipop?" He pulled a red treat from his grubby pocket and held it out to Jen.

"No, I don't want a... Um, can I?" She turned to Phage and smiled sweetly.

"Sure." Phage turned back to the man and asked, "So they supply you with lollipops to placate the kids?"

"Yep," he chortled. "And I've got real chocolate for the grown-ups. At least, they call it real. Even wine, if you'd prefer. Although it is British, so I'd take the choccies if I were you." He winked conspiratorially.

"We'll take the chocolates," I told him.

"Thought you might. But gotta do the business first. You folks got things ready?"

"Sorry, no. We forgot. Been rather busy."

"Isn't everyone? Can you go get it?"

"It's a he. Francis," I told him.

"Nice name. And look, folks, I'm sorry about this. I know how much the old guy probably means to you, but I'm just doing my job. I'd rather not, but you know how it is. Any job's better than no job. Please don't give me any grief. I've had all kinds of foul language thrown my way today, plus a shoe, and I'm sick of it."

"We don't blame you," Phage told him. "It's just a shame, that's all."

"Sure is. All these classics being scrapped. But hey, if it makes for a better world, right? And besides, they've already ripped up half the roads, so it's not like they're trying to pull a fast one. But yeah, I get it. Real shame."

I nodded to the guy, then headed to the garage and started up Francis Ford, our old, reliable car. With a final flooring of the accelerator, I then released the clutch and drove in first down the short lane before turning off the engine beside everyone.

"Dad, what's happening?"

"We forgot to tell you, but you heard the news. They're scrapping nearly all the cars. And you know they've removed most motorways and major roads and planted them with trees. Well, it's our turn. Francis has to go."

"No, not Francis."

"Afraid so."

"Okay, everyone stand back. This will get incredibly loud, and it can be dangerous, so stay well away." The man nodded to me, then walked back to the vehicle and climbed up the ladder.

As we retreated up the lane, he got into the cab and began to maneuver the long extendable arm out until the grab swung over Francis. Slowly, and with well practiced moves, he lowered it over the car, then gripped tight without even smashing a window.

The old Ford was lifted up, then unceremoniously dropped into the open top of the container. Metal crunched, bits flew up high, glinting in the harsh light, then dropped back in, and in less than a minute silence returned.

The man climbed back down and beckoned with a finger. We scraped past the hedge to the back of the vehicle.

"There you go. All ready for recycling."

"That's a whole car?" asked Jen, impressed.

"Sure is. They can crunch up pretty small. See, that's five already on the back. I can get another ten maybe, then go back to the yard and drop them off before coming out for more. It's a busy day. There's fifty of these monsters just in Shropshire alone. Soon there won't be a car anywhere. Apart from for the bigwigs, of course. They get to keep theirs." His joviality faded and he frowned.

"So that's it, no more driving ever?" asked Jen.

"Your guess is as good as mine, missy. Oh, the payment will be in your bank by end of day. One thing the bosses do is keep their word about paying properly, and on time."

"Okay, thanks."

I led Phage and Jen away, but he called, "Don't you want the chocolates?"

He caught us up, retrieved a nice box of expensive, undoubtedly foul-tasting treats from the cab, and he must have had a cooler in there to stop them from melting, then handed them to Phage. "Enjoy," he beamed.

"Thank you," said Phage.

"Ah, almost forgot." He shuffled along the side of the container, then opened a hatch and pulled out a long hessian sack. "Don't forget this," he called.

"What is it?" asked Jen as he handed the six-foot package to her.

"It's your tree. They've got us doubling up on duties. Saves the fuel." He winked at Jen.

"I wondered when we'd get ours," she said as she took the wrapped sapling. "Loads of kids at school already had theirs. Think how many new trees there will be once everyone plants theirs."

"They reckon about forty million if everyone does it. Mind you, why wouldn't you?" he asked. "Guess you folks know the rules? That if you don't plant it somewhere, and send a photo in, then your electricity supply will be cut off. You have seven days," he warned. "I'll make a note of it." He tapped his tablet then beamed at us, satisfied.

"Can we plant it anywhere?" asked Jen.

"Sure! Pick a nice spot though, with plenty of space. You got a willow, and they grow pretty big." He turned his back then waved before hauling himself up into his cab.

We watched him drive on towards Job's from the safety of our gravel drive. I laughed when I pictured how that would go.

Not well, and a lollipop or chocolates wouldn't make him part freely with any of his vehicles, let alone ones that ran. Best thing was to keep well out of it. Job was a great guy, but boy did he have a temper.

"How about down in the paddock?" I asked Jen.

"What?" she asked, distracted.

"The willow. How about we plant it in the paddock?"

"Um, sure."

With Jen clutching her tree, whilst sucking on her lollipop, and Phage trying to pretend she wasn't interested in the crappy chocolates, and failing miserably because she was quite literally drooling despite knowing it would only lead to disappointment, we followed Woofer inside the house.

I slammed the door shut on the utter madness going on all around us.

Lunch Break

I felt dazed by the loss of the car. Pained by the morph. Disconsolate after revisiting my old life and tearing the raggedy bandages off wounds I vowed never to inspect. And confused by my extreme actions when it came to Jen.

So it felt surreal, bordering on trippy, to walk into the kitchen and find my two ladies chatting happily. They were putting the finishing touches to lunch a mere five minutes after I'd told them to go ahead while I got myself freshened up. Meaning, wiping away the signs of my tears and having a good long chat with myself in the mirror.

It consisted of telling myself to get a grip, to be strong for my family, and to never, ever lose the plot like that with Jen again. I still didn't know if I'd done the right thing or not. Maybe I had. Was that what she needed? Nip it in the bud before she began to believe she was superhuman and could go around pulverizing other kids whenever she felt disgruntled?

But she was a good girl, had just fought back against a bully, right? I thought it through and came to the conclusion that I'd taken the correct course of action. She needed to know what happened to other kids like her, and that there were levels of violence that were acceptable and levels that weren't.

Phage would know. She might have been new to parenthood, but she always knew what was right.

"You ready for your lunch now?" asked Phage with a questioning look in her eyes.

"I'm ready."

"Me too. I'm starving," groaned Jen with a greedy glance at the pile of sandwiches and a rumble of her tummy.

"I'll miss Francis," said Phage.

"So will I."

"Why did they take the car?" asked Jen as she snatched a sandwich the moment Phage placed them on the table.

"They're trying to ensure nobody pollutes. Too much bootleg fuel. The only way they can stop it is to scrap all the old vehicles."

"But they're scrapping the new electric ones too," spluttered Jen, bits of sandwich flying everywhere.

"Watch your manners. No talking with food in your mouth," I reminded her for the seven billionth time. "They've got new super-efficient vehicles now. You saw all the stuff on TV. Different batteries and engines and who knows what, but they cost next to nothing to run so everything else is gone. And they've removed at least half the roads in the country to ensure we never go back to how it was. Lots of countries have done the same now. Everyone hates it. Damn, pretty soon it'll be like when I was young. Mud tracks, wheels falling off your cart. Impossible to get anywhere."

"But we'll have a new car, right? Then we can go where we want?"

"Ha, good luck with that!" I snorted. "That's what the government says. They're paying everyone for their old cars, but it won't be anywhere near enough to buy a new, fancy, eco-friendly one. They cost a fortune. So, no, most people will be stuck. Same as we have been for decades. It's all a con."

"Come on, Soph. Why would they con us?"

"Why? So they can keep everyone in their place. At home. Spending all their time online. Spending all their money online too. They want us all to stay put so they can control us."

"Dad, that doesn't make sense. They want the country to be a success, so surely they want people traveling and spending money in shops? Tourists mean jobs. Travel means money."

"That's the past. Now it's different. Jen, this is just stuff you've heard. You never saw what it was like before. Everywhere was crowded. The amount of waste generated was unbelievable. Every house used to have a black bin, maybe two, plus the same of recycling full every week. When people traveled it got worse. Everything was packaged, all that wear and tear on roads, the maintenance, and the extra deliveries for food and stuff at tourist spots. It was crazy."

"So it's a good thing they stopped it then," she said around a mouthful of sandwich.

"No! What? That wasn't my point."

"And what was?" asked Phage, amused.

"Um, I've lost my train of thought now. Ah, yes, they want us at home so they can do whatever they want out there. Keep us monitored so nobody can get up to no good or question their authority. If people have no means of travel, then nobody can protest, organize marches, go teach the buggers a lesson. We're stuck. At their mercy. Just like it used to be. Mark my words, it will all end in tears. You've seen the riots. The whole world is up in arms. Look at America. They aren't standing for this crap. Or the Finnish. But don't get me started on the bloody French."

"Double forfeit!"

"Damn, okay, you got me there. But seriously, the Fins aren't standing for this, but a lot of countries are."

"That's because we don't have guns," said Jen.

"Hmm, maybe. Anyway, Francis is gone, so we'll wait and see. The main thing is we have our own power source so we can do what we want. We'll survive. We made do without the Internet and phones when the kill switch kicked in, and we can again. That was a lesson to us all."

"Speaking of lessons. Isn't someone meant to be in school?" Phage reminded Jen. She was looking at me, though. I was being scolded.

"Oops. Sorry. I just, you know, wanted to sort this out about the fight."

"Can I stay home today, then?" asked Jen brightly. "Hardly worth going now. School will be over soon."

"Yes, I already phoned this morning and said you were feeling sick. But no more time off. Are you two going to tell me what happened? Are you both okay? Was it awful?"

Jen and I exchanged a knowing look, then proceeded to tell Phage all about it. Jen left nothing out, neither did I. I explained to them both my feelings, my fears, my insecurities that stemmed from a life I'd long ago put behind me, and I did it for one reason.

We were a family.

And we had to hold on to that, no matter what.

When we'd finished, Phage was silent. We waited for her to process it all, then she turned to me, her face serious, and said, "You did the right thing. I'm with you on this."

"Thanks. But sorry for the theatrics. I don't know what came over me, acting so impulsively. And I've already apologized to Jen, but I want to say sorry again for shouting."

"That's fine. Soph, you're a kind man, and you are the perfect husband and father. You're allowed to raise your voice now and then when it's needed. And this was needed." Phage turned to Jen. "I hope you understand the sacrifice? How hard that was for your father to do? How much it hurt him to show you that? To act the way he did?"

"I understand. And I will never behave that way again. Promise. Those poor children. I still can't believe things like that are going on in our own country."

"It's done now. But Jen, now you know what this life of ours entails. How others are training to fulfill their notes. Never forget what has happened to some of the people you will face. The upbringing they've had, the things they've gone through. Never be callous or cruel. Remember that life is complicated, people are fragile and very complex, and their past is not your past. I'm sorry you had to learn all this, and I'm still not sure it was right to take you there, but it's done now and you know the reality of it. Now, can we please do something nice this afternoon? Something fun?"

"Like what?" asked Jen.

"I don't know. Hang out in the garden? Go for a walk. What about a barbecue?"

"A barbecue would be cool," said Jen, relieved the lecture was over.

"We've got chicken," said Phage.

"Have sausages?" asked a hopeful voice from under the table.

"Aha, so the crumb-catcher speaks," I laughed. "Yes, we have sausages."

Woofer poked his head out and asked, "Can eat now?"

"Later. It's too hot to cook yet. We'll have a late dinner once it cools down."

"Woofer so hungry. Feel ill. Need sausages."

"You'll live a few hours longer," I chuckled.

"He's so silly," laughed Jen.

"What's happening? I wish I could understand him all the time. It isn't fair," complained Phage.

"Woofer like talking to Phage. Is nice."

"He says he loves talking to you," I told her. "Maybe it's time to learn? Can you?"

"I could never get the hang of it. It's not a natural gift like it is for you and Jen. Even Mother. She tried to help me learn, but I was young and had other things I wanted to master. Then it was too late, as I left. I know lots of whispers, but I never found the time to master talking to the animals. It just isn't natural for me."

"Well, nobody's perfect," I said, smiling. "Except you."

"Yes, except you, Mum. And Dad's alright too." Jen reached out and kissed Phage on her glowing cheek. I don't think there was a prouder set of parents than us at that moment.

"Right, I need to clear my head if you both don't mind tidying up. It's been a long night and an even longer day. I need a doze in my chair, then I'll sort out for the barbecue. You two okay with that?"

"I'll tidy up. Mum can relax."

"Thanks," said Phage. "But somehow I never seem to have the time to just relax. Considering it's only the three of us, a lot sure does go on in this house."

"Ain't that the truth?" I stood, then bent and kissed the heads of my two queens. Phage smelled divine. Perfume, shampoo, slight scent of stables. Jen smelled of corruption and the decay of years, combined with the breaking of minds and bodies. I smiled at them both though, and knew I'd have to shower later to get the stink of the past out of me.

I could wash away the smell, but never the memories. Never the injuries they'd inflicted on my mind. The wounds had healed, but never the mental scars.

The bastards.

My tatty brown recliner was my own personal piece of paradise. A man needs his own spot, somewhere that smells like him, wraps around him. Cocoons him in a sense of familiarity and safety. Home within a home.

My sigh was deep and heartfelt as I sank into the faded chair that, just like me, had seen better days. Rough around the edges, with hard bits poking out, but still remnants of a softness inside. Worn, but hanging in there. Stubborn.

I kicked back and rested my head, the burden of my past easing as I closed my eyes and sank into a deep, dead sleep.

"Dad, wake up." Jen shook me gently by the shoulder.

I opened one eye and smiled at her. Her hair was still wet, she'd changed her clothes, and she smelled of apples and soap. "Hey, what's up?"

"You smell funky. I hadn't noticed until I got clean, but you smell bad. Even Woofer's gone to hide. You need a shower. And I'm hungry. Can we have dinner soon? And come on, it's lovely out. It's cooled right down. Better make the most of it."

"Oh, okay." Confused, I leant forward so the footrest tucked into the base of the chair, then heaved to my feet. I sniffed the air. "You're right. I stink."

"It's that place. It just smelled wrong. Corrupted. Take a shower. You'll feel better."

"Okay. Then we'll have the barbie."

Still dazed, and wondering why Jen had woken me just to shower, I nevertheless went upstairs and got myself cleaned up. After I'd finished, I even sprayed a little aftershave I'd been hoarding for more years than I cared to recall, and damn, but I felt like a new man.

With some fresh jeans and my usual shirt, I truly felt like the last day or so had been nothing but a dream.

With Bone Slicer secured against my thigh, I was once again complete. Ready for anything.

Almost.

Bleedin' Dwarves

"Surprise!" roared Phage, Jen, and Woofer, who then proceeded to run around the kitchen with his tail wagging. He was so excited, the poor guy morphed without even realizing and ended up in my arms, so took advantage and licked my face dementedly.

"Easy there," I laughed. "Come on, down you go."

"Soph likes cake?" he asked as I lowered him.

"What do you think?" asked Jen, excited. She was covered in flour and glowing with happiness.

"We thought you deserved it. And I managed to scrounge up proper flour. Look, it's even got your knife on it," said Phage, beaming.

"Wow! I wasn't expecting this. A cake. We don't normally do cake. But thank you, it looks amazing. And did Jen do the knife? Good job." I ruffled her hair in the way that always made her squirm, but she shook her head and cast a worried glance at Phage.

I turned and felt the full wrath of my wife's steely gaze. "I made the knife, Soph. I spent ages on it. All the time you were sleeping, while Jen did the cake."

"And a fine-looking cake, and knife, it is. Well done to both of you. Very, um, artistic." I looked down at the misshapen brown blob with what appeared to be a silver worm with dietary issues atop it, then glanced from Phage's stern face to Jen, who was stifling a laugh, and I couldn't help myself. First Jen tittered, then I sniggered, then we both burst out laughing and moved over to Phage and cuddled her.

"What's so funny? It's good, isn't it? Looks just like it."

"Yep, well done, Mum. You should go into the cake-making business," chortled Jen.

"Too right," I agreed. "You'd travel the world, making lifelike cakes for the rich and famous."

Phage studied the "cake" once again, then said, "Hmm, maybe it could do with a little more work. More icing maybe? Come on, let's tuck in. Soph, care to do the honors?"

"Sure. And thank you. Both of you. It might be a day late, but it was worth the wait if it tastes even a little better than it looks." I winked at Jen. She doubled over, laughing. Phage finally gave in and smiled, then joined us in our merriment.

"Okay, let's eviscerate this sucker." I pulled out my knife, ready to cut three, no, make that four, generous wedges.

"Dad!"

"What?"

"You can't use Bone Slicer. It's a magical elven knife forged ten thousand years ago."

"A knife is for one thing, and one thing only. Cutting stuff up." I sliced through the gooey mess, and when I pulled the knife free, it was as clean as a whistle. "See?"

"Now that is a knife I'd like in the kitchen," pined Phage. "No washing up needed."

"Hands off. And besides, remember nobody but me can even pick it up. It won't let you."

"What happens if we try?" asked Jen.

I shrugged. "No idea. But best not to find out. Right, who's for cake?"

"Woofer need cake before faint."

"So, Woofer needs some to stabilize his blood sugar levels. And everyone want a big piece?"

Everyone did, so I cut generous portions and dished it out. For a while there was silence while we slowly munched on our cake.

It was, without doubt, the worst thing I'd ever tasted. Even worse than eating dragon shit after a Marmite sandwich.

"Don't give up the day job, Mum," mumbled Jen as she tried to unstick her mouth enough to speak properly.

"You made the cake," I reminded her, then laughed.

"Mum gave me the ingredients."

"They said it was real flour," complained Phage.

"Then they saw you coming. Where'd you get it from?"

"The ubermarket. It's a new line. Said it was genuine."

"I think we need to start growing our own wheat." I placed the cake down. Suddenly it was heavy, and emitting fumes. That wasn't right. Not for cake.

"Hey, it's the thought that counts. So thank you."

"Woofer can have more?"

"Woofer likes it," I told Phage.

"Woofer likes dog bums," Phage reminded me.

"True. Hey, I know. Let's give a piece to Shey Redgold. Haven't seen him for a while. And he does love cake. Any cake," I added.

"Sweet. Does that mean I can finally come down and see his place?" asked Jen.

I turned to Phage. She shrugged.

"Okay, you can come. But you have to promise not to fiddle with his stuff. He's very particular about it, and he'll be an absolute nightmare if you mess things up."

"Do I have to come?" asked Phage.

"Yes, you do. And besides, he likes you."

"He's too moody down there. So bossy. And always complains. And besides, all that gold makes my head hurt. It's too shiny. Too much."

"Has he really got gold then?" asked Jen, eyes gleaming. "I figured he was just boasting when he says he hasn't got any, but really he means he does. What, a little dwarf bag of gold. Can I touch it?"

"No!" we both shouted. "Never touch it. Not unless he says you can. But trust me, he never will. And, er, well, I guess you'll see soon enough. Come on. Let's give the resident dwarf a slice of cake. He likes dwarf bread, so chances are he'll like this."

"Do not compare our cake to dwarf bread, Soph," phage warned. "There are insults, then there's just being downright rude."

I smiled at Jen before we all went off to offer Shey Redgold a prize worthy of any dwarf.

I unlocked the door under the stairs that led to the basement. Jen's eyes gleamed. Phage frowned. I took a deep breath.

"You look pretty," I whispered to her, then had a sneaky pinch of her bum.

"Oh, thank you!" Phage brushed at her hair and I got a waft of her familiar, intoxicating Phageness. Ah, bliss.

I winked at my wife, wishing we could go to bed. She licked her lips and pouted in that sultry way.

"Ugh, you guys. Come on, seriously?"

"Better than shouting, right?" I told her.

"No, I'd rather you yelled. Maybe stabbed me in my eyeballs."

"Okay, everyone ready? I'll open the door, turn the light on, put my basement boots on, oh, you should go grab some clean boots, you two. I'll wait."

They returned a minute later so we were good to go. "Now, don't touch, don't ask anything, and don't mention the war."

"What war?" asked Jen.

"Good girl."

"Huh?"

"Never mind. You ready?"

"Dad, it's just Shey Redgold. I've seen him loads since he got addicted to Neighbours. He was so sad when it ended. Wish they'd put it back on. Repeats aren't the same."

"I don't. He's better off in the basement. Can't cause any trouble then. Here we go." I opened the door, slipped my basement boots on, then pulled the cord for the bare bulb down below. Pale golden light gleamed up the ancient rickety steps.

"Oi, turn it off. It hurts my eyes. That's a crime, that is. A crime against dwarves. You hate me, is that it?"

I rolled my eyes at Jen, then nodded. With that, I descended the stairs into yellow madness. Phage and Jen followed right behind me.

"Oh, wow!" Jen stood on the carpet of gold and gawped.

"It's not real! Just my little joke," squeaked Shey Redgold hurriedly. "No, not real. Don't touch it! Watch that tower! Don't move that crown. Never look at that! That big pile is special, not that it's real or anythin', but don't touch it. Hey, are you sniffin' my gold? Gold that's just pretend."

Shey Redgold was sweating worse than a spit roast polar bear as he stroked his beard nervously. He kept shifting his battle-axe around in his belt loop whilst rubbing his chain mail with a fat gold coin he clung to like his life depended on it.

"Wow!" repeated Jen as she turned slowly in a circle and tried, unsuccessfully, to take it all in.

"Nice, innit? If it was real." He winked at me, seeming to relax a little, like his ruse was working a charm.

"It's... It's... Amazing! Look at it all. How come you never told me?" Phage asked Shey Redgold.

"Because it ain't real. And if it was, I wouldn't be goin' about tellin' all an' sundry 'bout it, now would I? Nah, that'd be daft. Do I look daft?" Shey Redgold, all four foot nothing of him, squared his wide shoulders and pulled his helmet low over bushy eyebrows. His tubby tummy bulged, his short legs were thigh high in a sea of gold, and I believe he was trying to glare.

"Can I answer that?" I asked, smirking.

"No!" everyone exclaimed.

"It's so cool. Can I touch it?" asked Jen as she bent.

"No!" we all said, panicked.

"Aw, why not? What's the point of gold if you can't touch it?"

A deep hush fell over the room. The only sound the tinkle of a million gold coins gasping.

I palm-slapped my head. Here we go.

"What's the point!? What's the point!?" Shey Redgold spluttered. "It's gold! Gold. G.O.L.D!"

"Yeah?"

"Is she a bit funny in the head?" Shey Redgold twirled a finger at his temple, nearly decapitating himself as he was holding his axe.

"No, and for anyone but a dwarf, it's a fair question," I told him.

"That's because you humans are all off yer bleedin' rockers. It's gold," he tried to explain again. "G.O.L.D. Gold."

"Why does he keep saying that?" frowned Jen.

"He's hoping that by saying it enough times, and spelling it, you'll suddenly be enlightened and understand that it's gold." I winked at her. Jen stifled a giggle.

"Oh, right. That makes sense then," she told him. Shey Redgold nodded, satisfied. "We brought you some cake. Me and Mum made it." Jen offered the cake and Shey's mouth opened wide, dumbfounded.

"For me? Really? Nobody ever brings me food."

"I always bring you food," I told him. "And you always say you hate human food and will get your own."

"I do hate it. But that smell, oh, it reminds me of bread. Real bread."

"Dwarf bread?" I inquired.

"Of course!" he snapped. "What other kind is worth mentioning? Gimme, gimme." Shey Redgold snatched the wedge of cake off the plate and sniffed tentatively. He sighed deeply, then with his eyes watering, and seemingly from happiness not fear, he took a nibble.

His cheeks flushed, his stomach gurgled like a boiling kettle, and he almost toppled over backwards as a look of pure bliss spread across his face then took a firm hold and hung on for dear life. Quickly, he took another bite, then another, then just stuffed the lot into his big gob and stood there, chewing and swallowing, making noises so embarrassing Jen's ears turned pink.

"Do you like it?" asked an astonished Jen, smiling sweetly at him. She was way out of her depth here, but I guess after what she'd been through, showing her something just a little less terrifying took her mind off the dark side. It was the right move.

"Like it? Like it?" bellowed the fake-chocolate-covered dwarf. "I love it! It's hard yet soft, and full of bits! You have to rip it with your teeth! It's got weird bitter nuggets, and tastes like it was run over by a camel with the hump. Geddit? What's not to like?"

"There you go," I told Phage. "You should write a cookbook. For dwarves only." Phage slapped me playfully, but I think I hurt her feelings. She sure as hell hurt my backside.

"Um, that's good, right?" Jen was definitely struggling to make sense of any of this.

"Amazin'. Any more?"

"Maybe tomorrow. You know what you're like if you eat too much human food." I told him.

"Goes right through me, it does. I remember this one time when I was inspectin' this crown for defects an' I got this weird feelin' in my tummy. Next thing you know, I was shi—"

"So, what have you been up to?" interrupted Phage as Jen giggled.

"Just the usual," shrugged Shey Redgold. "Counting, rearranging. Building. The usual."

"You mean you count all this?" asked Jen. "How often? And why? And what's with the towers? Can I wear a crown? Is that a real spoon? Why'd you want a gold spoon? Can we have some?"

The dwarf backed away like he'd been physically assaulted. "Have some?" he spluttered. "Are you mad? Is she mad?" he asked Phage. "She sounds mad."

"I'm not mad. Just asking."

"I'm a dwarf," he told Jen. "This is what dwarves do. It's mine. And yes, it's real," he admitted with a defeated sigh.

"Really? I'd never have guessed," said Jen.

"Good! Dwarves are cunnin' like that," he confided. "But it's our little secret," he whispered. "Ugh, so bright. Can you go now, please? Here's the plate back." Shey Redgold shoved the plate at Jen but she was preoccupied and it fell with a soft tinkle to a pile of gold. She picked it up then sighed as she stared at all the lovely trinkets.

"See you soon," she told him.

"Bye. And be good," I told him.

"Nice to see you again," said Phage sweetly, not meaning a word of it.

"Turn off that bleedin' light! It hurts my eyes. Don't know what's wrong with you all," he said gruffly.

After we got to the top of the stairs, I turned the light off, locked the door, secured the key with the others at my belt loop, then leaned back against it and sighed.

"That went well," I told them.

"Better than expected," agreed Phage.

"So much gold," sighed Jen as she wandered off in a daze to put the plate in the kitchen.

Emergency!

"Cuppa?" asked Phage, wiping the stress sweat from her lovely brow.

"Is the Pope Catholic?"

"Not anymore."

"Yeah, fair point. Yes to a cuppa though. And then maybe we can relax? Damn, it's been crazy since yesterday. What's going on?"

"You took our daughter off to terrify her, remember?"

"No, I didn't," I snapped. "Sorry, but I didn't know what else to do."

"I was joking. You did the right thing. She's different already. I can tell. It was exactly what she needed. A shock. Wake her up to the reality of it all."

"Maybe. It was rather harsh, though. It's not like me."

"Soph, kids sometimes bring out the worst in everyone. Parents lose their temper, get angry, say or do the wrong thing, just like their kids. But you didn't. You got angry because you had every right to be, and you did what you thought was best. I think it was for the best. You have my support."

"Thanks. Sometimes this parenting is so tough. I thought I had it nailed, but seemingly not."

"Think how I feel. It's a lot of pressure for me. You have all this experience, have done it so many times before. And I'm not having a go at you, I'm just telling you how it is. It's a lot to live up to."

"I know. We've had this conversation, but I'll tell you what I always tell you. How you handle things is amazing. You are doing a fantastic job. You're a great mother and a perfect woman. We love you."

"Love you too." Phage smiled as she placed our drinks on the table.

"She'll be alright, won't she?" I asked.

"Of course. It's just growing pains. I can't imagine how hard it is for her. Having to try to be normal. Hide who she really is. The one thing we never had to do was shy away from our Necro side."

"No, quite the opposite. It's better this way."

"Of course it is! Rather this than the alternative. At least going to school and having regular friends lets her understand what the normal world is like. Even if she won't ever be a true part of it when she's older, at least she can experience it for a while."

"What do you mean, I won't be part of it when I'm older?" asked Jen as she stepped into the room.

"You shouldn't be eavesdropping," I warned. "Never listen in on other people's conversations. You know that."

"Sorry. Didn't mean to. I'm a freak, aren't I?" The tears were about to fall, that much was clear. Too much had happened for her to process, and this was the last thing she needed to hear.

"Come here." Jen shuffled over. I grabbed her and sat her on my lap, then said, "You know life will be different for you. You can go out into the world and do whatever you want. Go wherever you wish, live any kind of life you choose. But no, you will never be like your friends, or live a life like theirs. It's a bad thing, but a very good thing too. You have a world of possibilities that isn't open to them. You can experience so much more, see so much more."

"Kill so many more," Jen sobbed. She buried her head in my chest. Her tears soaked my shirt.

I looked to Phage. She didn't know what to do. What could we do?

We had to let her get it out of her system. The stress of the last day, all I'd shown and told her. Jen stopped soon enough, then pulled away from me and said, "Sorry. Just feeling a bit delicate. Too much going on in my head."

Soph, you need to come, whispered a voice from far away yet somehow right beside me. I jumped to my feet, hand straight to my knife, and quickly checked the room.

"Dad, what are you doing?" asked a shocked Jen.

"What is it?" asked a concerned Phage.

I stood in the middle of our kitchen and held up my hand for silence. I listened, I waited, I got ready. Who was that? Where was he?

Come to me. There isn't much time. Hurry, but be prepared.

I turned, and caught a ripple in the air as reality kind of shifted sideways to allow space for the owner of the voice to appear.

Never before had I experienced prior warning of a morph about to happen. "Stay absolutely still," I warned my family, for fear of them moving into the space I knew would be occupied in a moment.

The air crackled as time slowed and my perception expanded. Everything vibrated with a deep magic, something foreign and exotic, yet as much a part of this world as tea and biscuits.

Tiny motes of black matter buzzed like flies in a vacuum. Angry, jagged. A violent swarm.

Gradually, as though I was watching in super slow motion, the particles took on the shape of a man. With a final *whoosh* of sheer willfulness, the disparate motes snapped into place like an impossible jigsaw and sound and light returned to the world.

"Mawr!" I shouted.

"Soph, my dear boy. Sorry for the rather dramatic entrance. Ah, I see your powers have grown. Tell me, this was the first time, right? The first time you were able to truly see a morph from an outsider's perspective."

"I... It..."

"No matter. No matter." Mawr turned as if looking behind him, then his attention snapped back to me and now Jen and Phage who had come beside me. "Oh, hello. So nice to meet you both at last. Sorry, no time for pleasantries.

There are, er, things happening. Soph, you know the way. Don't dawdle, but don't get into a tizzy either. Bring what you need. You'll be away for a while, just a day or two, so pack carefully. Then hurry to me."

"Mawr, I don't understand? What are you talking about?"

"No time, my lad. Just prepare for a little trip." Mawr turned his attention to Jen. "No school for you tomorrow. Looks like your holiday just got extended." From beneath his bushy wizard eyebrows, he winked. He turned to Phage. "And don't forget your gift." He smiled so sweetly at her, then turned back to me and said, "I have something for you. It's time. Don't forget to bring the dragon. And the, ah, what do you call it? Power pellets? Yes, and the dog, and I guess you'll bring the grumpy unicorn. Hurry, but you know, don't panic. There is still time. Leave early in the morning, but then, um, hurry. Gosh how confusing."

Mawr smiled at us, then time slowed again. I watched his body break into tiny parts then spread apart before vanishing.

Phage and I exchanged a worried glance. Woofer ran around the room, barking excitedly.

The window erupted in an explosion of shards of glass, followed by a dumb head and preceded by a long, sparkling horn.

"Did someone just call me?" asked Bernard.

"It's a fucking window, not a hole!" Phage and I shouted simultaneously.

"Forfeit!" jeered Jen, looking altogether too excited and pleased with herself.

"Ugh, what is happening?" I grumbled. "Why is everything so mad this year?"

Phage put her arm around me, moved her lips close to my ear, and whispered, "It's always like this. All the time. You just forget and pretend that you have a quiet life."

"Always?" I was genuinely confused.

"Always," she nodded.

"No, I don't think that's right," I told her, not convinced.

"Road trip," Jen hollered, then stood before us and asked, "Well? What do we need to pack?"

"Whoa there! We can't just all go and leave the house, and you have school. We aren't prepared. And it might be dangerous. Damn, I don't know what the hell Mawr was thinking. He can't spring something like this on us."

"So that was Mawr," mused Phage. "He seemed nice. Bit of a stereotype, but that's wizards for you."

"He's old school. Likes to stick to traditions. Big beard, even bigger eyebrows, silver hair, long robes. He even has a staff and a pointy hat."

"That's so cool" said Jen as she hopped about, almost beside herself.

"What are you so excited about?" I asked.

"We get to go on an adventure. Together. So cool. I can meet a real wizard. Um, no offense, Dad. Who knows what will happen? Plus, no school. So cool."

"Okay, go pack," I told her, but she was already out the door and banging up the stairs. "Don't forget, we aren't leaving until the morning."

"She's very excited," noted Phage.

"Guess we're going on a trip," I sighed.

"Looks that way," laughed Phage.

It was only then I recalled I still hadn't even opened my Necronote. I'd wasted the better part of a day and now this cryptic crap from Mawr.

Was it really only yesterday my note arrived? Seemed like a lifetime ago. Surely Phage wasn't right. It wasn't always like this, was it?

"You okay with this?" I asked her.

"Do I have a choice? You miss him, don't you?"

I nodded. "It's weird, I hadn't thought about him for centuries. Nothing. He did something to me to make me forget. Bloody wizard whispers. He said it was the right thing to do, so I could get on with my life. But after seeing him again, I can't stop thinking about the old bugger. Yes, I do miss him. Sounds silly, but I think of Mawr as family. Real family."

"That's perfectly understandable. He helped you when you needed it most. Was there for you. That's what family does. From what you've told me, he did more than your father did."

"Shit, yeah, lots more. I just wish he hadn't made me forget him. But ever since we met up again, there's been this nagging, like something is missing. There's more to be said, more to learn. Now I guess we're going to find out."

"I wouldn't count on it." Phage sipped her cooling tea and I did likewise. It calmed me somewhat after all the craziness.

"What do you mean?"

"You know what they're all like. These witches and wizards. They love their secrets. For instance, what did he mean by bring the gift?"

"He meant Malka, of course. I assumed you understood."

"No, I didn't. You sure?"

"Not a hundred percent, but that's what I thought he meant. Could be wrong. But it was like he knew you had her. Maybe that was the plan all along. I wouldn't put it past him. He's such a wily old sod."

"There you go then. Just like the witches. Just like Mother."

"You're right! They're a perfect match for each other. Although, I guess he likes his privacy too much these days. He did say he was married again for quite a while, but I guess these days he's happy where he is."

"I can't even picture Mother living with someone. Imagine being a man at that place with those witches glaring at you every day." Phage laughed.

I shuddered. "Damn, almost forgot again! I don't know where my head's at. I haven't even checked my note yet." I fished it out of my pocket, then held it in my hand, loathe to read it. It was real then. Once I got the location, it became an undeniable fact, something I could never turn away from.

"Oh, I'm so sorry. And you've already lost so much time." Phage twisted a tea towel like she could wring the dread out of it. I knew just how she felt.

"I've had worse birthdays." I smiled, but inside I felt like dying. As always, I acted brave for my family, but my guts churned and I felt sick.

"Now we have to visit Mawr. Talk about bad timing."

"Maybe. Or he knows exactly what's happening and this is all part of it."

"Part of what?"

"Of wizard and witch games. Fucking with things just because they can. Mawr's a great old guy, but they all love playing their damn games. You can bet he's up to something. Clearly is. Bringing you and Jen, Bernard and Tyr, not to mention Woofer? He either wants something or there's trouble afoot. Most likely both. Hell, what is with this year? It's enough just dealing with Jen."

"I think that particular problem might be partially fixed. Have you seen how she looks at you? How she's behaved since you both got back? She's like a different girl."

"Let's hope it lasts," I muttered as I pulled out my glasses and phone then reluctantly opened the Necronote. "Twig. Icicle. Right, let's see where I'm going this year." With trembling fingers, I loaded up the Necroapp and got the usual colored wheel of death. With a sigh, I turned my phone off then on again and repeated the process.

"You and technology really do have a love hate relationship, don't you?" laughed Phage, trying to lighten the mood.

"Yes. I hate it, and the tech loves that I do. Okay, wish me luck."

"Good luck."

With stress levels soaring, I typed in the locations with thick fingers not designed for such tiny keypads. I pressed the load button and the wheel of divine frustration spun and spun, just to wind me up. When I believed it had frozen, the app finally sprang into life and pinpointed the location. It marked the route options, giving times to travel, even highlighting any known roadblocks or closures, and helpfully showed which roads were either dug up and replanted or waiting to be eradicated.

I frowned as I stared at the map, something nagging at me. As it zoomed in slowly, I read the destination and my heart not just sank, but fell to the bottom of an ocean of misery then got ripped apart by a shiver of bloodthirsty sharks. Then, they shat out what remained, and my last vestiges of hope drifted around the globe for eternity.

The app zoomed in once more, and switched to satellite images of a place supposedly screened against such surveillance. The details were crisp, clear, precise. I saw the enclave, the orchards, the vegetable plots, the various roofs of the houses, even the supposedly secret forest that kept them all safe.

A red flag marked the communal building as my destination. There was no mistake, no way to make this not happen.

I groaned, then shut down the app, removed my glasses, and pocketed my phone. My eyes met Phage's.

"What is it? It's bad, isn't it?" I nodded. "Worse than you thought?" Again, I nodded. "Can you tell me?"

"I... Honestly, I better not. I want to. I really do. But you know the rules. You can't talk about where you're going. Talk of notes is forbidden. I can't risk anything bad happening to you or Jen because I blabbed. But I'm not sure you'll ever forgive me if I don't tell you. Phage, I can't decide what to do."

"Is there a way to help? How can we bypass the rules but not break them?"

"And risk getting us all into more trouble than we're already in? Maybe that's not a good idea. I'm stumped." I rubbed at my stubble, ran my fingers through my hair, anything to distract me from this utter nightmare.

"You could suggest places to go for a trip and I could guess," ventured Phage.

"That's pushing it, and you know it. Phage, please understand that what's on my note is the worst I have ever been given in my entire life. I don't know who the mark is, but this could be the end for me. Truly, this might be it."

"You can beat anyone," she told me firmly, nodding. She squeezed my shoulder and stood close now there was no chance of seeing the location or reading my note.

"I can. But that's not what this is about. I know the place I have to go, but I don't know who I am meant to execute. It could be a number of people. But if it is one person in particular, or one of the others in the group, then I won't be able to do it."

"Why not?"

"Because it would be the ruin of us all. Of me. Of our family. There are some things I will not do, ever. I'd rather this be the end of it all than perform certain acts, kill certain people. Do you understand?"

"Soph, you're scaring me. What are you saying?" Tears were already spilling from my wife's beautiful eyes, running over lips I'd kissed so many times yet could never get enough of.

"I'm saying that please understand if it comes to it, I will lay down my life to save you and Jen from a lifetime of hurt. And don't blame the person who took my life. I did it willingly. I knew what I was doing and they aren't to blame. Understand me, Phage, and remember my words. You mustn't blame them. It isn't their fault. Some things are unavoidable, and neither party is to blame."

"You're really frightening me now. You can't die. You won't. We can't live without you."

"You can, and you will. You know the risks every year, same as I do when you go to fulfill your note. There's always a danger. The main thing is Jen grows up knowing we both loved her and did our best. That's all we can do. So, if this is it for me, don't blame the one who finally put an end to me. I chose. I made the decision, and I let it happen. But, and I know I've said more than I should have, it might not come to that. There are a lot of questions still to be answered, and I don't know who my mark is, so I might have said all this for nothing and scared you unnecessarily. I'm sorry, but there was no other way. I had to warn you. Better said now than when on the road with Jen. She definitely doesn't need to hear any of this. Promise me. You won't say a word to her. If this is it, I don't want her worrying."

"Promise."

"I'm so sorry I told you any of this. But you need to know. I know it's a lot to take in, but I had to explain. Don't think bad of me whatever happens, but I promise you I will try to do the right thing. I promise."

"I believe you. I trust you implicitly. I love you and trust you like nobody else in the whole word. You're our rock, Soph. The foundation of our little family. Please don't leave us." Phage fell into my arms, sprawled across me as I sat, numb with shock, at my kitchen table in my own perfect house in my own perfect world where I had more than I had ever dreamed possible.

"That means so much. More than you will ever know. It will be alright. We'll get through this. We always do. But just in case. Know I did what I thought was honorable. Never blame anyone else. All of us Necros have it so hard. Sometimes, and listen to me, Phage." I lifted her chin gently with my hand so our eyes were locked. "Sometimes the decisions we have to make are impossible. There is no right or wrong, just degrees of misery. I mean this. Don't blame anyone apart from the note senders. It's their twisted games that made us all like this. Nobody else's fault." I smiled at her and she nodded. I did the only thing I could and held my wife close while my daughter banged about upstairs excitedly as she prepared for the road trip from hell.

This might be the last time I did any of this. The final curtain call. Never to return, never to see any of it again once we left in the morning.

My heart sank at the thought. This was different to every other year. Each time I'd left to fulfill a note, I knew I'd return. My faith unshakable. Now that had vanished.

After all, what man with any dignity could slay the mother of his wife, the grandmother of his daughter? Sure, everyone might get the urge to kill their mother-in-law, but no man with any self-respect would ever commit such a heinous act.

If my mark was Pethach, witch bitch extraordinaire, then I would not do it. I'd never be able to look my family in the eye again. It would tear us apart. Maybe not instantly, but slowly, over time, it would break our perfect bubble and destroy us.

If it came to that, I'd sacrifice myself. Not for Peth's sake, but for that of my family.

As we always had, and hopefully always would, we rallied eventually. Phage was all cried out, my tears wouldn't come as I was being strong, at least on the outside.

We got ourselves together, drank another cup of tea, and once again I placated Phage. Maybe I should have remained silent. I didn't know. Was it better to give her some warning that something truly terrible might happen, and our family unit destroyed, or best to keep her in the dark and not mention a word?

This felt right, but I hated having to burden her with this amount of stress. She'd be wondering, trying to figure out what the deal was, yet I knew I couldn't tell her, mustn't even hint at what it might be. If she thought I had to go assassinate her mother, what then? Nobody should have to make such a choice. If I told her, she'd be racked with guilt for the rest of her life knowing she'd chosen. I wouldn't put that on her. Never.

But it might not be Peth. It could be another witch, or a stranger who'd arrive. The truth was I plain didn't know. I wouldn't kill Peth, no way. She was a bitch of the highest order, but I would not do it.

Even if I chose my life over hers, what were the chances of me succeeding? She was so damn powerful and had all her sisters behind her. And yet one of their own had been killed a few years back by that redhead, and Phage had nearly died trying to protect her. They weren't invulnerable, and that rankled Peth no end. These days they were more vigilant, more guarded, and had beefed-up wards in place, but there was always a way.

But I would not seek a way to destroy her, and only play these games so far.

Surely they knew that? The Necrobastards at the heart of this. Sure, my cold heart could do it, but what then? My broken, remaining humanity would be forfeit. I'd become something else. Something base. Evil. I couldn't ever be with my family if I killed one of our own, and I couldn't live with myself if I betrayed a friendship.

But a stranger, or someone not close to us? Yes, I would kill them. And if it came to it and Peth tried to intervene, I'd do what was necessary to stop her, but never go so far as to kill her. I could live with Peth not talking to me ever again, but never go so far as to destroy the love my family felt for me. And the love so deep it made my heart ache that I felt for Phage and Jen.

"I need some fresh air, and I want to spend a little time with the animals. Will you be okay?"

"I'll be fine. Sorry for the outburst. I don't even know what this is about, but I trust you, and know you'll do the right thing, whatever that is. And we will always stand by you."

"I know. See you later, okay? We'll have a nice evening before we set off tomorrow."

I left her alone while I went to clear my head.

Would she still stand by me if it was Peth I killed? Would anyone? What kind of man would put his wife in that position? Not me. Not ever.

Zoo Time

The garden was empty without Wonjin. I didn't like it. I dared not go to the Necropub as the Brewer was still gone, and I liked that even less. Where was he? Was he even still alive?

I headed straight for the zoo. A distraction was what I needed. Something normal, at least for this sorry, heavily burdened Necro. I'd been neglecting everyone and wanted to do the rounds and catch up. If we were going to be gone for a few days—I had to keep that dream alive—then I'd best do it now, just in case anything even crazier happened, which was a distinct possibility.

Staying positive was important. It could be anyone at the witch enclave. It would be a stranger, an intruder, or as simple as me having to make the decision. I had to remind myself Necronotes weren't always a death sentence. Our masters enjoyed playing their games and often it was a test. Will you kill or save? As long as you made the right choice, you were in the clear. As long as you did.

I passed the chickens, although there wasn't much to be said to the girls apart from to congratulate them on their egg-laying skills. But just to stay connected we had a quick gossip about the state of straw, and the exciting news that one of them had grown most of her feathers back now after molting badly.

Chat complete, I headed down to the collection of barns, sheds, and enclosures that constituted the zoo. My sanctuary, and the animals'. I hadn't had the time to hang out with them as much as I'd have liked over the last few years. There was always something to interrupt us. Sure, I still visited and looked after them, but it hadn't felt the same. I decided to spend some quality time with everyone today, because soon enough you could bet that would all change. I also had to ensure everyone was set up properly for a few days without us all. Or a lifetime without me.

I could have asked Job and Shae to feed the animals and let anyone out who needed to be let out, but ever since they'd got all loved up they were a bloody nightmare of smooching and altogether weirdness and, frankly, I couldn't face it at the moment.

I entered the open-ended main barn split into various stalls and rooms where some animals liked to hunker down, while others had free rein and could go out into the paddock if they wished.

The straw-strewn floors were clean and fresh as always, and everyone was happy. This was no prison of a zoo; nobody was here against their will. They could leave any time they chose, but over the years it had become a family of disparate races, breeds, and creatures bonding over a communal trust. Although there was the odd accident, when say a snake ate a rat, or a rat ate a guinea pig, they mostly put aside their differences for the sake of warm beds, plenty of food, and freedom from judgment or persecution out there in the wider world. A world where even Necro animals were punished unjustly, or simply found it hard to settle into a life with others of their kind who lacked the insights and heightened intelligence being Necro afforded. Just like for humans, it was hard, but there were rewards.

"Hey Rupert, how they hanging?" I asked the large billy goat cheerily.

"Same as always," he replied morosely. "Low and full." He shook his head, the spiraling horns as dangerous as Bernard's single rod of power. His long beard shone as he often licked it to keep it clean, just in case any nannies happened to appear.

"Yeah, sorry about that," I told the depressed goat. "I've put the feelers out for a lady friend for you. The moment I hear something, I'll be on it."

"Wish I was," he sighed. "Haven't been on it for decades. I'm bursting here."

Nasty mental images crowded my mind. I grunted, and focused on his stall to distract myself. "Got everything you need, apart from a lady friend?" I pre-empted.

"Suppose. It'd be nice to have a new hairbrush for my beard."

"Okay. Anything else?"

"A mirror?"

"Sure. I'm away for a few days, but then I'll sort you out. See ya." I waved cheerily as I moved to the next stall.

"Frank, my old mate. What's new?"

"Global warming. Nanobots. TikTok. No, wait, that was decades ago. Um, give me a clue. No, don't. Um, jet packs? Are they a thing now?"

"Afraid not. They keep promising, but they never deliver. Bastards."

"Yeah, bloody bastards. Hey, did you see the one about the horse that bit the ear off that lady? It was all over the web. So funny," Frank cackled.

He was a dark horse, literally. Never mind that I could fit him in the palm of my hand. He was a hooligan, loved the macabre, and would smite you as soon as look at you. He always had extra special care and home comforts to keep him on side.

Frank could do you some serious damage if he put his mind to it, so it paid to be extra nice to the little guy. A small horse with the ability to morph short distances was not to be underestimated. Trust me, many a man has had his laughter choked off once he finds Frank in his underwear nibbling on some low hanging fruit that is strictly forbidden.

"You all good? Need anything? I'm away for a few days, so wanted to check. Catch up."

"Nah, I'm good. You got your note, eh?"

"Yes."

"Shame. But hey, look on the bright side. At least you get to have an adventure."

"I could skip it. I'd be happy to."

"What, and just hang around with nothing to do? No crazy antics? You'd be bored shitless. Trust me, I know."

"What do you mean? You're always buggering off for weeks at a time, up to no good." I had no idea where he went or what he did, but I just knew it involved a lot of trouble and probably an awful lot of even more mini-Franks out there somewhere.

"Gotta keep the juices flowing," he said, winking and whinnying.

"Sure." I waved as he just keeled over into his bedding and was snoring before I hit the next stall. Frank did like to sleep a lot when he wasn't telling bad jokes or eating. I think that was about all he did do when at home.

I continued doing the rounds, spending a few minutes with everyone. The number of animals wasn't as high as it had been in previous years, as the last few decades had seen so much upheaval in the world. Not to mention having Jen to focus on. We simply didn't have the time, or energy, to help as many as I would have liked.

But they still found us, or we found them. There were always the lost, the hurt, the mentally damaged to bring into the fold and care for. This was too big a part of my life to contemplate ever giving up. Hopefully, if travel improved, although it wasn't likely, or things out in the world at large merely settled down, I could spend more time traveling to bring home animals I got news of through the Necrovine. Offer them the chance to live out their years free of molestation and knowing they were loved.

After the main barn, there were several smaller buildings that housed animals that for whatever reason preferred to stay in buildings that were secured. Scared hedgehogs, freaked-out monkeys, psychotic sloths, even a clinically depressed pygmy hippo—which came with a whole host of challenges. They all got what they needed. Some lifted my spirits, others made me want to go out and kill the bastards that had inflicted so much pain on them, and several merely depressed the hell out of me because they were just wired that way and would never change.

Stripe, the goblin who preferred to be a badger, was snoring loudly under a bush as I went from one building to another. No point waking him; I'd return soon enough.

Reluctantly, I set off to see Bernard and his family, then thought better of it and skipped the inevitable moaning. I already had a window to board up later, and I knew I'd lose my cool with him. We needed him for the trip, so I'd leave Phage to deal with our unfathomable unicorn later and give him the good news. Instead, I went to tell Tyr the news and to see what Rocky wanted to do.

Tyr and Rocky were, surprisingly, on the ground in the small copse at the base of Sanctuary. The earth was now compacted and hard as concrete thanks to years of being pounded by a growing dragon and his cohort. No vegetation grew, but the trees were hanging on in there, seemingly unperturbed by the ridiculous summers. Although, I was sure it wasn't quite as hot as it had been in recent years. Maybe things were finally changing.

"Hey guys. What you up to?"

"Rocky has new game. We play. Soph want to join in?"

"It's a lot of fun," agreed Rocky.

"What's the game?" I asked, intrigued. Tyr wasn't the kind of creature that was interested in games. He was a serious fellow these days, not like when a wyrmling. I missed those times.

"Tyr morphs and I have to catch the creature he drops when he returns before it hits the ground."

"Is much fun," hissed Tyr. "Tyr burns rabbits and birds or pulls skin off when flying, then drops."

"Oh, right, um, that explains all the bones, I guess. I'll pass. Listen, the whole family has to go on a trip. Hopefully only for a few days, but we need Tyr to come with us. To watch over us all."

Tyr was instantly all ears. He turned his large body and his head snapped forward on thick muscles until his breath was hot on my cheek. He stared at me with intense, unblinking eyes, as he asked, "Jen goes with Soph and Phage? Away from home?"

"Yes, and it's the first time since, er, yesterday."

"Was different," nodded Tyr. "Tyr watched, listened. Soph showed best friend Jen old school. Not good place," he said, his words more snakelike than they'd ever been. If you didn't know him, it would send chills down your spine.

"You stayed after you dropped off my pack?"

"Yes. Tyr guards Jen. And Soph. Both sad. Tyr worried, so watched over you."

"Oh, well, thank you. But this time I would like to request your assistance. Remember Mawr, the man in the woods we visited when you were younger?"

"Tyr remember everything." He studied me, unblinking.

"He wants us to go visit him. Seems like there's a problem. And he asked for you to come, along with Jen and Phage. So, will you catch us up? Meet us there? We're leaving early in the morning."

"Tyr will fly high and watch over family. Keep safe. Mawr nice wizard. But lots of secrets."

"What secrets?"

"Tyr not tell secrets. Tyr not told. But saw. Is not place."

"But if it would help your family, you should say."

"Tyr knows this. Mawr nice man. Helped Tyr and Soph learn about dragons. Has many secrets but only one is important for family. If need to, will tell."

"Okay," I guardedly agreed. "It's good that you can keep a secret. I guess. Right, I just wanted to let you know what was happening."

"Soph?"

"Yes?"

"Tyr knew was going away. Am dragon. Big as the bus now. Very wise. Can see future."

"Yeah, I keep forgetting. But I also came to tell Rocky. We can't take you with us as we'll be on the road for a while, and it might be a problem if anyone sees you. Can you stay here and guard the other animals? Keep them safe?"

Rocky's chest puffed out with pride and he lifted his head high as he said, "It will be an honor. I will make you proud."

"I'm already proud of you. But thank you." With a nod to them both, I left. Time to find somewhere quiet and have a think about all that had happened since yesterday. And decide what to do regarding my note.

I got halfway up the garden when I grumbled, "Fuck that! No more thinking. No more second guessing. What will happen will happen regardless of my moping. Enjoy the day, Soph. Have fun with your family. Tomorrow's another day."

So that's exactly what I did.

Road Trip

"Road Trip!" shouted Jen as she almost fell down the stairs.

I caught a large holdall that came hurtling towards my head, dropped it at my feet, then was assaulted by several pairs of shoes, a bra, a rainbow of t-shirts, a pair of jeans, a stack of books, and other assorted teenage "important" things as they burst from various bags.

Jen thumped down the stairs behind them all, riding the steps on her duvet like a one-woman Winter Olympics wannabe.

"Sorry," she mumbled as her feet crashed into my shins, sending me into the pile I was already currently swamped under.

I fought, and won, my freedom then hauled Jen to her feet and stared at the mess around us. "You can't take most of that," I told her. "We're going to quickly visit an old friend because he needs me, then we'll go visit Grandma. You don't need bedding, or all that make-up, or..." I trailed off as Jen began stuffing everything back into her holdalls. I knew when I was beaten.

"Uh-huh. Yeah. Right."

"You aren't listening to me, are you?"

"You bet. Sounds great. Thanks."

"I know when I'm beaten," I chuckled, then left her to it.

Several hours and many more trips upstairs later, we were finally ready to go. This was not how I was used to going about things. I was methodical, traveled light, always ready well in advance, and I never dicked around at the last minute.

Such were the joys of traveling alone and by bicycle. Simplicity was forced upon you. The most important things were spare inner tubes and tobacco—everything else was secondary. I patted my pocket to ensure my pipe was there. Satisfied, I tapped my foot while I waited for the two angels in my life to get their fucking act together and stop messing about.

Didn't they know I had someone to kill? Didn't they know Mawr said this was relatively urgent? Didn't they know I was stressed to fuck and desperately trying to figure out what the hell to do, and how to accomplish this without my world falling apart entirely?

I needed some answers, but I wouldn't find them for days yet. And what would they be? Surely they could read all that in my sad, wrinkly eyes?

No, they couldn't. Because I always tried to hide my fears from them. To put on a brave, strong face so they'd never doubt I'd be there to protect them. So they could feel safe and secure and not have to worry about me. Especially Jen. Phage could most definitely take care of herself, I knew that, but I still did my utmost to be strong around her. Even though I had often shared my fears and insecurities when alone at night.

But only to a degree. She was, and I had to keep reminding myself of this, so much younger than me it wasn't even funny. A measly fifty-odd years on the planet. Little more than a blink of an eye. And half of that without me. But boy had we packed a lot into the years we'd been together.

"What are you smiling about?" asked Jen as she dragged an oversized pack across the yard.

"Just thinking about your mother," I told her, reaching down and hauling the bag up over my shoulder. I dumped it into the back of the cart with the rest, then looked around nervously. "Where is she?"

"Here I am." Phage appeared looking like a vision on legs. Tight black vest, fitted dark jeans, a lightweight coat slung over her shoulder, her bronzed skin glistening with freshly applied sunscreen. She put a straw hat on at a jaunty angle, adjusted it, then beamed brightly.

"Come on then, what are you waiting for? We have to go."

I said nothing, just bowed my head dutifully and clambered onto the front bench of the cart. Jen hopped into the rear to join Woofer, Phage led Bernard through the gate, closed it behind her, then joined me. She took the reins and we were finally off.

"Is she asleep already?" I whispered as I turned to find Jen curled up on a pile of blankets on top of the packs, snoring like we'd been away for months.

"You tired her out. She's exhausted."

"Fair enough. That just means we can talk about grown-up stuff without her hearing."

"Like what?" piped up our sneaky daughter.

"I thought you were asleep?"

"I was."

"It's the sixth sense all children have," laughed Phage. "If they think there's some juicy gossip, they're suddenly all ears."

"You just go back to sleep. This will take a while."

"How long?"

"That depends on Bernard," I told her.

"I'm tired," our unfathomably anxious unicorn complained.

"We haven't even started yet!"

"What?" asked Phage.

"Sorry, I was talking to Bernard," I told her.

"My legs are sore. What's for lunch? Are we there yet?"

"No, we aren't."

"Aren't what?" asked Phage again.

"What is for lunch?" shouted Jen from the back as we took the turn at the end of our lane and onto the road.

This was going to be a very long trip.

"Can you tell me anything more?" asked Phage kindly once we got going.

"I wish I could. I really do. Okay, I think I can say a few things, but please bear in mind what I said yesterday about my note."

"Of course. Please, Soph, I'm getting very worried."

"Not as worried as I am." I took a deep breath then said, "Okay, after Mawr's, we're heading straight to your mother's. Understand? Mawr's first, then your mother's."

"What? You mean Mawr is on your note? No, don't answer that. I know you can't. But why mother's?"

I held the gaze of my wife, much as I wanted to look away, amazed I could look her in the eye at all. I saw the realization dawn, the horror that passed across her face, the sheer injustice of it all. I nodded my head.

"You mean...? No, surely not?"

"I don't know, and that's the truth. We're going to your mother's. What comes after is anyone's guess. You know how these things work. You get a location, that's all. After that, you're on your own. You decide. It never tells you who, or when, and some places are busier than others. Lots of people. Understand?"

Phage nodded, mute, unable to form words. All she managed was a tiny grunt

"So I will have to see what happens. But as I said yesterday, and I'm choosing my words carefully here, I would never, ever ask you to make a choice. It won't come to that, as I've already made it for us all. I refuse to sour the memory you and Jen have of me. I would never hurt our own family. Never. I won't destroy the life that brought you into this world and let our daughter be possible. Never. Damn, this is hard without breaking the rules. Do you understand me, Phage? Am I making myself perfectly clear so there is no doubt in your mind that I absolutely will not do it if it comes to that?"

"Oh, my sweet darling." The tears gushed like they could drown the world. Phage understood perfectly well what I was saying, so cried for the sheer unfairness of it all.

She tensed, clenched her jaw, then wiped at her red face and told me, "Do what you have to so you can stay with us. There must be a way. Another way. I can't lose you. I won't."

"Phage, I don't know who my mark is, remember that. But I will not take the life of anyone in our family. Ever. That is unforgivable, and the choice isn't yours. It's mine. You can't make that call."

"I think I could. If I had to. How could we lose you? We couldn't. But after? That would be too much. It's beyond barbaric."

"It won't come to that, I'm sure. There are a lot of people in a lot of places, and some might be very bad people. Oh, hell, this is ridiculous. Trying to talk about this without breaking rules is idiotic, but I can't risk it. Do you understand, really, what I'm saying?" I asked again, knowing I had to be sure.

"I do," she said, burying her head into my shoulder. "You know I love you more than anything, don't you?" she whimpered. "That you saved me from that other life, and our world is the only one I care about. That this is what I want more than anything, and if I had to choose, then I would. You know that, right?"

"You don't have to choose. I won't let you. I decide this, Phage. Only me. It's my duty as a father and a husband. Maybe that sounds old-fashioned, but I won't let you carry this burden. If this is our last time together as a family, let's make the most of it and not let this beat us." I turned to look at Jen and Woofer sleeping. "After all, if these are my final days on earth, it's all been worth it. All of it." I smiled at Phage and wrapped my arms around her.

It was a long time before we released each other, and before the tears dried up.

When they did, I found that we'd stopped outside a very familiar place.

"Bernard," I exclaimed, brightening instantly, "you know me so well. Great job!"

"What's the big deal?" asked Phage, smiling as she knew how much I needed this. That it was part of my ritual, same as hers was getting the best Indian food this side of Mumbai.

"You're so funny," I told her, rubbing my hands together.

"What's happening?" asked Jen from the back.

"Are there sausages? Woofer like sausages."

"Really, you should have said," I told him.

"Woofer not say?"

"Only like a hundred times a day," snorted Jen. She yawned and stretched as Woofer leapt up and began hunting for the missing meat-fest.

"I wish I could hear the animals all the time," complained Phage. "It's so frustrating."

"Trust me, you aren't missing much. I can sum it all up in two words." I pointed at Woofer. "Sausages." I pointed at Bernard. "Moaning."

"Sausages! Hooray." Woofer sniffed the cart deck like the demented fool he undoubtedly was. We howled at his antics, and all was right in the world. Especially now we were at Pam's slice of paradise. Better known as Necrosmoke.

"Nice," I sighed.

"So lame," laughed Jen.

I didn't say anything, but I definitely preferred my yearly trip when alone. What kind of man brings his child along for his yearly murder spree?

I knew why, even though until now I hadn't even considered leaving them behind.

Because this was family, and it was Pethach's domain. And frankly, I didn't trust her. I wanted Jen and Phage close, even if that meant walking into the lion's den with them. I could protect them better with me than left at home when I had to go to Witch Bitch Central.

It wasn't just Pethach. I knew she wouldn't harm either of them, but it was the other witches. If things went sour, I didn't know how they'd react or what retribution they would seek. They were not all nice old hippy witches. Many were dark, and fucking dangerous.

But were the witches more dangerous than me?

Guess I'd find out.

"Come on, Dad, what are you doing?"

"Sorry, just thinking. Oh, this is just what I need."

My spirits lifted as I shoved Jen through the door and the annoying bell jangled.

Necroboobs

"Who said boobs? I didn't mention boobs. Why are you all talking about boobs?"

The three women in Necrosmoke all looked at me like I'd gone extra daft. I hadn't. I was merely as daft as usual.

"Is he alright?" Jen asked Phage.

"No, he's a man."

"Got that right," said Pam, beaming from behind the counter. She flicked a plait, leaned forward so her hands pushed up against her considerable chest area, although I hardly noticed, forcing her cleavage almost out the top of the low-cut vest she wore just to annoy all the men and make all the women drool. Or was it the other way around?

"Hello person," I said, walking casually across the room and checking out the ever-changing gear that Pam stocked as she tried to keep up with the latest smoking trends and the constant morphing of the rules regards plastic, batteries, harmful substances, and people's preferences. I didn't envy her.

"What's wrong with Dad? Is he ill?" Jen whispered.

"No more than any other man. This is how they act when they're pretending that they don't like boobs. When you're older, you'll understand."

"Oh, I get it already," said Jen. "The boys at my school are obsessed with any girl once she starts wearing a bra."

"Can't hear you. Can't hear you," I sang. "And fine, we like boobs. But I was only messing about. Just lightening the mood. Hey Pam. How's it going? You still writing your book?"

"Oh, you're writing a book?" asked Jen, intrigued.

"Hey everyone. This is a nice surprise. Jen, how's school? And, er, why aren't you there? And ignore your dad. He thinks he's being funny because I have lovely boobs."

"You do have big ones," admitted Jen.

"And school? What gives?" asked Pam again.

"A funny wizard called Mawr appeared in the kitchen and told us to go see him. And Dad's got his you-know-what. Oh, and yesterday I got into big trouble for beating up a bully, so I got punished. Now I'm here."

"Gosh! Well, sounds like your folks have it under control." Pam raised an eyebrow in query at Phage and I, but we both shook our heads meaning not to pursue it. Pam understood.

"Where's the pipes?" asked Jen as she looked around the room, nonplussed.

"Pam went over to the dark side and stopped selling them. Now it's battery controlled crap. You suck on a box and smoke melons instead," I explained.

"Hey, don't listen to him," laughed Pam. "And it's not batteries these days. They brought out a wind-up range as batteries are like gold now. And we have solar, which charge in fifteen minutes and are guaranteed to last a full day. Pretty neat."

"That's not bad," I agreed. "But my pipe needs no winding and lasts for centuries.

"And it will also kill mere mortals, so there is that," chided Pam.

"Hey, don't shoot the messenger. You're the pusher, selling it to me."

"Not selling, giving," Pam reminded me. "You get it free, remember?"

"How could I forget?" I gave Pam my best wink, then leaned on the counter and asked, "So, how is the book going?"

"Yes, what's it about?" asked Jen as she and Phage came and rested on the counter too. It was getting somewhat crowded, and it felt odd them both being in what I thought of as my world, but it was nice to bring Jen to one of my haunts too.

"Oh, that." Pam waved it away with a hand and laughed lightly. "It's getting there slowly. I'm not even sure exactly what it's about yet. But it keeps me amused. So, what's up? You really heading to meet a mystery wizard? Shouldn't you be off, er..." Pam glanced at Jen then trailed off.

"She knows about notes now, Pam," I told her. "About how we all get them."

"She does?"

"I do. And it's horrible." Jen pulled a yucky face and scowled.

"It sure is, kiddo. Don't ever forget it. But what, you going to help your dad out, are you?" Pam looked at Phage and me for guidance or explanation. Where did we start?

"Don't be silly. I told you, we're going to meet a wizard."

"He's an old friend," I explained. "Said he needed to see us all. Even Woofer. Damn, where is he? I forgot about him."

"Woofer here," he spluttered as he appeared in the middle of the room, a string of sausages hanging from his mouth.

"Where did you get them?" asked Phage.

"Woofer found them." He gobbled several pink meat tubes, eyes darting, concerned Phage might try to pull them from his guts like a magician.

"What did he say?"

"That he found them," Jen told her.

"You did not," scolded Phage. "You stole them. Naughty dog!"

Woofer's ears flattened, his tail thudded morosely, and he hung his head low. He kept eating the sausages though. We watched for the full five seconds it took him to devour the lot, then he licked his lips, smiled sheepishly, and asked, "Woofer not really bad dog?"

"What did he say? Damn, I need to be able to understand them all." Phage was becoming flustered. Woofer's antics since he became Necrowoofer had been stressing her out because there was so much more to talk about, plus he got into a lot more bother.

"He asked if you were going to beat him again with your belt then lock him in a cupboard," I told her as I winked at Jen and she stifled a giggle.

"Oh Woofer, I would never do that." Phage rushed over to him and bent to cradle his neck and stroke his head. Woofer wagged happily, but as Phage stood he morphed and was gone.

"He's been doing that a lot," I told Pam. "Did I tell you about what we did? About the power he now has?"

"You told me. And watch out, Jen, or he'll be showing up in school and getting you into trouble. Speaking of which, shouldn't you be there? What was this about you being naughty and beating up a bully?"

"It's a long story," Jen mumbled.

"It sure is," I agreed. "So, any news? What's been happening? You know all the gossip. Spill it."

Pam smiled as she beckoned us closer, eager as a beaver at a sawmill. "Oh, you aren't going to believe what some of the guys have been telling me."

"Go on." Phage was practically drooling already.

"I hope it's juicy," I said, at this point realizing we really didn't get out that much.

"They're crushing all the cars. All of them." Pam stood back, arms crossed, pleased with herself.

"We know. They did ours," Jen told her.

"Oh." Pam frowned. "Um, everyone has to plant a tree. Look, here's mine." Pam lifted up a sorry specimen from behind the counter.

"We know. We got ours too. You should put that in water until you get home. Plant it today or it might die," I told her.

"Damn, you guys know all the gossip. Okay, they're digging up half of all the roads. Cutting everything down to three lanes at most. Or is it two? You know that already, don't you?" she sighed.

"Sure do," Jen told her. "Anything else?" she asked.

"Aha, this is a really good one. You know we have Dark Wednesday now?"

"I hate it," pouted Jen.

"Me too. But guess what? They're gonna roll out total blackouts for a week at a time. Really cut down on the use. Stop us relying on it so much. I can't blame them really. The cost of electricity is so ridiculous nowadays that I hardly use it anyway."

"That's not fair. Why can't they just let us use it when we want?" Jen stamped her foot and did a proper teenage pout. She was getting very good at it.

"Because it costs a fortune to produce," said Pam. "If we can't drive, we only need it for light and heat, and in the summer nobody needs heating. It doesn't get dark until ten and it's light when we get up, so there's no need for it."

"Apart from dishwashers and washing machines and charging batteries for power tools and for seeing in dark places and cooking and TV and computers and phones." I counted them off on my fingers until I ran out, then used Jen's.

"Yeah, yeah, don't be so bloody backward," said Pam. "We should save energy however we can."

"You were selling a shop load of things that ran off batteries until recently," I reminded her.

"Yes, but only because I could," she said, laughing.

"It really is like the old days now," I told Jen. "Next they'll uninvent bicycles, stop producing make-up, and everyone will have to use bits of old tires for shoes. And," I added ominously, "a man will come around and take your phone off you."

"No way." Jen clutched her jacket tight where she kept her phone hidden. She wasn't a big user, plus she had no credit, but she could use it for emergencies. I got the sneaking suspicion she put credit on it herself now and then when her minuscule data allowance ran out.

"Pam's right though. The cost is ridiculous. It's through the roof and goes up every year. I don't know how people cope."

"Mostly they don't," said Pam. "Most of my customers can hardly afford to run the lights, let alone washing machines. You guys are lucky to have solar and wind."

"Don't I know it? Okay, sort me out, Pam."

She gave me a wink and flung her other plait over her shoulder. "What, here? Now?"

"Watch it, there are young girls present," I warned.

"And his wife," said Phage, not quite smiling, not quite punching Pam in the face.

"Hey, just a joke amongst friends." Pam held both hands up and backed away from the counter a little. She doled out my yearly tobacco allowance, wrapped it nicely, tied it with string, then slid it across the counter.

"Thanks. You're the best."

"Be careful out there," she said, waving us off.

"We will," said Jen as she skipped out the door to the grating sound of an already complaining Bernard.

We headed off at a steady, if slow, pace through the surprising amount of traffic. Bikes of all sorts, horses, buggies, carts, plenty of people on foot, and even a few go-carts and other more unusual homemade contraptions. There wasn't a single car on the roads, not even any buses. It was becoming stranger by the day. Soon this would be all Jen knew, until one day memories of cars and the like would fade completely.

The sun beat down, a cruel mistress as always. We hid under umbrellas while Jen shaded herself in the back under the canopy I'd rigged up.

"Um, where's Woofer?" she called from the rear.

"Damn, he's a bloody nightmare with all this morphing. God knows what he's getting up to."

We each checked behind us, and then I spied Woofer running for his life down the road. A red-faced butcher in his bloodied apron, wielding a cleaver, puffed after him. Woofer had a large chunk of meat in his mouth and he wasn't about to give it up.

When he reached us, he jumped onto my lap and shouted, "Drive! Drive!"

I burst out laughing even though he should have been told off.

"I don't need to understand his words to know he meant he was sorry," said Phage.

"Yeah, that's exactly what he said," I told her, winking at Woofer and rubbing his head as he tore chunks of meat off in my lap.

I'd had worse, and at least I hadn't killed it to get covered in gore.

Road of Destruction

Shrewsbury was quiet, out of town was apocalyptic. Several main arterial routes were undergoing massive transformations, and the one we were on had half of the road closed entirely. There was no denying it any longer. The rumors were definitely true. In what seemed like an utterly pointless move, they were turning a three-laner into a slow single lane in each direction, if there'd been much traffic.

The entire left-hand side was in the process of being ripped up. Huge machines with weird grinding rollers that crushed the surface and the sub-base into small chippings belched black smoke as they rumbled along, spitting out the offending mess to the side of the road, forming steep embankments.

Trucks, machines, and men were everywhere, not that you could see much through the cloud of noxious dust. The roar of the engines made hearing one another impossible, and I had to question the environmental impact of destroying a perfectly good road in the name of eco progression. Surely it was better to leave it as it was and let it slowly break down, rather than cause this kind of mess?

The new transport policies had been in full effect for a while now, and there had been massive backlash. But with our cars being crushed and fuel and energy prices so high they were basically unaffordable, there weren't exactly huge public protests. And besides, the major cities enforced strict, and very draconian, rules about gatherings. Most people were on the side of the government anyway.

Soon these snakes of dead earth that criss-crossed the country, and the globe, would be minimal at best, the country returned to a more pristine state. All that was needed now we'd been thrown right back into the dark ages.

I didn't like it one bit. It smelled of dictatorship, of things having finally gone too far. Where was the choice? The freedom? The fucking hope? Motorways were mostly to be left intact for the supply chain to function, but hundreds of other main roads were to become narrow, tree-lined wildlife havens. But it didn't stop there.

As Bernard took us past the chaos, several miles down the road we were presented with the vision our overlords had for our countryside.

"It's going to be alright, I think," said Phage as we studied the end result.

"They've just covered it all with earth and stuck trees on it," I said, nonplussed.

"And they're sowing wild meadow seed everywhere they're reclaiming. It will make a massive difference to wildlife and the quality of the air. Soon, it'll be beautiful."

"Can we come and see once it's flowering?" asked Jen as she squeezed between us on the bench.

"Sure," said Phage.

"I just don't get it," I told them both. "On the wider scale of things, ripping up the roads and sowing seeds or planting trees will make minimal difference. Why not just use the existing verges for that? It's nonsense."

"Dad, you're so out of touch. It's a waste of land, and land's precious. The roads that basically nobody will use now take up loads of space, and look, they flatten it out, make ponds and pockets of forests, then the steep banks protect it. It'll be amazing. I think it's cool. And," she continued, "they can give a little land back to the farmers. Now we're almost self sufficient in food, we need as much space as possible to grow things. It's already made a difference. People are saying we might have actually made the air and the environment nicer than it was before we began messing it up. Not just here. All over the world!"

"And you don't think it's just a way to control us?" I asked, glancing at Phage to make sure I was within our agreed rules when discussing such sensitive issues. We'd promised never to force our opinions on her malleable mind, to always respect her opinions and let her make her own decisions.

"Nope. I think the world is a better place now and we need to respect it. Treat it kindly and not keep trashing it. That's why they've implemented the two child restriction. I mean, China only let you have one child for decades, so it isn't that strict really. Things had to change as there's hardly any oil left anyway, and there's no way to provide energy for everyone without it ruining the planet."

"Especially now they did away with nuclear."

"And that's an even better thing. No more risk of whole countries being deadly. No more terrorists blowing them up. It's good stuff, Dad. Right Mum?"

"I think so. I don't agree with everything that's happened, and I envy Soph having experienced all that driving and being able to go where he liked for a while, but yes, we had to do something drastic before it was too late."

"Okay, you two eco warriors, how about this then? Why no proper chocolate?" I grinned as they both pulled a sour face. Jen jumped on my back and pretend strangled me as they both laughed.

"That's not fair, Soph. Below the belt," chided Phage. "Get him, Jen. Teach your father a lesson for reminding us how much we miss chocolate."

"Oh, I wish we still had it," sighed Jen as she slid off me and sat back down.

"See, it's not all good."

"Woofer like chocolate?" he asked as he clambered over Jen and lay across all three of us, tail wagging because of the excitement.

"You would love it, but it's dangerous for dogs, and besides, if there was any these two would eat it even before you got a look in. But seriously, this just all seems to have gone a little too far. It's like they don't want anyone doing anything. Going anywhere at all."

"And they don't, Dad, that's the point. They want us to stop ruining things so they've done what they had to so it will happen. It's all about local now. That's what we've always been taught in school. You buy local and help support your community and the local farms. That way, everyone's happy." Jen gazed off into the distance, staring at the green hills of England and the massive swathe of reclaimed road that would become a dense forest in a few decades.

"You're thinking about chocolate, aren't you?" I asked, knowing for a fact Phage would be too.

"How'd you know?"

"Because you're both drooling worse than Woofer with a bowl of sausages," I laughed.

"Woofer have sausages?" He jumped up, vaulted Jen, then figured the sausages were up front so scrambled back over, sat on my lap, and stared into my eyes with longing.

"Not right now. Maybe later?"

"Woofer love sausages."

"Really? I never knew." I winked at Jen and she giggled at our old joke.

Bernard trotted along, silent and steady. I think that was the eeriest thing about the trip so far. His silence. It was more unnerving than any of this.

Maybe I was too cynical. Maybe this was for the best. Repairing past mistakes, putting the world back into a semblance of order. A sensible approach to the wrongs wrought by those who either knew no better, or plain didn't care. On the other hand, maybe I wasn't being cynical enough.

As we slowly ate up the miles, my thoughts turned to more pressing problems. My Necronote and the fact we had to visit Mawr first. And that I'd brought my bloody family with me on this. But what choice did I have? Whatever happened, there was a real risk they would lose either me or Peth in a few days. I couldn't let that happen without them seeing her one last time if it came to that.

A selfish act, or a sensible one? For Necros, things were never that black and white. We survived in the murky in-between where answers were seldom clear and motivations were always convoluted, often utterly deluded.

"Bernard, can we get a move on, please? You're walking like you've got a carrot up your arse."

"Maybe I have," he snapped, then slowed further.

"Have you?" I used all my will power to look anywhere but his looming behind.

"No."

"Please Bernard. Just go a little faster and then we can have a rest in a while," soothed Phage.

"Tell her I'm doing my best," sighed the most annoying thing about this new world I was stuck with.

"He says he's doing his best," I told Phage.

"What's wrong? Are you feeling okay?" Phage called.

"Just not in the mood. It's too hot and too dusty and you're all too heavy. Why should I be treated like this when you lot are just sitting there?"

He had a point, but it was one we'd been over endless times. I explained what he'd said to Phage and she worded it better than I ever could.

"You're part of the family. That means sometimes you have to help out in ways you don't particularly enjoy. But be honest, you like the responsibility. Knowing we're relying on you. Because we are. You're what makes trips like this possible, and we appreciate it. We appreciate you."

"Thank you, Phage. At least someone understands how important I am."

"Hey, I was just about to say the same thing!" I wasn't. "You are a great help, and if you'd stop bloody complaining it would be an even greater help."

"Soph!" Phage gave me a look.

"What?"

"That's not how you do it. Be nice."

"Fine. Bernard, get the fucking carrot out of your arse and hurry up. We need to get to Mawr's."

"Forfeit!" called Jen from the rear, full of glee. I was dreading her actually getting it together and deciding what they'd be.

"Fine, if that's what you want," snapped Bernard.

Phage grabbed hold of me for support as the world turned rainbow and reality as most know it suddenly became much harder to explain. In fact, it got thrown out of the window and replaced with wonky weird.

We went supersonic. I was caught off guard and slid off my seat into the cart with Phage on top of me, while Jen giggled about chocolate and Woofer jabbered about how he could smell sausages, while the world whipped by in a blur.

Before I could right myself, we slammed to an almost dead stop. Phage rolled sideways, I cracked my head on the underside of the bench, and Woofer sat on my heaving chest.

"We're here," said the grumpy unicorn.

"I bet we bloody aren't."

Scrambling to my feet, I hauled up Jen and Phage then stood and smiled as I peered at a dense hedge on a small road in the heart of England.

He was right. We really were at the entrance to Mawr's own private slice of paradise.

"Thank you, I think," I called to Bernard.

"One question," said Bernard as I jumped down and moved to the hedge.

"What's that?"

"How am I supposed to fit through there? I'm not getting all scratched up, and the cart is too big."

"I... Maybe you could... How about if we..."

"Look, the hedge is moving," shouted Jen excitedly. She vaulted off the cart and ran over as the hedge parted like it would do anything rather than have to listen to Bernard moan.

I turned to him and smiled. "There you go, problem solved."

"One of them," he replied, not even cheered a little by the sight of the cool forest that welcomed us.

"Yes, one of them." I glared at the downer of a mode of transport, but I couldn't help feeling buoyed by the thought of seeing Mawr again.

I hoped it wouldn't be the last time.

"Come on everyone, let's get into the shade. The forest is awesome. It's cool, there's a stream, and it's not far to Mawr's from here."

I'd expected some excitement, maybe cheering, but even Woofer had his head down and wouldn't meet my eyes.

"Dad, it looks scary." Jen chewed at her lower lip and played with a strand of hair.

"What? No, honestly it's lovely. Come on." I turned to the large opening and, as my eyes adjusted to the gloomy interior, I understood their reticence.

Where once had been a beautiful, emerald green carpet of moss, it was now brown and dead. The trees were wilting, hardly a leaf in sight, and thus there wasn't the shade I'd expected. Fat streaks of harsh sunlight pierced the dead ground, incinerating life that had grown slowly over centuries.

"Something's very wrong here," I told them. "Don't come in, just wait. I'll check it out. Maybe this is why Mawr called us."

I ducked through the hedge, my hand resting on the elven wood of Bone Slicer's handle. A comforter I'd grown accustomed to and now welcomed. It grounded me, made me feel whole even though I hated the reliance on something so alien.

Inside the woodland I spied the familiar path, but it was weak, faded, like the very essence of the place had been sucked dry. No birds sang, no bees buzzed. The gentle, meandering stream was dark and sluggish, seemingly having lost its way.

But what struck me the most was the sheer wrongness of it all. The energy was messy, haphazard, hints of broken whispers on a cruel breeze that came and went without rhyme or reason. The forest was listless, the trees were sick, the very ground was polluted with the antithesis of an almost holy, spiritual energy that reflected Mawr himself.

This was his secret world, one only those invited could enter. If it was dying, that could only mean one thing.

I hurried back out into what felt like a clean and wholesome world and told the others what I thought. No point hiding my suspicions, as it was better for Jen to be forewarned if things were bad once we reached Mawr.

"We better hurry up, then," Jen said with a nod.

"I'm so proud of you," I told her. "You're so grown up sometimes. Thank you. Phage, you good with this?"

"Of course. He might need us. He called for us, so there's certainly something amiss. Come on, let's hurry."

Woofer was subdued and kept close to me as I entered Mawr's forest once more. He whined quietly and kept his ears and tail low, but although it felt wrong in here it wasn't exactly malevolent. As though the world was fading from glory into accelerated old age.

Bernard came through, huffing and puffing like he was dragging one of the road crushers rather than an empty cart. I was dubious about how we'd make it to Mawr, but the forest still held power, and was still accommodating.

"Watch the path," I whispered to Jen as I put my arm around her.

She glanced at me curiously, then looked where I was pointing. Directly ahead, the twisted path, little wider than a person, began to stretch.

"They're moving!" Jen clapped her hands silently with glee as the trees gently slid aside, allowing the path to expand until it could accommodate the cart and Bernard's fat, possibly carrot-stuffed, arse.

"Whatever's happened here, there's still a lot of Mawr's power in operation," I told her. I turned to Phage and asked, "Can you tell what the problem is? Can you read this? Understand what's wrong?"

"A little," she shrugged. "I can feel his magic. There are a lot of whispers here that have built up over the years, but something definitely isn't right. It's not a sickness as such, more like neglect. No, that's not right either. If he left it alone, it would just return to being a regular forest. It's almost like the the place is sad. Not ill, just unhappy. It's so closely tied up to Mawr, same as the woodland surrounding the witches is, that it reflects his mental state, his focus, his ability to maintain whispers. I think that's it. The forest is depressed. And there's something else. Like it wants to tell us a secret but it can't. All of us. It needs to. But honestly, I'm not the best at this, so I might not be right."

"Then let's go and find out. But I think you're right. The forest is depressed."

"Can you get a sad forest?" asked Jen.

"Everything's connected, my little apple," I told her. "The entire world. Trees and the way they interact with each other and with the ground, with fungi and insects and the weather, is incredible. You should look it up. Trees really do talk to each other in their own way. They communicate via the fungal roots and filaments and warn each other about things. Crazy, but true. And anyway, you don't need the science to know that. You can feel it. A healthy forest is a true wonder. It's a living, breathing organism, and you mother is right. This forest is seriously fed up."

Bernard had already moved ahead, uninterested in taking part in the conversation. Woofer was still quiet, too. They were both clearly sensitive to the needs and wants of this otherworldly environment and chose to act with all due caution.

As Bernard weaved his way around trees and across dirty streams, so the path narrowed after his passing, leaving us walking through a marvel of an ever-changing landscape that still welcomed us, if in a more subdued way than the last time I'd had the pleasure of visiting.

By the time we reached the edge of the trees, all of us were quiet and introspective. Energy was sapped, mental faculties dulled, each step more listless than the last. I would have been worried we'd be trapped in there forever if my mind had been capable of such concerns.

But we made it, and it was with a cheer and a whoop that we stepped from the half-gloom of a dying world into a bright, cheery clearing. Birds still sang, and chickens pecked at the ground. A wizened old wizard waved at us with his gnarly staff clutched tight and held above his shaggy great head.

"At least he's not dead," I noted.

"Dad!"

"What? Just saying. I was worried for a while back there."

"So was I," admitted Phage.

"Me too," said Jen with a cheesy grin.

"Woofer not like sad trees."

"And I don't like the smell in there," added Bernard, never one to miss out on a good moan. He'd been bottling it up for a while, so I was certain there was more to come.

We waved at Mawr, then rushed into the light.

Old Friends

"My dear boy, so good to see you."

"Great to see you, too. You had me scared, getting in touch out of the blue like that. I hope we aren't too late for whatever the problem is?"

"No, of course not. And apologies for the call. But you're here now, and that's so nice." Mawr embraced me warmly and I returned the hug. It was like cuddling a hairy tree. He was all bone and smelly hair. He reeked of tobacco smoke. I liked it.

We broke apart and I stood back and smiled warmly, even though it was clear something was amiss. His lined face was dry and cracked, and his hair was so brittle I feared it could snap off. Even his insanely bushy eyebrows hung limp, and the beard was ghastly.

"Now, who are these two fine ladies you brought with you? I thought you were bringing your wife and daughter, but one seems to be your wife, and the other," he smiled warmly at Jen, "is certainly too old to be your young daughter. So grown up."

"He's funny," giggled Jen. "You're funny," she told him. "And I am Jen, his daughter. And this is Mum."

"Hi," said Phage, smiling but clearly confused by Mawr's appearance and the whole situation.

"Lovely to meet you both properly. Apologies once more for appearing at your home like that. Now, do we hug or do we shake hands?" Mawr kicked at the ground with his head bowed a little, clearly uncomfortable, which was a surprise.

"Hug?" ventured Jen.

"Hug," agreed Phage.

Both moved in for an awkward cuddle. Mawr pulled them both close and sighed happily as they embraced. A little light returned to his face.

"What's with the forest?" I asked as Mawr reluctantly gave them some space to breathe.

"All in good time. Nothing to worry about. Just an old man feeling rather sorry for himself and reminiscing. Were you scared?" he asked Jen.

"No! It was a bit creepy, but I wasn't scared."

"Had Woofer to protect her. Woofer great guard dog. Have sausages?"

"Ah, the infamous Woofer." Mawr bent and ruffled his proud head. "I understand you are no longer an ordinary dog. That you have superpowers?"

Woofer nodded gravely. "Can morph and run real fast and will live forever. Get to see Jen be grown woman and marry Tyr."

"What!?" blurted Jen, face reddening. "I'm not marrying him. Don't be silly."

"What's happening?" asked a frustrated Phage.

"Your delightful dog appears to believe Jen and Tyr are to be married," Mawr told her.

"Oh, that again. No, Woofer, that's just Tyr saying things. They won't be married. Just friends."

"Oh. Okay," he replied happily. "Have sausages?" he asked Mawr again.

"You are a hungry fellow, aren't you? Yes, I have sausages. Plenty, in fact. Shall we all have some later on? Maybe with pots and some vegetables from the garden?"

"Pots?" asked Jen with a frown.

"Potatoes" explained Mawr.

"Woofer not want vegetables."

"You have to eat your greens," I told him.

"Shall I just go and hide myself away?" sighed Bernard. "Maybe I can drag this heavy cart around for eternity while nobody bothers to talk to me or make introductions."

I shook my head, but Mawr smiled at Bernard then beckoned for him to follow with a crook of the finger. Amazingly, Bernard trotted after him, head high and proud. A little way off, Mawr whispered into Bernard's ear then unhitched him from the cart. Bernard whispered to Mawr in return, then headed off towards the stables, seemingly satisfied.

Mawr hurried back, a spring in his step, and asked, "Now, where were we?"

"Get sausages for Woofer?"

"Later, remember?"

"This is beyond frustrating," complained Phage. It was getting harder and harder for her now Jen was older and could converse with the animals too. Her impatience growing year after year.

"Then learn how to listen to him," Mawr told her.

"I've tried. For years when I was younger, but it just never worked. The only time I hear animals is after having the powder."

"Ah, yes, I have heard of the powder you concocted. A risky business, but it certainly worked for Woofer."

"You seem to know a lot about our business," I told him.

"As I told you last time we met, I like to stay informed about people I care for. It is my understanding you've had some rather epic, some might say historic, adventures of late." Mawr's gaze drifted to my side where Bone Slicer was tucked away.

"You could say that," I grumbled. "I'd rather be dozing in my chair, though."

"The same Soph as always! Never happier than when he's grumbling or sleeping." Mawr clutched his belly as he laughed, finding his own joke funnier than it was. At least according to me. I did other things apart from grumble and sleep. I swore a lot.

"He does love to sleep and grumble," snorted Jen as she looked around the grounds of Mawr's home.

"Going to give everyone the tour?" I asked, knowing Mawr would get to the point of our trip in his own sweet time. One thing an old wizard liked to do is draw out the anticipation, milk every event for all it was worth.

"Of course. I'd be delighted. Oh, I can't tell you how happy I am to see you all. What a treat." Mawr offered his hand and Jen took it, then he led the way off to his vegetable plot which, thankfully, was in much better condition than the forest.

When they moved off a little, I told Phage, "He's acting weird. He's too happy to see us. What gives?"

"Maybe he's just lonely. Living out here all alone for so long, it must be hard."

"He likes it. And he has some action when he wants it. The witches love a bit of old wizard sexy times." I gyrated my hips as I ogled my wife.

"Soph!"

"What? It's true. He's had flings and wives over the years. He told me. Even children. But I think the kids were a long time ago now."

"I wonder why he said it was urgent. He's not acting like there's anything particularly wrong."

"Oh, there definitely is." I glanced at the sick woods. "Something is definitely up. If the woods reflect his mood, his mind, then he's either really sick, or depressed as fuck. He'll tell us when he's ready. Let him take his time. He likes to talk."

"I gathered that."

We held hands and went to join the others. I wondered where Tyr was. He'd been unusually quiet, not making a single appearance for the whole trip so far. I'd expected him to be excited to meet Mawr again, but seemingly he had better things to do.

"Dad, look at all the vegetables Mawr's got. We should start growing more. You never grow this much."

"It's certainly impressive," I agreed. "Maybe you could start helping grow things, spread the compost, and weeding, and sowing the seeds, and watering every day, and picking what you grow then washing it, and removing slugs," I told her.

"I didn't mean that! I meant for you and Mum. Be a nice hobby."

"Hey, we grow veg! Just not as much as Mawr," said Phage.

"Besides, I have the animals to look after, and your mother does, too. Plus the gardens, and the house. And you."

"But look at his tomatoes!"

"We'll try harder," I promised. "As long as you help."

"I will."

Mawr beamed with pride at his endeavors, and he certainly did have green fingers. The vegetables brimmed with life and abundance, which made the forest seem doubly sad.

He caught my glance into the gloom and said, "Yes, it's not happy. But I'm sure it will recover now I have visitors. Come, let me show you the outdoor kitchen, and then I can show you my home. Oh, there are fruit trees too, with apricots and peaches and plums and cherries. Come see."

We dutifully wandered around his land, admiring the trees and the naturalized gardens—even the weeds looked great under the dappled light of the large orchard. Jen and Woofer ran around excitedly, seemingly fine after the bumpy trip.

Phage and I mostly tagged along behind, letting them enjoy their time together.

"It's like they've known each other for years," I told her.

"It is. They get along well. And he seems nice. A bit wizardy with the hair and the eyebrows, but I like it. It suits him."

"Yeah, he's a true wizard through and through. Knows a thing or two. I wonder what the deal is with him and Peth. Remember she was asking after him a while back. Saying she knew him, but he'd been missing for years. You'd think she could find him here. He's been here for so long now."

"It's a hidden world, same as Mother's is. If you don't have permission, you can't get in or even find it."

"Not even if you've got her power?"

"Nope. It's obvious Mawr's got plenty of magic at his disposal."

"How can you tell?"

"I just can. Call it witch intuition. Not that I am one," she added hurriedly, but we both knew that wasn't the case. Not really.

Once Mawr had shown Jen just about every nook and cranny of his slice of England, and I'd been tasked by Jen with creating an outdoor kitchen, planting more fruit trees, sowing buckets of seeds, and definitely constructing a large fire pit so she could get a cauldron, Phage finally grabbed Jen. They left us alone while they went to sort out the cart and fuss over Bernard. I didn't doubt he was still acting like the grumpy twat he was.

Mawr and I ducked into the gloomy interior of his small home and sat at the table near the crackling fire that somehow didn't make the room too hot though it certainly made it smoky

"Thank you for coming, old friend," he sighed.

"My pleasure. You okay? What's the panic then? Why did you say we all had to come? And why now of all times? You know I have my note, that I shouldn't be with Jen at a time like this. Although, it's unavoidable this time," I said guardedly.

"Yes, I can sense this is rather closer to home than you'd like."

"It is. But what gives?"

"Apologies for the bad timing, but it's been eating away at me. I needed to deal with this now before I backed out again. Oh, Soph, I don't even know where to start. But please, forgive me. Forgive me for imposing at such a bad time, when I know you have to prepare and be composed, but this simply could not wait. And I, well, I knew it was now or never. That just in case, and I know it won't, anything happened to you, then I would never forgive myself. So please forgive me."

"Forgive you for what? Come on, tell me."

Mawr coughed harshly and twisted his gnarled hands together, then shifted books and various crystals and other wizard paraphernalia around the table. Suddenly, his head snapped up, his pale, powerful blue eyes locked on mine, and he blurted, "Phage is my daughter. Jen is my granddaughter."

"What? Is this a joke? How?"

Mawr raised an eyebrow. "You know how these things work."

"Seriously? You got it on with Peth? That's why she was looking for you the other year?"

"She was? Ah, that explains it. Yes, she finally found me last year."

"You can't be her father. That's nuts. She never knew?"

"No. Surely she would have told you if she did."

"Of course. Sorry, this is just too confusing. Are you going to tell her?"

"I am. That's why I needed to see you. It's made me sick with worry. My magic is weak, my focus gone, my wards close to collapsing. This must be done, and I simply couldn't wait a moment longer. Please forgive me."

"Wow, look at this place," shouted Jen as she barged inside. "It's like a hobbit house. So cool. Is that a real skull? Can I touch it? What's this? Is that a real wand? How do you get it to work?"

"Not a word," warned Mawr as he pointed a crooked finger at me. "Let's eat, then give us time alone. I will tell her today and then you can be on your way. I assume I don't need to ask where you are going?"

"No, you don't."

Mawr studied me for the longest time, then nodded his understanding. "I hope it isn't her. It's doubtful. But just in case, let me warn you. Be careful."

"If it comes to that, I won't do it," I told him.

He smiled sadly, from a place of untold experience and more than his share of grief and loss, then told me, "You are a man of honor. And you know what is right. Be well, Soph, and be safe. This won't be our last meeting. My magic may have faltered, but I still know things. See things. This isn't the end for you, my dear friend."

We glanced up at Phage and Jen back by the door. Phage had her arms on Jen's shoulders to stop her running about and interrupting us, but we both smiled at her and Mawr said, "Now, let me show you all the fun things we have in here, then we can have an early dinner of sausages."

"Sausages!" shouted Woofer as he barreled through the door, ensuring the time for a quiet chat was definitely over.

Secrets

Late lunch, early dinner, whatever it was, was an enjoyable experience. Mawr cooked at his open-air kitchen while Woofer sat drooling, watching his every move. Jen helped out while Phage and I wandered around, hung out with Bernard, and laid the table.

As much as I needed to share the news with Phage, to forewarn her, I knew it would be better coming direct from the man himself. There was no time to think it through though, to get it all straight in my head, as Phage was talkative, excited about meeting Mawr, and distracted by the constant calling of Jen to come look at this cool thing or that awesome thing.

As sausages sizzled, Tyr finally made an appearance. He circled high above, announcing his arrival with a loud screech. After showing off, he settled in the middle of the open clearing, folded his wings, then looked around with his steely gaze.

Jen ran over, calling as she went, then hugged him around the neck as Tyr bristled with love. His tail thumped the grass, vibrating the ground like dwarves were hard at work beneath our feet.

Mawr left his sausages for a moment with strict instructions to Woofer to keep an eye on them but not eat them or he'd be turned into a frog, and we went to greet Tyr.

"He looks so big when you see him away from home," noted Phage.

"That's because he's bloody massive and still only thirteen. He'll double that in the next decade, then slow right down but keep growing for centuries."

"Think Sanctuary will hold his weight?"

"Of course. Job over-engineered it so much it will take five dragons."

As we neared, Tyr turned his head our way and hissed, "Tyr is here."

"Yes, we know," I laughed.

"Hello Tyr. Where have you been?" asked Phage.

"Tyr hunt. And hide from drones. So many now. Make head hurt more than ever. Are new. Dangerous. Got strange things inside."

"Like what?" I asked.

"Not know. But weapons maybe. Feel like weapons."

"That's not good," I said.

"Is bad," he agreed. "Forest sick. Not like Tyr. Hard to find family."

"Yes, sorry about that," Mawr told him. "But it's getting better already. Look."

We turned to the trees and he was right. New life was forming. A green canopy where it had been patchy and limp. Now it shone. Even the ground seemed to sparkle a little.

"How did that happen?" asked Jen.

"Because you are all here to keep a lonely old wizard company," he told her as he patted my smiling daughter's shoulder. "Now, Tyr, how are you? I see you have grown somewhat since our last meeting. When you were here before, you sat on my table. Now you can't fit inside my house. Have you been feeding when you shouldn't be?"

"Tyr had to feed. And protect Soph and Phage. Kill bad men, feed a little. Grow," he admitted.

"Yes, well, I suppose rules are to be broken. Are you behaving otherwise? Keeping your family safe and maintaining your bond?" Mawr inspected Tyr as he spoke, clearly delighted with the way he was shaping up. It was hard not to be impressed by his size and color, and the graceful movements. He was the epitome of a healthy dragon. Not that I had anything to compare it to.

"Tyr always close to Jen. Love her and all family. Can fly to sun, am strong, can hunt on own, even have new home. Is Sanctuary."

"A sanctuary is very important," agreed Mawr.

"What's he saying?" whispered Phage.

"Tell you later," I replied.

"Our neighbor built him a huge place to live. We called it Sanctuary," I explained. "Jen uses it a lot, too. She rides Tyr now, and likes to terrify her parents by acting like a monkey, swinging from the platforms."

"My, that all sounds perfect," beamed Mawr. "Now, my sausages are ready to burn. Excuse me. Oh, Phage, I can show you if it would be acceptable?"

"Show me what?"

"How to communicate with the animals. With all Necro creatures. It's easy."

"I wish it was," she grumbled. "I've tried so many times, but it won't work. It's my blind spot."

"Come, you are a clever, accomplished Necro. You can learn. I will teach you after we eat. Excuse me."

"He's nice, but he won't be able to," Phage told me.

"Don't be so negative. He's wise, and old, and knows a thing or two even Peth doesn't. Give it a chance."

"I will. How great would that be, Tyr?"

"Yes, would like that." He nodded, so she knew he'd replied.

Mawr called to us, so we left Tyr to rest while we went to eat.

"Remember, it's not about expecting to see their lips move or for them to suddenly talk in a posh English accent. It's more subtle than that. And sorry, my dear, if I am telling you things you already know, but this needs to be understood before it can be mastered."

"That's fine. A refresher wouldn't hurt. I just never seemed to click with it before, and god knows, Mother tried. In her own way."

"Then that is excellent news. Unfortunately for you, many Necros with the gift of zoolinguism are born with it. But you can learn. And you will. Talking to an animal is like reading every small expression and sound then letting your Necro mind interpret the results. Even though, and excuse me while I laugh," Mawr broke off to chuckle into his cupped hands, "it really is a telepathic skill when you strip back the layers and get to the heart of the matter. You merely find the elusive connection. That wavelength that all Necro animals, and in fact all creatures, communicate on. You lock it in, so to speak, like you lock onto a target, and once you find that spot, that feeling inside yourself, then the way is open to you. You can talk to them silently, although most talk out loud as they find the sound resonates and you are better understood. Is that all clear?"

"Yes, in a makes-no-sense-but-what-does way. Let's sum this up. You talk to other animals by reading their bodies and focusing on their thoughts, but really it's all telepathic in the end, and sound is merely to make it more likely to be understood properly?"

"I think you've got it!" Mawr slammed his staff into the ground with excitement, while I remained silent and merely sat, watching and smiling. "Although, and sorry for the confusion, many Necro animals do actually speak out loud, too. Take Woofer, and certainly Tyr, for example. They use their mouths as much as their minds."

"They certainly use their mouths a lot. Not sure about their minds," I butted in, unable to help myself.

"Yes, thank you, Soph." Mawr frowned at me so I covered my mouth to signal I'd be quiet. "Tyr has very advanced use of his mouth, same as Woofer, and so do other animals, so they use sound as well as thought. But no matter, this is all just the magic behind what actually happens. You will find that when you communicate, you do so naturally and just like talking to another person, so no need to worry about any of that."

"Good, because it makes no sense." Phage smiled sweetly at Mawr, and you could see his heart melting. He was like a proud father holding his newborn daughter, which in a way he was.

"Now, as I said, the real secret is merely finding that spot inside your head that can understand another Necro. Forget about average animals not connected to the Necroverse like we are. That will come in time, but only if you practice. But this will happen fast. You've experienced it before, I believe, when you have taken the powder?"

"Yes, but it always wears off. And I always see their mouths move."

"What about when you're looking the other way, or they are?" Mawr raised an eyebrow.

"Oh, well... Yes, gosh, I suppose it's just like talking to a person then. I still hear them!"

"Bravo. Now, shall we begin?"

"I thought we had."

"No, we haven't."

"Oh." There was an awkward silence as they stared at each other, then Phage blurted, "Gosh, yes, let's begin. I feel like a young girl again, being taught my lessons by Mother."

"To me, you are a child still. All of you. Even Soph. But no matter, the younger the student, the better they are able to adapt. Now, close your eyes."

Phage closed her eyes. With a look of sheer malevolence, Mawr whipped his staff around and slapped it down hard across Phage's thighs.

"Ow!"

"Silence. Be still, no distractions. Go deep inside, and search for the spot. A tiny ball of understanding curled up tight, ready to unfurl. Go to it and remove the outer shell. Reveal the truth. The heart of the Necromind."

As the lesson continued, so Phage's legs got more sore and my interest waned. I was never one for such teachings, had no stomach or inclination for magic like Mawr or Peth. To them it was life itself. To me, and to some extent Phage, although she was rather adept in many things, it was more a distraction from everyday life we could do without. A reminder of what was wrong with our lives, rather than a celebration of what was good and joyous.

I admitted I was pig-headed about it, and knew Phage enjoyed some aspects of the magic, but she was content with our life so never spent much time practicing, or trying to develop her skills beyond what was needed to remain alive each year.

Give me a knife over a wand any day. A fucking sharp one.

"Woofer move mouth when talking?" He sat in front of me, wagging his tail happily. Oh, to be a dog.

"Um, kind of. A bit. Sometimes. What do you think? Are you moving your lips? Are you talking out loud to me?"

"Woofer not know. Just talk. Not think. Can hear sound, so am talking in proper words?"

"It's not that simple," I tried to explain, finding the whole concept pretty hard to get my head around even now. "Your lips move a bit, sometimes, and you make sounds, and I understand them, but there's more to it than that. It's the connection through the Necroverse."

"Okay. Woofer understand. Will go explain to Phage."

I smiled as I watched him lope through the long grass back to Phage and Mawr. It obviously hadn't entered his head that he couldn't explain it until Phage could hear him. And she wouldn't be able to hear him until his explanation was too late.

"Woofer, thank you!" I heard her shout. Phage bent and hugged him, then jumped up and down and called, "I heard him. I can do it!"

Woofer ran laps of the orchard, barking, just barking, and Phage's arms dropped to her sides in disappointment.

Not wanting to spoil her moment, I ran over and told her, "He's just barking, so don't think it's a lack of understanding. But you heard him earlier?"

"I did. I did! Just like when I take the powder. Oh, Soph, this will be wonderful."

"Don't count on it," I told her. "Woofer does like to talk."

"Woofer very good at talking. Know lots of words. More than ten," he panted.

"Yes, you do," Phage giggled. "But you can't count, and that's okay, as you are so very special in other ways."

"Woofer is special," he agreed, running off, presumably to find Jen and share the news.

"Good job, Mawr. Seems you worked your magic on your daughter."

My heart froze, my hand slapped over my mouth, but it was too late.

Phage's smile slid off her pretty face, leaving puzzlement behind. She searched my eyes for answers, then turned to Mawr and asked, "Daughter? What does he mean?" then immediately turned back to me. "What do you mean, daughter? You knew and never said?"

"I only found out today. He told me earlier, said he would tell you today too. It's why we're here, Phage. Why the forest is sick. He's feeling bad and needed to tell you. Try to make amends."

"Make amends! Are you fucking kidding me?" Phage snapped around to face Mawr and spat, "Make amends? Go on then, make up for me never having a father around. Make up for me having to live with an insane witch and her bunch of even more deranged cronies. Make amends for me never having a childhood, or love, or affection, or cuddles, or bedtime stories. Of being taught how to kill before I even had my first period. Being shown how to stab someone in a hundred different ways before I ever heard a pop song or went on a date or visited a funfair or got to have a sleepover with my friends. Not that I had any. Can you do that? Can you?"

Phage didn't wait for an answer. With her face red and tears built up over a lifetime of loss and resentment slowly falling, she stormed off across the clearing and into the sick woods.

"That did not go well," sighed Mawr.

"What did you expect? You played us all, and I don't know whether to apologize for telling her, or smack you for ever denying her a father. You could have helped. Seen her grow. Been part of it. Experienced the joy of raising your own child to womanhood."

"I couldn't. I wish I'd had the opportunity, but I didn't know until it was far too late. Pethach and I never kept in touch. In fact, I made sure not to as our relationship did not end well. I knew she had a child at some point but, frankly, it never crossed my mind it was mine. Why would it?"

"Because you slept with her? Come on, of course you would have wondered."

"I did," he sighed. "So I asked, and she laughed at me and said no, there had been many others and I was not the father."

"And you couldn't tell the truth? Not with all your magic and whispers and bullshit?"

"I never even tried to look at her like that. I never saw the child at all. This is the first time I've set eyes on my daughter. And my beautiful, adorable grandchild. I made a terrible mess of things, Soph. A terrible mess. I'm not making excuses, but you have to understand, Peth never told me. Not until this year. She tracked me down and told me bluntly about Phage. No apology, just told me."

"But you figured she might be yours, right? I'm getting the sneaking suspicion that me meeting Phage was no accident. That you had a hand in it. Am I correct?"

"I may have planted a seed in your mind. Maybe I reached out into the Necroverse with the best whisper I ever created and had you go there. To meet the woman I suspected might be my daughter. To do what I had been too much of a coward to do."

"What's that?"

"My dear boy, to protect her, of course. To save her from that life and give her all she deserved. You were always like a son to me. Now I have a daughter too. I am so sorry."

"I'm not the one you should be apologizing to, although thanks for telling me the truth."

"It's the least I can do. Now, if you will excuse me." Mawr moved slowly, timidly, across his land and followed Phage into the woods. For once, he actually looked his age. Beyond old. Beyond what was natural. With the weight of the world on his bony shoulders.

Judging by the shouts and screams, it didn't go well at first, but soon it quietened and all I could do was wait.

Wondrous Times

Jen was still off with Tyr when Mawr emerged from the woods an hour later. Phage trailed behind. I had no idea how it had gone, or if we'd ever return here as a family.

Unsure what to do, I waited by a plum tree bursting with sweet fruit, and watched the wasps stealing the irresistible juice.

Mawr, lost in thought and oblivious to his surroundings, stopped and smiled at me when he got close. "It is done," he nodded.

"All good?"

"I think so. It will take some time, as I expected, as I hoped, but I believe I may one day earn the right to be called her father."

"You are my father," Phage assured him as she arrived. "Sorry for running off like that," she told me.

"Are you okay? This is a lot to take in. About the biggest news a person can get."

"I... I think I am," she said, smiling brightly. "Mawr explained it all. How they met, had a... a fling, I guess?" she asked Mawr.

"Yes, a fling. A wild, energetic, maddening fling."

"Too much information," protested Phage, shaking her head and covering her ears.

"Definitely," I agreed.

"Ah, apologies. Yes, of course, you don't want to hear that. Have I done the right thing?" he asked, wringing his hands. "Should I have told you?"

"Yes, over forty years ago! What's done is done. I understand, Mawr, I really do. Mother is a hard woman to love, or even get to know. She's had many children, but there's never been a father for any of us. I have many sisters but don't know them. They all leave her."

"Yes, a complicated woman. But this is a complex world, is it not?"

"Only as complicated as you make it. I wish you'd tried harder. Once you knew she had a child, you should have forced the issue. Come and checked for yourself. You say you asked and she told you I wasn't yours, but you didn't come to see for yourself."

"I know, and I have no excuses. I have reasons, but they are the reasons of a coward. I believed I was doing the right thing. That it was better, easier for me, I suppose, to not know, as there was no way I could ever be a proper part of your life. As you say, you have many siblings, but there was no father to guide you. Peth would never have allowed me to be present."

"But you would have known, and you could have seen me sometimes."

"Yes, you are right. I failed you. I failed myself."

"Mother is a difficult woman, and you probably regretted the whole thing."

"I did not," Mawr said firmly. "I don't regret it at all."

"No?" I asked, shocked.

"No. Peth is a fine, if hard woman. She has a very dark and sad past, which is why she is how she is. I do not regret our time together. Especially now I have you in my life?" he ventured nervously.

"You do."

"Wonderful! That makes me so happy. The forest will be singing by this evening. You have lifted the spirits of this old man to new heights. I am overjoyed. Please forgive me. Understand, I only knew recently for certain when your mother told me. I don't even know why she did. Maybe getting softer, finally."

"She has mellowed a lot lately. She's been spending time with us, trying to relax. We even had a snowball fight, if you can imagine it."

"No, never!" chuckled Mawr. "With Pethach, Queen Witch Bitch?" Mawr's eyes widened in shock and he almost dropped his staff.

"It's okay. We've all called her much worse."

"For sure," I agreed. "Much."

"Then I can be your father? Be a grandfather? Help in any way I can? Be part of your life?"

"One step at a time. But I think so, yes." Phage frowned in concentration for a moment, then seemingly made her mind up and flung herself at an unprepared Mawr. This time he did drop his staff, as they clung to each other for all they were worth.

"Cuddle time!" roared Jen as she dashed across the grass, having arrived without us noticing. She grinned at me, then jumped at her grandfather and mother and hugged them both.

"Ah, what the hell?" I reached out and joined the cuddle huddle.

"Jen, your mother has something to tell you," I told her as I took in the scent of Phage's shampoo, Jen's aroma of sulfur after her time with Tyr, and Mawr's wizard stink.

It smelled like family, with a new, yet very old addition.

"What's that?" she mumbled, her head buried in Mawr's cloak.

"This pongy old wizard is your grandfather. He's my father," Phage told her.

"I knew it! I knew he was. So cool. Can you teach me magic? How do you use your staff? Have you got a spare wand?"

I groaned, Phage groaned louder, Mawr snorted, and Woofer ran circuits around us, barking.

"He's just barking," I told Phage.

"I know."

Night was approaching. That special time when the world becomes hushed, secretive, and still. It was well past Jen's bedtime, but the fire was roaring, the animals were all snoring, and the cocoa, a rare treat indeed, was hot and milky, so nobody wanted to go anywhere.

Bats darted past above our heads, the *click, click, click* of their sonar always a comfort when sitting out under the vast sky.

Smoke from the fire, and the pipes of Mawr and I, kept the bugs away, and although the heat wasn't needed it helped Tyr to sleep well. It also provided a sense of comfort for us insecure humans. A primal thing. Fire meant safety, security, the ability to see danger approach. We sat close together, the sense of family strong.

Jen accepted her new relative without the need for much explanation, just happy to have a cool, gnarly wizard in her life. Hopefully for good.

Mawr just sat there smiling when he wasn't talking. If a man could be happier, I'd never seen or experienced it.

Phage kept glancing at her father, trying to take him in, study the man who was now her blood. I watched Phage carefully, worried this was too much for her, but I had to remind myself she was strong and had coped with much worse. That this wasn't a loss, but a good thing, if rather belated.

I wasn't sure how I felt, as my emotions were conflicted. I loved Mawr, but this was a pretty crappy thing to have done. But life was complex, same as people, and sometimes we fucked up. Mawr fucked up big time, but none of us were perfect. The older you get, the more chances for doing stupid things. It's inevitable.

"Can you do real magic?" asked Jen as she licked her cocoa mustache, eyes dancing with reflected firelight, still on a high from the trip and the revelations. Mawr was the first old wizard she'd met, a *proper* wizard, as she kept calling him, and she had more questions than even he had answers.

"And what constitutes *real* magic?" he asked with an impressive eyebrow wiggle. "Morphing? Riding dragons? Talking to dogs? Changing into animals? Whispers?"

"No, not that. That's just boring regular stuff. I mean real magic. Spells, and bolts of fire from your staff. That kind of thing."

"Don't be silly, Jen," chided Phage.

"Like this, you mean?" Mawr's hand shot forward, staff gripped tight, and he pointed it towards the forest in one fluid motion. White fire shot from the tip in a deathly silent blaze of wondrous glory. The bolt split, then arced between the trees, venturing deeper and deeper, then burst into glorious technicolor, sending multiple bright lights whizzing off in every direction like Guy Fawkes Night.

"Wow! That is so cool. Dad, can you do that?"

"Left my staff at home," I laughed. "And I haven't had enough practice."

"Do it again. Do it again," pleaded Jen as she sat staring at Mawr with adoration and wonder.

"I don't want to scare the birds. But how about this?" Mawr planted his staff in the ground between his feet then mumbled incoherent whispers. As he spoke, miniature dragons of all hues drifted from the flames like ash on the wind, but they had purpose and glided silently over to him.

He said a single word under his breath and they circled his head, spitting tiny flames at each other in mock battle. Jen clapped and laughed while Phage and I gasped. A true feat of magic with no harm behind it, just some fun direct from the Necroverse.

"Can you teach me?" Jen asked eagerly as the dragons silently drifted back into the crackling flames.

"Maybe when you are older, if your parents deem it apt."

"Can I, Mum? Dad?"

"As your grandfather said, when you are older," said Phage as she looked to me and I nodded my approval.

"So cool."

"You called me grandfather," said Mawr quietly as he wiped at his eyes.

"Yes. I did." Phage smiled, then stood and told Jen, "Time for bed. I think you've had enough excitement for one day. We have to get up early tomorrow to go visit your grandmother, so off to bed with you."

"Goodnight, Grandfather. Gosh, that sounds stuffy. What can I call you?"

"Mawr?" he ventured.

"No, a proper name like you're part of the family," insisted Jen. She chewed her lips, then brightened and said, "Boppa. I'm going to call you Boppa."

Before anyone could inquire as to why, she kissed Phage, then me, hugged a teary "Boppa", then dashed off to the hobbit house to flake out on the pile of blankets by the fire.

"She'll be asleep in seconds," I told Phage.

"And she hasn't brushed her teeth or had a wash," she reminded me.

"Once won't hurt."

"Boppa. I like it," sniffled Mawr.

"Admit it, you'd say that if she called you Twisty Fuckhead," I laughed.

"I believe I probably would," he nodded in agreement.

"I like Boppa better," said Phage.

"Yes, so do I," agreed Mawr.

We sat up late into the night, getting to know each other as a family, uncovering the secrets, learning more about Mawr's whispers that sent me to Phage that first time, so I could look after her, get her away from there, and be a family. At least he'd done that right, something to help out his kin.

We learned this and much more that night. Not all good, but not all bad either.

That's the way it should be.

New Additions

The early start was a no-go. Which wasn't good for my nerves or my bowels. I loved my family, but I hated not being in complete control at a time like this.

Making my own decisions, moving when I wanted, doing what I wanted, swearing when I wanted, was what I needed when on Necronote time.

Hanging around for children, wives, and hosts to emerge from their slumbers and get their fucking act together was exactly the opposite of that. After mooching about and enjoying the cool dawn air, I got my frustration in check, realized I still had days and days left before my deadline, and decided to chill the fuck out and enjoy what might be the last few precious hours with my family.

Please don't let it be so. But please don't make me destroy this family either, were the thoughts that snapped like angry dragons at my resolve and deadly intent.

Mind made up, I relaxed. No point rushing this, as what was I going to do once we arrived anyway? This would play out however it was meant to, but it was clear I wasn't going to merely walk into Peth's domain and find some brooding stranger there who I had to eradicate. That would be too bloody easy. No, this would be a total stressor, and until then I should enjoy the company of my family and friends. Especially now we had a new addition.

Part of me wanted to be furious with Mawr for keeping such a secret, but I wasn't. Being of a certain age brought a deeper insight into the complexity of life and family, and I was a newborn in comparison to the old wizard.

He did what he thought was right, but he'd also been scared. Maybe terrified to get involved, fearing loss or rejection. Or maybe he was just too set in his ways to force the issue with Peth and demand the truth. After all, raising a child is no easy feat, and he'd done it more than enough times already.

He'd accepted Peth's denial because it suited him for whatever reason, and he was right that even if he'd pushed her and got the truth when Phage was young, his involvement would have been minimal and infrequent. You did not screw with Peth and her way of doing things.

It rankled that I'd been manipulated into meeting my love, though. But only superficially. He had been looking out for her, just in case she was his own flesh and blood. And I had got her away from there, kept her safe, tried my best to bring joy into her heart and give her all the love I had to give.

That had been a true act of kindness and affection in its own right, so I simply could not hold a grudge against Mawr. Especially after all he'd done for me when I was a reckless young man.

He'd saved me, and I'd always owe him for that.

And besides, I told myself, having him as a grandparent would be great. I liked him. He held a vast amount of information in that wrinkly head of his, and it would even out things for Jen having a fun, more open grandfather as opposed to a very closed, uptight, serious grandmother.

If she lived.

"Play ball with Woofer?" asked the wagging Lab sat in front of me, ever hopeful.

"Hey buddy. So you're finally awake? I could play ball. But listen, you have to let the ball go so I can throw it, okay?"

"Okay," he agreed eagerly.

"Right, um, so where's the ball?"

Woofer frowned in confusion, then opened his mouth wide and stared at the ground, clearly expecting it to fall from his mouth. "Not here?" he inquired, puzzled.

"No, it isn't," I laughed, my mood already lifted. "Come on, let's go find it. It must be here somewhere."

We set off around the grounds, searching for his elusive ball. It was nice to stretch my legs and spend some time with him, and the morning was truly joyous. Birds sang, bees buzzed, already busy collecting pollen and nectar, and there was even a slight morning dew which was rarer than gold these days.

"Found it!" I called in triumph and nabbed the orange ball before Woofer could get it. He bounded over, excitement building, and I threw it across the clearing. He shot after it, joyous in the hunt, as happy as any animal had ever been. Content to be lost in the moment and focused on what made him happy.

I smiled as he snatched up the ball with expert timing on the rebound and turned sharply to race back with his prize.

"Good job. Now, listen carefully," I told him seriously. Woofer's ears pricked to attention and he stood stiff, ready for my wise words. "You must let go of the ball. I know it's difficult, as you love it, but you love chasing it more, right?" Woofer nodded, keen. "Okay, so here we go." I took a deep breath and commanded, "Drop the ball!" in my best dog trainer voice.

Woofer paused, thought about it, then his tail wagged manically as he ran around me, grunting and shoving the ball at my legs, smearing me with dirt and having the best time ever.

"What are we going to do with you, Woofer?" I asked, happy to know some things would probably never change.

And then, miracle of miracles, Woofer dropped the ball, stepped back several paces, and eyed it with incredible focus.

"Okay, I'm going to reach down and pick it up now. Hold steady, you can do it. Congratulations for making it this far." Knowing what would happen, I nevertheless bent to retrieve the ball, waiting for him to snatch it away.

My fingers touched the hard plastic. I cupped it in my hand, then lifted it aloft in astonished triumph.

"I got it! I actually got it!"

"Throw. Throw," he pleaded, close to having an utter meltdown, so deep was his excitement.

I threw the ball back into the orchard and he tore after it once more, again catching it on the rebound. He was back in a flash, panting and happy, and before I even asked he dropped it, backed away, and eyed it intently.

I bent again and grabbed it quick. Woofer remained still, eyes on the ball. Another throw, and he sprinted away yet again.

Moments later he returned, and the same thing was repeated.

Over, and over, and over we played our game. Woofer was unstoppable. Having finally, after all these years, got the whole point of fetch and release, he appeared to have become utterly consumed by the repetitive act.

He ran, he caught, he fetched, he dropped, he waited. Then he ran again.

We both became lost to our game. There was nothing else. Just a man and his dog having fun in the morning, doing what dogs and people did.

"Are you alright?" asked Phage, appearing beside me without warning.

"Damn, where'd you come from?" I asked, wiping the sweat from my eyes with my sleeve.

Phage frowned. "I just walked across the clearing. But I've been watching you guys play for at least half an hour. How long have you been out here?"

"Depends what time it is. I didn't notice, though." I bent and picked up the ball, then threw it for Woofer again. He tore off, oblivious to Phage.

"It's mid-morning." Phage smiled, a puzzled look on her face. "Are you okay?"

"Yes, I'm great, thanks. Did you see? Woofer finally learned how to play fetch properly. He's so crazy." I grinned at Phage then moved to hug her, but Woofer barked and nudged the ball forward with his nose. "One minute." I threw the ball then reached for Phage.

Woofer barked again.

I threw the ball.

"Soph, I think you need to stop. You're soaked in sweat, it's horrendously hot out here, and Woofer looks like he might have a heart attack. You too. Have you got sunscreen on?"

"No, I forgot. I didn't realize we'd been playing for so long. But, ugh, my arm is very tired and Woofer does look exhausted. So, how did you sleep?"

Woofer barked again.

"Last throw, so make the most of it," I warned him.

"I slept like a log. Amazingly. Jen's still out cold. And I don't know where Mawr is."

Woofer returned and dumped the ball, but I wagged a finger at him. He barked once, then staggered off to the water bowl Mawr had put out for him.

"He's probably gone to inspect the forest. I can't believe how different it is already."

We both studied the trees; things had moved on apace since yesterday. The healing process had accelerated, and I didn't doubt that in a day or two it would be healthier than it had ever been.

"You think this is all down to him telling me he's my father?"

"I'm sure of it. How are you about this? Yesterday was a lot to take in. This going to work?"

Phage beamed. "I think it is. I've been mulling it over this morning, just lying there, wondering, trying to put it all into place, and yes, I believe this will work."

"He's a good guy. One of the best. I know he screwed this up, but maybe this has worked out for the best."

"I'm not so sure about that. But you might be right. Once again, my bitch of a mother has ruined things. What is wrong with her? Why does she act this way?"

"Mawr said a little about it. That her past is complicated and it's the way she was brought up," I said.

"But that's not an excuse. I was brought up by her, and look at me."

"I know, you broke the mold. Look, I don't have the answers, don't pretend to know what's for the best, but what if you had known he was your father from being a baby? What then? He wouldn't live with you, you'd hardly see him. Would that be better or worse?"

"Soph, it would have been better. I could have visited, stayed here sometimes. Been a part of his life, and him mine."

"And what would life at home have been like? Knowing Peth kept him away?"

"Worse," she admitted.

"It's complicated, right? And these truly old Necros, they have a different perspective. They see things so differently. It's hard to put yourself in their shoes and know what you'd do."

"Even for you?"

"Yes. You know I've had other children, and you know about Adina. She's my daughter, Phage. A daughter I'd believed was lost to me. Maybe even dead. When I saw her again, knew she was alive, it was beyond hard. But I'm not part of her life, and she isn't part of mine. Does that make me a bad person?"

"That isn't the same thing. She was taken from you. She's grown up now. She never grew up with you."

"I'm not making excuses for him, but isn't that similar to Mawr's situation? He was denied his child, just like me. But unlike me, he's trying to connect now, be part of your life. I'm not doing that with Adina. And why? Because that time is past. It would hurt us both too much, and it's too much to ask of either of us. It pains me so much that I lost her, but now it's too late."

"Soph, I'm so sorry. I know this has been hard for you. That you dwell on the past so much and miss her and your boy so badly. It kills me to know you lost so much."

"And I never tried to find her, Phage. I let her mother and her go and never tried to get them back. Not really. Not hard enough."

"You tried, but you couldn't. I understand."

"I'm sorry, but you don't. You can't. This is all so hard to explain, and it's so complex, but we have it so lucky. We are a family, together, and would never dream of taking our girl away from the other. For Necros like Peth and Mawr, things are undeniably more complicated. They come from such different times, where life was brutal and losing children was expected. The norm. They have a different outlook, and they grew up in ways we can't even imagine. I mean, Jen, and even you, can't really imagine how it was for me before the digital age. The world was so different. And even I can't imagine the life Peth had."

"And all of that is why I have decided to let him in, be part of our family." Phage smiled warmly, clearly delighted now she'd had time to think of it, yet still with doubts, as should be expected. "I like him. I forgive him. I want him to be my father. If Mother doesn't like it, then she can go to hell."

"Good. That's good. I agree. I think you made the right choice, but I'll stand by you whatever you decide. Jen loves him already. Especially as he's a *proper* wizard."

"You have your own gifts," she consoled, patting me on the head like a good boy and grinning devilishly.

"Why, thank you. But seriously, I understand how monumental this is. I mean, Mawr is your father. It's unbelievable. He got us together. He wants to be part of our lives. It's late for it to happen, but it is a good thing."

"I know. I'm pleased, truly, but it doesn't seem real yet. Like a dream. There's too much to think about. Too much to go over. I don't know if I should be hitting him or hugging him."

"You'll figure it out. For now, just be glad that you accept him as your dad. The rest will come with time. You can't be expected to be totally happy about it. Just bear in mind, and I hate that I'm saying this, that your mother had her reasons. That she did what she thought was best. She's so old, Phage. We have to make allowances."

"Hmm, maybe. But she's done so much wrong that it isn't easy. And now we have to go there. And you have your note." She left it hanging, knowing we were skirting danger.

"Yes, we do. But Jen will always have her grandmother if I have anything to do with it. We'll find a way."

"I want her to have her father, too. More than anything. You hear me? More than anything."

"I hear you. Come on, let's go wake sleeping beauty. And I'm sure Bernard needs a good moan, so we better wake him up so he can get started. If we leave it too late, he'll be playing catch-up all day and we won't get a minute's peace. You just wait." I rubbed my hands together with glee. "You're going to hate that you understand him now. He'll drive you mad in an hour."

"Don't be silly. I still can't believe I can hear them now. It's so nice. And Mawr did that for me."

"With a little help from Woofer," I reminded her.

"Yes, Woofer helped a lot. Where is he?"

We looked towards the house. He was keeled over, legs twitching as he chased balls in his sleep.

"I think he might have overdone it," I noted.

"You too. Go get a shower. You stink."

"Yes ma'am."

"Come on, we really do have to go. At this rate, it'll be tomorrow before we get going. Move it, slow coach," I told Jen.

"Aw, do we have to? I want to stay with Boppa."

"Why Boppa?" I asked, intrigued.

"Dunno," shrugged Jen. "Just sounded right. "All cuddly and like a grandpa, but different somehow."

"I have never once been called cuddly in all my years," said Mawr, face serious. Jen blanched, but then he smiled and held his arms wide.

She dashed over and hugged him tight. He enveloped her in his large wizard garb, staff still clutched tightly. Such a strange sight, but a welcome one.

"Miss you already, Boppa," said Jen as she battled the tangle of smoke-infused robes.

"And I miss you too. All of you. Phage, it has been a pleasure to meet you. What a fine woman you are, and I am immensely proud of all you have accomplished. Please don't think too badly of me, and please let me know the moment you are home and safe. I have always worried, but now I will worry even more."

"We will. And it truly was lovely to meet you, Father." Phage smiled awkwardly, the words clearly strange on her tongue.

"Oh, that makes my heart sing. You give me so much. Have blessed me with your kindness. Please do forgive this old man his terrible sins."

"I told you, I already have. I just need a little time to think this through, but it has been great. And Jen loves her Boppa, right?"

"Sure do! Hey Woofer, come on, sleepy." Woofer's ears twitched, and he reluctantly roused himself from his slumber and came over to say goodbye.

"Nice sausages," he said by way of thanks.

"Glad you liked them," said Mawr. "And keep this between us," he whispered, "but I snuck a nice large pack of them in with your provisions."

"Woofer love Boppa." He licked Mawr's hand and wagged happily.

"See you soon," I said, then grabbed his shoulders and stared into his eyes. "Thanks for everything. I mean that."

Mawr clasped my forearms and nodded. "No, thank you. Be safe. Do what you must."

"I will."

"Safe travels, Bernard," Mawr told him.

"Thank you. I'll be fine. I always am."

"Then that's a good thing, is it not?" he asked, eyebrows raised.

"Suppose," grumbled Bernard.

I shook my head at the grumpy unicorn, then we piled into the cart.

"Oh, one more thing," called Mawr. "Phage, a moment?"

Phage rejoined Mawr and I watched as he spoke a few words then she pulled the matchbox containing Malka from her shirt pocket. She slid it open and Mawr peered inside, smiled, then nodded to Phage. They exchanged a few more words then Phage got back into the cart.

"Everything okay?" I asked.

"Yes, he just wanted to have a look at her." Phage shrugged.

"Wizards!"

"Yep."

"What were you doing?" asked our nosy daughter.

"Just saying goodbye. Right, off we go, Bernard."

With plenty of waves and shouts of farewell, we were sucked in by the happy trees and heading in the direction Mawr instructed.

Soon the forest wrapped us in its welcome embrace, back to being a place of joy and growth, of contentment and satisfaction.

Mawr was happy.

The Stories We Tell

The journey continued in a frustrating manner. Bernard was still miserable, the roads were crap, and often congested with carts and a plethora of unstable contraptions, and I couldn't get my brain to switch off.

I hated dragging my family into this, but I'd hate myself more if something happened and they were stuck at home without saying goodbye to either me or Peth.

Trying to appear in control, calm and confident, was difficult when the same thoughts swirled in my head like an endless whirlpool. My usual sense of purpose and utter confidence in my abilities was waning by the minute, replaced with an ennui, an almost pathological desire to just give it all up and let this cruelty be done with. I wouldn't, of course, but it was only Jen and Phage that kept me going.

Without them, I don't know what I'd do, but bringing them was still a mistake as much as the right thing. It was the not knowing that was getting to me. Not knowing who the mark was, when I would find out, and if my most beautiful women would be safe when the shit inevitably hit the fan. After everything I'd learned over the centuries, I was at an utter loss.

The heat, the dust, the bugs, and the humidity were not helping my mood, but I sucked it up, remained calm on the outside, and reminded myself that whatever I was feeling, it wasn't their fault.

Drones watched our every move, spies that were out in record numbers to ensure the populace were behaving. Tyr was right, they looked different. Even the matt-black casing was menacing, and there appeared to be small munitions chambers and muzzles spaced at regular intervals around the middle. It was impossible to get a close inspection, but they certainly gave off a fascist vibe.

Big Brother was most definitely watching, and it left people on the road uneasy. Everyone we met had something to say about the state of the roads, the insanity of crushing cars, the bloody cheek of being forced to plant a tree, and the endless list of tribulations the country, and the world, was currently experiencing.

Nobody was coping. Heating fuel costs and rationing meant most people couldn't have hot water on a regular basis, electricity prices were crippling everyone, even though we'd grown accustomed to using next to nothing now. The drones buzzing about, watching us, set everyone's jaws to grinding—every conversation was interrupted as people looked to the sky and scowled. The mood was dark, the sun harsh. Tempers were fraying.

People were hungry, dissatisfied, and the older the man or woman, the more pissed off they were. It was the loss of what they'd known, what they'd expected to always have. Now everyone was fighting just to keep a roof over their heads and their children fed and clothed.

Scowling at a particularly insistent drone, I was jolted when Bernard came to a sighing halt. He had little choice in the matter. The Shire horse confronting us snorted, then neighed as it shook out its long, thick mane. The impressive creature lowered his head and moved forward a few steps, pulling the cart where a man lay sleeping with ease. Nonplussed, I watched with interest.

Once they were nose and nose, the Shire horse towering over Bernard who merely stared vacantly, doing nothing, the larger creature snorted loudly. Bernard jumped back a step at the sudden gust.

"As jittery as ever, I see," grinned the horse.

"I'm not jittery. I'm just cautious," Bernard told the stranger.

"Still getting that daft horn stuck?" asked the Shire.

"Daft? What's daft about it? I'm a unicorn. We have horns. You're just jealous."

I smiled at a confused Phage, genuinely pleased to have a distraction, then jumped down and reached out my hand for her. She took it with an uncertain smile, then joined me beside the two very different animals.

Jen was comatose in the cart, so I figured it was best to leave her to rest. With her body going through so many changes, she slept so much these days it was amazing she got anything done.

"Aren't you going to introduce us to your friend?" I asked Bernard, giving a nod to the big fella.

"He's not my friend. I don't know who he is. All I know is he's in my way." Bernard tried to sound tough, but he merely sounded petulant.

"Bernard, my buddy, don't tell me you've forgotten old Samuel? Really? After all we've been through?"

Bernard was confused, that was clear, but he lifted his head proudly, almost impaled Samuel, and told him, "We've never met. I'd remember. Although, if it was a very long time ago, it might have slipped my mind."

"Always the joker. Okay, have it your way. But you can't seriously tell me you don't recall the time we made that trip all the way over to Sussex and you got your horn stuck right up in that wall and there were those soldiers and wild men on either side itching to get busy killing each other. So much fun. You nearly killed their king, remember? I yanked you out, saved you. You must remember that?" The horse paused, deep in thought, then grinned widely and added, "Okay, I bit your arse and you jumped back, and then you turned around and there was the king. Moments later, he had an arrow through the eye and that was that. Bit of a letdown, if I'm honest."

"Is he talking abut the Battle of Hastings?" I asked Phage.

"I think so. Ssh, I want to listen."

"It might ring a bell. Vaguely. Was that you? What was the name again?"

"Samuel. Oh boy, you are such a kidder. So, what's new? What you been up to lately?"

"Lately?" I asked. "That was over a thousand years ago."

"I know. Okay, I don't. Never really keep track of time. That's for you humans. But yes, it was a while ago. Who are you?" asked Samuel, standing up straight and lifting his head so he loomed over me.

"I'm Soph. This is Phage. We're with Bernard. Or he's with us."

"They're with me," moaned Bernard. "Make me trudge around the country pulling a cart. It's demeaning."

"What's wrong with you?" boomed Samuel. "I love pulling carts. And ploughs. All that good stuff. Keeps you fit. You need the exercise, Bernard old mate. Looking a bit loose around the waistline." Samuel indicated Bernard's tummy with his eyes and shook his head. "Need to get some good loads in there. Start pulling it around the fields. That'll sort you out."

"I have no idea what you're talking about," replied an indignant Bernard. "I'm the same size I was all those years ago. Fit as ever."

"Suit yourself. So, what's new?"

"Um, not much. Just the usual."

"In all this time?" Samuel lowered his head again and asked, "You've forgotten, haven't you?"

"No. I just can't remember."

"I love this guy." Samuel winked at us; Phage tittered like a schoolgirl.

"Bernard has a family now. A lovely mate, and a young foal too. She's a real warrior," I told Samuel.

"Good for you! Still got it in you then? Nice job. And what else? Any cool battles?"

"No. Just doing my work, dragging the cart."

"Bernard, we have been on countless adventures," admonished Phage. "We've been all over the country. Fighting wizards, destroying witches, battling all kinds of strange things."

"Have we? Oh, that's nice." He turned his attention back to Samuel and said, "Guess I've done a few things."

"Yeah, me too. This one's a bit of a dimwit and he won't be around for long, but I've got my eyes on this up-and-coming Necro who has these amazing abilities. Once he's more mature, I'll be off to go introduce myself and live with him. He doesn't know it yet, but it'll happen. Well, anyway, great seeing you again. Maybe we'll meet up again in another thousand years?" I nodded. "See you around. Nice to meet you both."

Samuel snorted, then skirted around us and headed off with the man still dozing fitfully in the cart.

Phage and I stared at Bernard, waiting.

"What?"

"Don't you have anything to say?" asked Phage. "That nice friend of yours came to say hello, and it turns out you had all kinds of adventures with him."

"He was making it up," grumbled Bernard, then he looked away from us and began to move.

Phage and I exchanged a glance, then jumped back into the cart and continued down the narrow road where piles of lifted Tarmac and sub base grew more frequent, like miniature mountains, testament to times past.

"Do you think we should pull over?" I asked Phage.

"Let Bernard have a rest?"

"Yes. That was weird, wasn't it? It isn't just me?"

"No, definitely weird. He acted very strange. Do you think he's alright?"

"I'm not sure. It's hard to tell. Sometimes he's just moody."

Phage cupped her hands around her mouth and whispered so Bernard couldn't hear. "He's always a sweetie when we're alone. Hardly even grumbles. I think he's sad. Maybe even depressed. Or that made him realize things."

"Like what?" I glanced up to see if Bernard was listening, but his head was down and he didn't seem to be taking any notice of us.

"Quite how long he's been alive. That he's forgotten so much of it. Forgotten his own life."

"I had a conversation with him about that a while back. He didn't seem bothered. Explained it as animals being different to humans. That someone his age had to forget things as there isn't room in the head for all those memories. Even your mother is the same. It makes sense."

"Yes, I guess. But still, that wasn't normal."

"Nothing's normal when it comes to Bernard," I told her with a wink.

"I heard that," sulked Bernard.

"Of course you did," I sighed. "How about a rest? You fancy pulling up somewhere and taking a breather, Bernard?"

"I suppose so," he said glumly.

"Okay, you pick the spot. Just tell us when you want to stretch your legs."

"I don't want them any longer. They're just the right size."

"No, I meant... Ah, forget it!" I rolled my eyes at Phage. She stifled a giggle and put her arm around me. She was such a strong woman. After the revelations from Mawr, she was holding up surprisingly well.

It was the anger. That's what was fueling her. That, or she finally had some sense of completeness. That she finally knew who she was. But there would always be vitriol and resentment towards her mother. Peth had done too much over the years for it to ever be any different.

We sat in companionable silence while Bernard trudged along, seemingly lost to his own thoughts. Soon, we were off what remained of the main road and onto smaller, less well-traveled routes that would soon form the backbone of the country once more.

Bernard, miraculously, seemed to remember the way, and it wasn't very long before he took the turn off into what appeared to outsiders to be nothing but dense undergrowth.

This was, just like Mawr's private paradise, a closed route into another world. Nobody without permission could enter, certainly none would ever leave. Special invite only.

Once we were inside this private forest and traveling the narrow, purposely convoluted and twisting dirt track, the atmosphere changed. It wasn't that it was dark and menacing, merely that it was different. There was a weight to the air, even though there was a lightness too.

A promise of magic.

A foreboding of magic.

Whispers of death to trespassers.

Guarantees of safe passage to friends.

Heavy with the whispers of countless generations. Witches down the ages who had added their own words to the spells and wards that kept their slice of England hidden from the world.

No drones or cameras were present here. It had been overlooked by the world, and the witches wanted it that way. Even Necrodrones couldn't enter. This was their domain, and theirs only. Private, secretive, and deadly to all but those Peth trusted implicitly, or who she deigned to invite for her own selfish needs and wants.

I had no doubts about Pethach. She was mellowing of late, had begun to show interest in Jen, and was becoming closer to Phage, but she was, first and foremost, a witch. Not a mother. Not a grandmother. Not even a sister or a woman.

She was a witch in her heart.

Magic came before all else.

How this must hurt Phage. I knew it did. Although she was resigned to her mother's wildness, her dabbling in the darkness of the Necroverse, and her aloofness, it would always cut deep and leave her feeling like an outsider here.

Maybe that was what Peth wanted? To remain a thing apart, so she never had to get too close and risk getting hurt? Or was I giving her the benefit of the doubt, and really she was nothing but a cold, hard-hearted bitch full of self-interest and didn't give a shit?

Time would tell. Time would reveal all. It always did.

Lost in thought, it took a shake of my shoulder to rouse me from my reverie.

"Bernard's stopped," Phage told me. "You were miles away.

"Sorry. Just thinking about you." I pecked Phage on the cheek.

She smiled and asked, "Good things?"

"Always. When it comes to you and Jen, my thoughts are always good thoughts."

"Gosh, what did I do to deserve you?"

"Just lucky, I guess."

Happy to be together, we hopped down and began to sort out the grumpy unicorn.

"How can she still be sleeping?" I wondered. "We set up camp hours ago, we got firewood, lit the fire, got Bernard comfortable, played with Woofer, and even cooked sausages to tempt her, but she's still fast asleep."

"She's a growing girl, and you know what teenagers are like. But it's probably the stress of it all. Too much excitement. There was that, er, incident at home, and then Mawr. That's a lot for a young girl to handle. And don't look so surprised," Phage said, smiling, "she just takes after you."

"I do like to sleep," I admitted.

"It's what you do best," agreed Phage.

I bit the end off a rather charred sausage whilst avoiding looking at Woofer, and tried not to let the woods get to me. I'd had enough magic to last me a lifetime with Mawr; this I could do without.

"Ugh, this place gives me the creeps."

"I think it's nice." Phage cuddled up close; I shook my head in wonder.

"You are one amazing lady, you know that?"

"I know. I wish we could just stay here and not go to Mother's. Why must it always be like this?"

"Can you just trust me on this, please?"

"I do. With all my heart."

There was so much we could have said, but we didn't. It put a strain on things, as we weren't ones to keep secrets, but the risk was too great.

"Let's try to get Bernard to talk to us," I said, changing the subject before our thoughts turned too dark.

"Yes, good idea. Poor thing's so unhappy."

"Don't let him fool you. He does this sometimes just to get attention. But I think you're right, he's not himself after meeting Samuel. Not that he was happy before. I wonder what else those guys got up to. Bet they did all kinds of crazy stuff. If Bernard was at the Battle of Hastings, no wonder it's still a large part of our history. What else has he screwed up?"

"Ssh, he'll hear you."

"Not likely. Look at the daft oaf."

We giggled like kids as we watched Bernard's legs kick while he lay opposite us by the fire, snoring even louder than Jen.

As was his norm, Bernard performed one somnambulist kick too many and woke himself up. He sniffed, he frowned, he grunted, and he snorted, then his gaze turned to us.

"How you doing?" I asked, kindly.

"Felt worse," he mumbled.

"Really?"

"No."

"What's wrong? You can tell us. We're your family."

"You wouldn't understand." Bernard did a weird back-and-forth rock, then righted himself and stood. His usual shine was dulled, the horn hardly sparkling at all. Poor guy was either depressed as hell or coming down with something. Considering he'd never been ill a day in his life, it had to be a mental issue.

"We would, buddy. You can tell us anything. It was meeting Samuel, wasn't it?"

"I think so. He knew me from all that time ago. He could remember. Why couldn't I?"

"That's a good question," Phage told him sincerely. "Why do you think that is?"

"Because he's smarter."

"No, that isn't it at all. It's because he hasn't lived as long as you. Hasn't had as fulfilling a life, so there's less for him to have to recall. And anyway, he might remember you two being friends, but I bet there's lots of more recent stuff he's forgotten. Everyone's only got a finite amount of memory."

"That's what I told Soph," Bernard said, eyes brightening.

"There you go then." Phage smiled at him, but gave me a smug look.

"Phage is right. Samuel probably can't even remember what he had for breakfast."

"Neither can I." Bernard's head hung low.

"What!? You have the same bloody thing every day. Always have."

"Stop it!" hissed Phage.

"Oh, yes, right. Sorry. Bernard, do you remember how we met? I have a hard job recalling as it was so long ago. My memory isn't so great either. It's tough when you live a long time. Stuff gets pushed out. I remember bits, but not all of it. How about you?" I was gambling here. If he couldn't recall, it would sink him lower into his mire of misery, but if he could recount our first meeting it might lift his spirits.

"I remember," he said, voice dour and sullen.

"Don't sound too happy about it." I tried not to take it personally, but it was about as personal as you got.

"It's not that, it's just that I remember what things were like before we met, too. You know I had a hard time back then. But this is recent history, not proper old stuff. I might have lots of other families, even more children. I lived all these other lives, did all these things, and now it's gone. It's pointless. What's the point in doing things if you forget them? May as well not bother."

"Because life is the present. You enjoy the present, live it to the fullest, and then you don't need to remember. You just know that you always lived in the here and now and it was good. The best time is always now."

"Blimey, that was deep," I told Phage, impressed and inspired, knowing I had to take her words to heart.

"Not just a pretty face." Phage turned her attention back to Bernard. "Why don't you tell me the story? I've never heard it."

"I told you, didn't I?" I asked, sure I had.

"Nope. You two like to keep your secrets."

"Then it's over to you, Bernard. Don't miss out the juicy bits." I smiled cheerily, but even that didn't perk him up.

"If you think it will help?" he said.

"We do," said Phage, full of encouragement.

Bernard studied us with mournful eyes, his long lashes completing the picture of a despondent creature. "Now, let me see. It was back before there were only a handful of cars and most of the roads were like this track in the woods. Industry was polluting the air like you wouldn't believe. Towns and cities were thick with smog. Filthy places. Dark and noisy and you could hardly breathe. It was the coal. Everyone burned it. Factories used it for everything. When you walked down the streets, you could hardly see what was in front of you."

"It was a grim time," I agreed. "Makes the pollution problems of recent years seem like fresh country air."

"I'd just lost the previous man I lived with. He died."

"Oh, I'm so sorry," said Phage.

"You all die." Bernard shrugged, like it meant nothing, but I knew the truth. He was hurting when I met him. Hurting real bad.

"I was rather lost. I don't mean direction-wise, I mean at a loss what to do."

"And you didn't know where you were," I added with a smirk.

"Shut up!" Phage ordered.

"Yes, do that," Bernard chimed in. "Now, this had happened many times before. Either humans died, or I didn't like them, or I got bored and wandered off, or sometimes I went for a little walk and I, er, well, you know."

"You couldn't find your way home, could you?" asked Phage, understanding but not making fun.

"Not always. But I'd been with this man for a long time. Hundreds and hundreds of years. It was very sad at the end. He couldn't stand it, so one day decided to put an end to things. I didn't understand what he was doing until it was too late. He wasn't himself."

"Go on," Phage encouraged.

I kept quiet about the fact the guy had obviously lost the plot and tied a noose around his neck, secured it to a beam in Bernard's stable, then told the poor thing to run like he was chasing his own rainbow. Before Bernard knew it, the man was swinging from the rope and Bernard was left with serious guilt issues. Maybe Bernard didn't recall that; maybe he didn't want to.

"Things were a blur for a while. I just wandered about the place, not knowing what to do. It's lonely being what I am. There are so few of us. At some point, I met Soph. He was, er, not like he is now," said Bernard cautiously as he glanced my way.

"You can tell her. We don't have any secrets," I told him.

"Like me, Soph had lost his way. His son was dead, his wife and daughter had left, and he was very sad. Sadder than me. He'd left his home because it wasn't a home without them, and he was wandering the same as I was. We met in a field."

"We did. A damn field! After what happened, I was very low, and couldn't get my act together at all. I think I tried to outrun the notes, the pain, the heartache. But it always found me eventually. All of it. Those were dark times."

"Gosh, then it's a good thing you two found each other."

"Go on, tell her," I said, my spirits lifting just at the thought of how we met."

"Do I have to?" moaned Bernard.

"Yes."

"What? What is it?" Phage looked from me to Bernard, excited to hear a lighter part of the tale.

"I was, er, just wandering about the countryside, wondering what to do, where to go, not paying attention, and all of a sudden I was stuck. I lifted my head, but my horn was suddenly very heavy and I was confronted with this monstrous sight."

"Hey, no need for name-calling," I chortled.

"Staring at me, or, you know, right in front of my eyes, was a massive—"

"Careful!" I chuckled.

"—gigantic, bare bottom. It was Soph's," he added, in case Phage didn't get it.

"No. Really? How?" Phage laughed at the thought, but it only got worse.

"I'd kind of got my horn stuck through his belt, and Soph had been having a massive stinky poo, so his trousers were around his ankles. I got everything tangled up, then lifted him up so he was hanging from my horn upside down with this disgusting, truly huge bum right in my face." Bernard guffawed, a deep belly laugh, and as he did so the shine returned to his coat and horn. His large, pale eyes danced with merriment long overdue.

"That didn't really happen! No way?" Phage looked at me and asked, "Seriously? He hung you upside down with your bum hanging out. Had you, er, finished?"

"Yes, I'd finished," I laughed. "I was all clean and everything. Just about to pull up the old trousers and next thing I knew I was upside down and staring at the legs of this horse. Or so I thought. Bernard dropped me, I scrambled to sort myself out, and when I turned around I got the shock of my life. A bloody unicorn, staring at me, moaning about how fat my arse was."

"It was very big," noted Bernard. "Huge. Almost as big as yours, Phage."

I cringed as I shuffled rapidly away as the air went cold and Phage's eyes turned to ice and fire simultaneously. Yes, that's possible of all women if you talk about their bums that way. I know, I have seen it many times and never learned my lesson until the last century or so.

"That was a joke," said Bernard hurriedly. "You have a perfect behind that any horse or unicorn would be proud of. Um, no, wait, that doesn't sound better. You don't have a bum like a horse. You, er..."

"Quit while you're ahead, I would," I told him, my eyes streaming with mirth.

"Yes, good advice. And well done for telling a joke. I think." Phage couldn't help it, she burst out laughing too.

"Sorry. Now, where was I?" Bernard stroked his long nose, then fell over because he can't do that. While we absolutely did not laugh, he managed to regain his feet and a smudge of composure, then continued. "Once Soph had his trousers up and I'd disinfected my horn, we—"

"Two jokes in one day!" I interjected. "It's a miracle."

"—introduced ourselves. He was in awe of me, naturally."

"Naturally," agreed Phage, smiling, and nudging me in the ribs.

"I told him about recent events—"

"In great detail," I nudged Phage right back.

"—and he explained what had befallen him. We talked for hours, and we shared his meal."

"You mean you ate it all and complained there wasn't enough?"

"It was tiny. I'm big."

"I'm pretty big myself," I grumbled.

"After that, we were inseparable. We did everything together. We shared all our worries, talked a lot, and then when we were feeling better because we had a friend, we went house hunting."

"House hunting?" asked Phage.

"It's true, apart from the talking a lot bit. Bernard, you were the same as you are now. You hardly said a word some days. After the initial outburst when we first met, you went back to being quiet, like you are now."

"Did I? Am I? I always thought of myself as a bit of a chatterbox."

"Oh, okay. But yes, Phage, we went house hunting. Bernard helped me scour the land for our first home together. It certainly made life easier being able to race about the place. Plus, there weren't estate agents like now, so it was a lot of going to villages and towns and asking the locals. Took a while, but not as long as it would have otherwise. Of course, that was before you, long before, but we've been together ever since."

"Ever since the day I saw Soph's fat arse," agreed Bernard.

"That was a lovely story," Phage told Bernard. "Thank you for sharing. It means a lot to me. And I'm glad you both found each other."

"Me too," agreed Bernard eagerly.

Phage nudged me in the ribs again. "Oh, yes, absolutely. Me too. And Bernard, I know I joke about with you. You know, the window thing, but in all truthfulness, I don't know how I would have made it through without you. You were there for me in my darkest, loneliest hours, and for that I will always love you. My friend. My family."

It was rare I felt emotional towards Bernard, but before I could stop myself I was hugging his neck while I shed a few tears for what was lost and what was gained.

"You're a true friend," I whispered into his ear. He smelled of magic and candy floss and funfairs and rainbows and straw. The most enduring scent I'd ever known besides my own stench of foulness. Bernard was, and always would be, pure of heart and deed. No matter what he did, it was always for the right reasons. I loved him for it.

"And you were there for me," said Bernard, his ear twitching. "Can we go home now?" he grumbled.

"Same old Bernard." Never one to miss out on some hug action, Phage came over and embraced us both.

"Hey, what's going on? What time is it?" asked Jen as she emerged from the blankets. Her hair was tousled adorably, her face cute as anything, slack and friendly, still full of the calmness of sleep.

"Guess it's time to cook more sausages." I moved to the fire to sort out food for my daughter. Woofer ran around excitedly, woken by the promise of food.

I'd come a long way since those dark days when Bernard and I first met, and I would never stop reminding myself how fortunate I was.

Never.

Death in the Woods

Although, perversely, I was itching to arrive at Witch Bitch HQ, I knew being there would do nothing but aggravate my already raw nerves. So as the evening drew in, it made sense to suggest we sleep in the woods and take our time. Why I'd insisted on rushing from Mawr's, I had no idea. Maybe that was for Phage's sake as much as mine. Or maybe I'd naively assumed my stress levels would lower once away from the old wizard's machinations.

It hadn't worked.

Now I was stuck between waiting here, or twiddling my thumbs at Peth's. I wouldn't be lucky enough for it to all be over the day we arrived there, so why not camp out here and enjoy another night with my beloved? There was no reason not to.

Phage was delighted by my suggestion. Jen too. Although she was looking forward to seeing Grandma, I think she would have been happy whatever we did. Anything was better than school.

We set up an awning attached to the cart for shelter and so we could all snuggle down to sleep later. Jen helped build up the fire, and even insisted on doing most of the cooking. We ate yet more sausages with spiral pasta and veggies along with boiled eggs combined with various bits and pieces Phage had the foresight to pack. I could have done with more meat, but trying to bring perishables like that with the weather so intense was asking for food poisoning.

I had all I wanted anyway, especially as my adorable wife had snuck in enough wine to keep a ship full of sailors happy for the longest of voyages. As long as they didn't mind the taste. It was still as rancid as it had ever been. England would never win awards for wine production, but they'd get a gold for crap vinegar with a high alcohol content.

Jen was wiped out before the bats came out to dance. Woofer and Bernard were the same. Tyr was on the wing, practicing night time hunting, and would have to find a place to sleep somewhere else. Dragons weren't allowed in Peth's realm. She strictly forbade it.

So it was just Phage and me, sitting in companionable silence beside the crackling fire. We spoke little, as the only things to be said were too hard to say, so we simply huddled together and hoped there'd be many more nights like this one.

"Tyr see man."

I was on instant high alert. Phage jumped like she'd been struck by lightning, and was on her feet with her knife drawn the same time as me.

"What was that?" she whispered.

"Tyr. He's warning us."

"I didn't get what he said. But I felt something. His presence."

"It's because it's all new. Wait a minute, let me talk to him." Phage nodded, then crept away from the fire towards where Jen and the others were sleeping under the tarp. I moved in the other direction. No point making ourselves an easy target.

"Man gets close," warned Tyr.

"Where is he?" I asked. "And thanks for watching over us."

"Is Tyr's job. Always watching. Man come down path, from east. Is very close. Not friend. Is bad."

"How so?"

"Just is."

"Okay, thanks. Stay close, but you know you can't get in here, right?"

"Tyr could now. Is strong. But cause pain. Be no use anyway." I felt him shrug, then return to sentry duty. I got a picture of the man through Tyr's extraordinary senses. He was right. This was someone full of evil intent. Bastard on legs.

I circled the fire, well out of the light, and eased close to the others. Phage saw me coming and relaxed as I nodded to her. Jen was fast asleep, but Woofer was up, nose twitching, ears flat.

I bent down and whispered to him, "Well done for waking up. There's a man here and he isn't our friend. I want you to stay close to Jen and ensure nothing happens to her. But you must be quiet. He might leave us alone and go past, but I don't think he will. Don't leave Jen," I repeated.

"Woofer good guard. Not let Jen get hurt."

"Good boy." Standing, I whispered to Phage what Tyr had said, then suggested we split up so we stood a better chance of dealing with this guy if he tried anything. She agreed, so she slid off into the woods to circle behind the trespasser while I remained with Jen.

Bone Slicer was warm in my hand, his energy rising as if keen for a fight. I honestly couldn't tell if that was true, or me broadcasting. Either way, no sneak in the night would harm my little girl. I'd tear his foul heart out before I let that happen.

Peering around the side of the tarpaulin, I caught my first glimpse of him. A sneak alright. He wore a dark hooded cloak right out of fucking Robin Hood, but this was no champion of the people. He was bad, I could sense it. I might not practice magic, but I wasn't immune to the power drawn from the Necroverse, and my Necrosenses were telling me this guy was out to do us harm.

Keeping absolutely still, I watched the man creep along the path then stop dead in his tracks. He cocked his head to the side then faced our camp. We hadn't tried to disguise the fire, as this was private property and he shouldn't have been here, but it was a stupid oversight and one we would pay dearly for.

It was a mere few years ago when that redhead had almost killed Phage as she'd somehow managed to bypass the wards and whispers that should have kept her out of here. Why hadn't we been more cautious? Hurried to arrive while it was still light?

Because bloody Peth had assured us that they'd increased security so nobody uninvited could enter, that was why. Words would be had. Harsh ones.

The man reached to his side and pulled out a knife. He was still in shadow, but the night held some light, although darkness was falling fast. He eased forward, crouched low, and constantly stopped to listen. From his position, there was no way he could see much of the fire, and certainly not if we were there, but it was a brave approach nonetheless. That, or he was an idiot.

I didn't think so. There was something about his movements, the looseness of his limbs. A fluidity that told me this man was confident in his abilities and merely being sensible, even though he believed he could take us regardless of his approach.

The closer he got, the calmer I became. My focus sharpened, senses heightened, breathing became slow and steady as my heart rate lowered. I was no caveman, panicking and adrenaline coursing to give me an edge. I was approaching the zone and felt relaxed, confident, and sure of myself. Zero emotions.

My family were still there in my mind, I was here to protect them, but the emotional attachment faded into the background as my instinct to kill surfaced.

Bone Slicer was itching for a fight. I had to shift him behind my back as the runes flared and the entire blade shone silver. "Be still," I warned the elven blade, and damned if it didn't wink out of sight entirely, the glow vanishing instantly.

The intruder gave up all pretense of secrecy and straightened his back then strode into camp like he owned the place. I held my position. Waiting. Watching.

The weapon he gripped was a simple knife, nothing special, but he handled it with dexterity and confidence as he skirted the fire, investigating the blankets, pots and pans, and mugs. He even lifted the bottle of wine and sniffed it, then muttered as he threw it down. Guess he wasn't a fan of British booze either.

I bristled as I felt a presence approach, and turned sharply but silently. Phage nodded to me and I mirrored the gesture then turned back to the man and motioned with my left hand behind my back for her to wait with Jen while I confronted him.

I stepped from the tarpaulin and walked towards the fire. The moment I did so, the hooded fucker stood stock still, his back to me. He either had supernatural hearing, or he sensed me, knew where I'd been all along and had a flair for the dramatic.

Shit like that didn't bother me. It was neither impressive nor clever. Just another dickhead trying to intimidate his opponent.

Once I felt the heat of the fire, I stopped and waited. He spun fluidly to confront me, then lifted his head up high so I got a glimpse of his face, still deep in the shadow cast by his hood. His teeth glinted as he smiled. The teeth were crooked but very white. Maybe he'd had work done?

"We don't want any trouble," I told him quietly. "There's a young girl sleeping, so I'd appreciate it if you were on your way and left her dreaming."

"Hmm," he pondered, "what should I do? Walk away and not look back? Or kill all of you and get to live another year? Decisions, decisions." His grin widened as he chortled at his own sour words.

Could this be the one I'd come to kill? Was this the mark? But we weren't at Peth's, and that didn't feel right. So what then? Did he have a note with my name on it? It had never happened before, but there was a first time for everything. Something else?

"Oh, gosh, you don't understand, do you? Think I'm here because of a Necronote, is that it? You couldn't be more wrong. No, I'm here for you, Necrosoph, but not because of any note."

"You want me, then let's take this away from my daughter. Are you a man, or a snake with no honor?"

"I have honor!" he spat. "More than you. But I'm not going to leave. You die, you wife too, then the girl. And the fucking animals. All of you. You hear me? All of you." He cackled, a raw throaty laugh that left me sure he wasn't stable. Who would be if they could do such a thing?

I sighed, lost to the moment. Unafraid, a pure being born and bred for the fight. Enraptured by the highs and lows of taking another's life and feeling nothing but a slight sense of loss of self. For that little bit of hope it took from me each and every time. Hope of salvation, of forgiveness, of recovery from so many sins I'd truly lost count.

"You showed the kind of man you are. I'll ask one question, not that it matters," I told him. "Why are you here?"

"Because I'm better than you! I heard the stories. News travels even in these days. Fucking superstar, aren't you? I've come to take the life of the infamous Soph. The first to travel further than the most respected witches, to defy the odds and witness the birth of the Necronotes. To ride a fucking dragon and fight the elves on home territory. But most of all, I'm here for that." He lowered his gaze to Bone Slicer.

I laughed. A genuine, hearty laugh that bubbled up inside and refused to be silenced. He pulled back his hood and glared at me in annoyance. I don't know what I was expecting, but his face was just another face amongst the hundreds I'd killed. I wouldn't even recall it by morning. Sunken eyes, thick beard, and lines around his thin lips. A man who liked to travel, had seen his fair share of weather, but was old, maybe older than me.

The years had taught him nothing but bitterness and resentment. What a waste of resources. Three centuries of feeding, clothing, and housing this sorry excuse for a human being. He'd learned nothing but how to kill, how to wallow in self-pity and crave things that any man in his right mind would run a mile from, rather than towards.

"What's so funny?" he snapped. "You get all this glory. Fame. People whispering your name like you're a god. Look at you, cocky and grinning like you aren't scared. I know you are."

"I'm not."

"You... you should be. I've killed nigh on a thousand men and seen sights you wouldn't believe, but nobody knows my name."

"That's a good thing. Why would you want them to? I never asked for any other Necro to know about me, and sure as hell wish they didn't. And let's be truthful here. You just heard gossip in a few places where pathetic Necros hang out, boasting about shit they should be ashamed of, and telling tall tales. But hey, if you want the fucking knife, then take it." I tossed Bone Slicer to the ground between us.

"You coward. You'd give up such a prize so readily?"

I shrugged. "It's a knife. If you want it so bad, take it. But it won't bring glory or acclaim. If people do know your name, so what? Why would that make any difference to who you are? Do you need other's recognition to make you whole? Why aren't your actions and thoughts enough? Why care what others think? They don't count. Only your own thoughts do."

"They need to know there's a real Necro better than you. All those stories about what you've seen and done, it makes me sick. I'm better than you. And now when I confront you, it seems it's all been a lie. You're a coward."

"I'm no coward, but no fool either. If a simple knife means you'll leave, then you can have it. But it won't change what you see in the mirror. The difference between you and me is I genuinely don't give a shit what you think of me. I'll sleep just as well either way. So, take it and leave."

"Ha! I knew it! You're nothing. Nothing! A sad loser hiding behind his family. What, you'd rather be with them than using all the power you supposedly have? So sad."

"The only sad thing is that you think being a Necro is more important or exciting than playing catch with your kid or cuddling someone you love."

"I've been there and done that countless times. It's nice, but sure, using my powers and showing everyone what losers they are is much more exciting."

I shook my head at this poor creature. How could he be so lost, so misguided? He didn't even have youth as an excuse. He wasn't alone, though. Many Necros reveled in the magic, the excuse to kill. Their loss.

"Go on then. Take it and fuck off."

He grinned as he glanced quickly at the knife. His intentions were clear. He'd take it, believing I was weak, then kill me and my family.

It was tough trying to stifle my grin, but I managed it and hid my smile behind a cough. Unable to wait a moment longer, he bent, keeping his eyes on me, then glanced at his prize and snatched it up with a greedy, trembling hand. He stood, triumphant.

The smugness was short-lived. His eyes went wide in shock, rapidly morphing to a scream of utter anguish as Bone Slicer's wrath was unleashed.

"Guess now we know what happens if anyone else tries to hold my knife," I chuckled as his screams reached new heights. "You hear that, you twisted fuck? It's my knife. Mine! I earned it. Enjoy."

Firelight bounced gleefully off the shining knife, the runes glowing, almost singing with joy at the chance to injure.

Bone Slicer sank through flesh and bone, searing away the meat on his hand so rapidly there was hardly time to follow what happened. The thief's grip remained fastened around the hilt, even as he shook his arm, trying to dislodge the knife. Skin hung in tatters from his fingers as flesh bubbled and spat, the silver inferno rising up past the wrist and roasting the muscle of his forearm.

There was an audible twang as tendons snapped. The hand hung loose as any remaining control was lost. Bone Slicer swung of its own accord on the limp hand in a menacing arc.

With fear etched across his face, the terrified wannabe batted at his forearm with his left hand to try to halt the momentum.

As the fingers around the handle blackened, nothing but bone now, Bone Slicer took on a deeper luster and the arc of the pendulum increased until it forced his arm to bend at the elbow. The blade swished across his thigh muscle with a majestic sweep.

For a moment there was silence, nothing but the crackling of the fire. He looked down as the blade once again hung limp at his side, clutched by nothing but a skeletal, shaking hand. A cut opened in his dark jeans where the impossibly sharp blade had slid across, revealing a gaping wound right to the bone.

As if waiting to build pressure, blood finally spurted from the incision, hissing as it arced into the fire. Flames roared, then shot up into the sky, lighting the scene in macabre shadow and fierce orange light.

"Happy now?" I asked, holding his gaze steadily as his mouth opened and closed in wordless screams like a landed fish. "Not so fucking brave now, are you? Kill my fucking family, would you? Hurt them? Destroy a little girl's life so you could tell tales in the pub!"

I strode across to him and whispered, "Come," as I held out my hand. Bone Slicer tugged away from finger bones that dropped to the trampled ground, and snapped into my palm. The familiarity was as comforting as stroking Phage's warm thigh, and with it came a pleasant glow throughout my body as the energy built in my arm and I zinged like I was Wolverine. The knife was as much a part of me as my own fingers.

Runes shone, the impossible edge grinned devilishly with red firelight as the man howled and his entire forearm crumbled to dust, leaving a raw, bloodied stump just below the elbow.

As Bone Slicer squirmed in my hand, I cut across the man's stump, slicing away the raggedy edges and leaving behind a clean cut. The freshly exposed wound pumped arterial blood as I hopped aside. Just for the hell of it, I slammed a left-hander into his nose, pulverizing cartilage with that ever-so-satisfying crunch I was more familiar with than my wife's underwear drawer.

This wizard wannabe took the hit surprisingly well. He grunted between screams but remained on his feet. Morphing quickly, I came up behind him, ready to slit his throat and be done. But even in his sorry state he had other ideas and, sensing my move, he stumbled aside, rolled across the ground, and came up facing me. Reaching over to his right hip, he pulled his knife with his left hand as he murmured quiet whispers.

Dark Necromatter crawled around his bloodied stump and swirled over his nose. With an audible *crick*, his nose popped back into place and the arm sealed over, stemming the tide of crimson.

"You tricked me! I'll kill you slow for this."

"Okay stumpy, whatever you say," I sighed, knowing he wouldn't stop until he was doubly dead.

"You don't know who you're fucking with," he spat, focusing half on me, half on his whispers to bring himself back to fighting fitness.

"In case you've forgotten, you're the one who started this. I'm defending myself and my family. Hey, you sure you don't want this?" I asked, waving Bone Slicer and grinning.

He jumped back, fearful, then cackled wickedly as he made a decision and sheathed his knife awkwardly. Reaching into an inside pocket, he pulled out a bloody wand of all things. As he did, so it glowed royal purple.

As all such things are, it was a prop of sorts, but imbued with his power just like Mawr's staff. A focal point, something to harness energy and direct it with better control than merely using whispers alone. That he would use it at all rankled, and made my beard bristle with annoyance. I fucking hated dicks like this. So full of themselves because they thought they were better than others because they had a nice stick.

Power direct from the Necroverse sloshed at his feet in a sickly puddle, thick and gelatinous. As his whispers deepened, it spread out then became nothing but air. Light as a feather, magic on the breeze. It spiraled and spun, entwining with his limbs, then he was encased in a whirlpool of this dark magic drawn from places none should venture for it always came with a price.

Faces of daemons howled and screamed from within the black mass. As the dark wizard tilted his head back and sucked in this power from another realm, he spread his arms, or one arm and a stump, and his body began to shine.

"Fuck this," I groaned, then threw Bone Slicer as hard as I could.

Time slowed as magic from one foreign realm met another. The dark magic almost held as the elven blade hit the power of the wizard's whispers, and it slowed until it was as though the knife's edge was trying to pierce molasses. The tip inched forward, magic crackled where the two forces met, but then my knife was through. It surged forward, and the impossibly honed tip touched the wand. The world erupted, and a massive explosion sent me flying backwards.

I landed on my arse as time sped up and reality hit home with the mother of all headaches. Bone Slicer screamed with joy inside my head as it swished once, cutting the wand in half, then embedded itself in the man's one remaining good hand.

A gasp, a morph, then almost doubled over with pain I reached him and yanked my knife free. The wizard slumped as he dropped the broken magical prop, so I wasted no time.

Holding Bone Slicer like an ice pick, I jabbed into his eyes, *pop, pop*. Both orbs burst in a limp splurge of aqueous humor that trickled past his cheeks and into his screaming mouth.

I booted him away with a sharp kick to the stomach, sending him sprawling to the ground. He attempted to gather up more whispers. Already he was chanting for the Necroverse to come to his aid, but not on my watch.

Utterly lost to it now, I slashed at his face manically, slicing away his lips, then his nose, and cheered with delight as an ear fell and got trapped in his hood.

Still not done, he beat at me with his damaged hand and his stump. I felt nothing; didn't care. As he kicked and bucked, I slammed down with Bone Slicer into his chest and dragged the blade past his sternum like the bone was melting aside, then felt the freedom of his stomach cavity.

Our faces were so close, I could smell his sour breath. He disgusted me.

Lower and lower I cut, like a deranged surgeon, until his entire torso opened up like a nice piece of chocolate cake with jam hidden inside. I sliced left then right, making a cross of his abdomen. Wild, and full of the joy the blood always brings, I plunged a hand deep inside the cavity and shoved my fist up into his chest.

As ribs cracked aside, I felt the warmth of his beating heart, then gripped it tight.

With an almighty grunt, I tore it free and sank back onto my haunches with his still pumping heart clenched tight in my fist. Veins and arteries trailed across the ground like spastic worms.

My eyes remained locked on his ruined face as he stilled, all life extinguished, then his heart finally gave up. For several seconds, I remained there, with my prize held aloft. Anger bubbled as I returned to my senses at least somewhat, so I scrambled to my feet and kicked him hard in the side of the head. A needless act of brutality, but what did one more nail in my coffin of humanity matter now?

Looking down, I stared for the longest time at the source of life squeezed into a messy pulp in my hand, then I felt a calming presence by my side and turned my head to see Phage reach out and lower my arm. She was crying.

I nodded, then threw the lump of foulness into the fire.

All I could hear was the blood thrumming in my ears and the far off sound of a dog howling and a little girl sobbing her heart out.

Was that something to do with me? Should I be concerned?

Pain, and a deep exhaustion, took me over. I welcomed the chance to escape as I fell onto the ravaged corpse that lay before me, testament to the madness within all men.

I never did get his name.

Apologies

"You killed him! He's dead!"

The screams of my daughter snapped me to consciousness. My head throbbed, my heart shriveled, and my guilt shone through above all else. Not for the deeds committed, but that I'd been so lost to the bloodlust that I hadn't given a second thought to what my darling daughter might witness.

I stifled a yell as I pushed from the ground, only to find my hand sank deep into the guts of the dead wizard. Intestines burst, coating my shirt in a foul mess of half-digested food and thick shit. I must have pierced his bladder and kidneys too, because a green slime and a spurt of rancid piss arced into the fire. It hissed as it hit. I snorted involuntarily, spluttering as I inhaled the stench of a human being's innards and the unmistakable punch to the nose of roasting flesh.

His arm was in the fire, so I ignored the grossness and dragged him away a little, then sank to my knees, exhausted, morbidly ashamed, yet joyous that I'd beat the bugger.

"You... you squashed his heart! You ripped it out and squashed it. Look at you! Look at him! How could you?" wailed Jen, her face contorted in a rictus of fear, disgust, and utter shock. She was bright red and tearing at her hair before she flung herself at Phage and sobbed into her chest.

If I'd ever felt lower in my life, I couldn't think when.

"Hush, it's okay," soothed Phage, shaking her head at me, telling me Jen was not cool with this.

"I'm sorry, you shouldn't have seen," I said, then groaned as I stood and moved closer.

Phage shook her head again, telling me to wait a while before touching Jen. She wasn't accusing me, we both knew how it went when in the throes of battle, but I had to admit, it was pretty gruesome.

Taking the hint, I sucked up the pain and dragged the body away into the woods while Jen remained in her mother's arms. Woofer trailed after me, quiet and oozing compassion. He knew what went on in my head, understood the fact I had to fight for my life. He wasn't happy, but that mostly concerned what it did to his family, not the act I'd committed.

Animals had a different outlook on violence. They were closer to their base instincts to survive at all costs, so didn't balk at the nastiness the way most humans did. But he wasn't exactly jumping for joy either.

"It's okay," I told him. "Jen will be fine soon. It's a shock, that's all."

"Jen will have to fight too? Like Soph and Phage?"

"Yes, I'm afraid she will. It breaks my heart to think of her doing what I did, but there's no other way."

"Woofer do it for her?" he offered bravely, hope in his eyes.

"Oh Woofer, if only it were that easy. No, your place is at home for the most part. Not out here fighting for your life. You've had your fair share of battles, so you need to let us handle this."

"Woofer fought before. Was good."

"Yes, you were. That was your first morph, wasn't it?"

"Woofer help Soph," he nodded.

"You sure did. Sorry about this. I know you hate the shouting and the upset. I do too. I wish with all my heart things were different. I get lost to it, boy. The bloodlust takes me over and I am nothing but a machine. Death. It's how we survive. Us Necros. We let the fight consume us and nothing else matters."

"Not even me?" whispered Jen.

I turned to find her and Phage standing back a little, clearly having listened to every word.

"Not when I'm lost to it, no," I admitted. I hated telling her that, but she needed to hear it at some point, understand what it truly felt like to fight for you life.

"Like an animal?"

"Yes, just like an animal. I am so sorry you saw that, Jen. Truly I am. I know you will think differently of me, that you now know the other side of your father. The darkness that's within me. But this is who I am."

"Who we are," corrected Phage. She turned to Jen and told her. "I'm the same. What your father did was certainly monstrous, and even uncalled for, but we both have a wild side to us. It's how we've made it this far. We let the bloodlust consume us. Everything else fades away until only the fight remains. We won't be beaten. We will win at all costs. When you get like that, nothing else matters. You are fighting for survival, nothing more."

"But he tore out that man's heart," wailed Jen. She turned to me. "You didn't need to do that. You could have stabbed him or something."

"I could," I admitted. "But I was angry, and not myself. He didn't deserve any better."

Then my daughter said the most profound words I had ever heard. "He may not have deserved better, but you did."

I was left speechless. Gentle tears fell for the faith my daughter still had in me. That she believed I deserved more for myself. She knew what such an act would do to me, and I shouldn't tarnish myself with unjustified barbarism.

"Come on, back to the fire. Let's leave your father alone for a moment." Phage smiled kindly at me, then led Jen away.

I stood over the body of a stranger yet again, and wondered if I truly did deserve more than this endless circle of death.

Maybe I had once. Now, I wasn't so sure.

For a brief moment, I wondered what to do with him, then remembered where I was. Let the witches deal with him. He shouldn't have been here. It was their oversight, so they could clean up the mess that was their doing.

After the high of battle, came a deep weariness, yet this night was far from over. More important than rest was my daughter, but I couldn't face her like this. I was covered in blood and gore, and smelled vile, so had to clean up and get myself changed.

In a daze, I wandered to the cart, said nothing to a watching Bernard, and stripped down then used the large water canister to clean myself up best I could. The water refreshed me and brought me back to myself somewhat, eradicating the worst of my crime. Once dressed in clean clothes, the foulness of my deeds faded further, until I could almost convince myself it never happened.

But it had, and for whatever reason, Phage had allowed Jen to see at least some of it. How much, I wasn't sure, but I was about to find out.

With a deep breath, and ignoring the sorrowful look Bernard gave me, I went to speak to my little girl.

"Hey, how you both doing?" I asked as I sat cross-legged opposite them by the fire.

Jen was cuddled in close to Phage. She wasn't crying, but she was shaking a little and looked so lost.

"We're a bit better," said Phage, her face tight.

"I'm okay, Dad. It was just a shock. I thought it was bad with those daemons the other day, but that didn't seem real somehow. This did. So gruesome. Seeing you like that scared me. I didn't recognize you."

"I know, and again, I'm so sorry. Please forgive me."

"Of course I do!" Jen sniffed, then wiped her nose with her sleeve. "I get it, I really do. But seeing it up close like that. It was... I don't know. Seeing the insides of a person, all the guts, and you with your arm inside him. You pulled out a person's heart, Dad."

"I know. I went too far."

"A heart! That's real. That's terrible. Who does that?" Jen held up her hand as I was about to reply. "Don't answer. I know. Necros, that's who. Us. You, Mum, and me. That's the kind of thing people like us do. But I don't want to do that. I don't want to be so consumed by a fight that I'd open up a person, no matter how horrid they are, and reach inside and tear out an actual heart. You looked happy. You were smiling as you held it up like you'd won a prize or something." Jen's head sank, letting her hair cover her eyes. She began to tremble again as Phage pulled her in close then looked at me with such deep sadness.

"We don't want you to be that kind of person either," I told her. "And please forgive me for saying this, Jen, and it truly is one of the hardest things I have ever said, but you have to be."

Jen's head shot up, and she glared at me. "I do not!"

"You do," agreed Phage, face full of sympathy but her words strong. "It's why I let you watch." Phage turned to me. "I'm sorry I let her see, but I thought it best. Our daughter has to know who we really are, to see what happens to us. She had to know, Soph, but I think I made a big mistake."

"You didn't make a mistake. You're right, she needs to understand the reality."

"This was another lesson?" Jen hissed, hurt and confused by a world she no longer understood.

"It was," agreed Phage. "You've learned so much these last few years, but it's never been real, has it? Now it is. Now you know exactly what we are. What you are."

"I am not like that!"

"Jen, my dear, darling daughter, you have to be. You must have that within you," I told her.

"No. Never. Why?"

"Because otherwise you won't make it past your twenty-first birthday," sobbed Phage. She hugged Jen as mother and daughter cried in each other's arms.

There was nothing I could do to make this better. So I waited for them to finish crying, hating every moment of it. Disgusted not only with myself, but with Phage too. What kind of parents were we? How could Phage make her own daughter watch me kill someone, then do that to him?

Were we truly that broken? The only thing that saved us was that we felt anything at all. That we understood how much this was to witness and maybe even understand. That this was not normal behavior. Had we scarred her for life? Children could be broken so easily by their parents. We both knew that. We'd both experienced the dark side of being Necro ourselves, yet here we were, maybe repeating the same mistakes inflicted on us.

Or had we? At least we knew how abnormal this all was. Held on to the everyday world and acknowledged we were different, and that this was barbarism of the worst kind.

But what other choice was there? Jen had to know, had to be made to believe that she must, absolutely must, find that darkness within that would allow her to kill another human being and live with what she'd done afterwards.

But at this age? Soldiers didn't learn to kill until their time to venture onto the battlefield was almost upon them, did they? Why did we think we knew better? That our little girl should see such things at the unripe age of thirteen? Not so long ago, we didn't want her to know anything about Necronotes. Now we were confronting her with the worst of it.

Was Phage wrong?

Was I?

I didn't have the answer. Some things parents do are by instinct alone, and if Phage believed this was right, then I had to support her decision. She knew Jen even better than I did. I sure as shit didn't know when it would ever be right to let my little girl truly understand she had to be a stone-cold killer or she'd die. She would absolutely, certainly die unless she found that hateful place within and reveled in the brutality.

"Will I really have to become like that?" asked Jen once the tears were all dried up.

"You will," I said. "I know it's an almost impossible concept to get your head around, but you will. You will have to kill people, Jen, and you need to lose yourself to it. Like you did with that bully. But only when it's you or them. Not for kicks," I warned. "Never when it isn't justified. If you saw all of that, then you know that I did all I could to stop it from happening. I would have given him anything if he'd have walked away. But he wouldn't have. No matter what I'd said or done, he would have tried to kill us all."

"He might not have."

"Oh yes he would. You know me, and you know I will never let anyone harm you. So, yes, I did what I had to. But I'm not proud of it, never proud, always hate it, but in the moment, when I am that other me, then yes, I revel in the madness that consumes me. It's the only way. Many don't have that, and you know what happens to them?"

"They die?"

"Yes, they do. You must let the wildness take over, be utterly confident that you will emerge the victor. No doubt, no hesitation, no second-guessing your own instincts. If something feels wrong, if you get a feeling, however small, then you trust your instincts and you believe. You believe with your whole heart that what you feel is right. Never be uncertain. Trust your gut, and do what you have to with utter, unshakable conviction."

Jen turned to Phage. "You have that too?

"I do," admitted Phage. "Just like your father. A terrible price to pay, and a terrible admission to yourself, that you not enjoy, but... what's the word? You admit that it's who you are, the other side of yourself, and you never, ever, like your father just told you, hold back. Does that make sense?"

"I think so. I think it does. I still don't want to do it, though."

"None of us do, honey," I told her. "None of us do."

There was nothing more to be said. It was done. Our girl finally understood the world she'd been born into.

There was no going back now. No return to a time of innocence. Jen had been baptized. Truly at one with the Necroverse.

Final Approach

We remained by the fire for the remainder of the night. Jen huddled up in blankets as she continued to shiver. Her eyes were vacant. Phage wrapped her in her arms and soothed our hurting child by stroking her hair and, once asleep, she remained that way until morning.

Phage dozed off, but her sleep was fitful, repeatedly jolting awake and scanning for intruders until she locked her eyes on me and smiled weakly before eventually succumbing to her dreams once more.

I didn't sleep a wink. It wasn't safe here.

Early morning saw us all getting about our business. Nobody spoke much, nothing was said of the previous night's events, and Jen looked terrible. The rest had not done her any good.

We needed to get away from the scene of my crime, so we cleared everything away, left our camp spotless, and were on our way as the sun rose.

The forest was a delight in the early morning. Birds sang, a joyous celebration of the day ahead, insects shook off the dew with manic flight, creatures of all kinds wandered across the path, unafraid and often curious, and even Bernard got so caught up in the positive vibrations that he forgot to moan for a full ten minutes.

As the sun warmed us with shafts of green-tinged light finding its way through the lush canopy of ancient oak, gnarly beech, and proud ash, everyone's spirits lifted.

"It's like yesterday was a dream," noted Jen as she smiled at me happily.

I nodded. "Sure is. What a day. It's glorious. This is what life's all about, eh?"

Jen's smile faded, my words evidently bringing it all back. But she shook her head, having undoubtedly made up her mind not to dwell on it, and the smile returned. "You're right. This is what life is about. Enjoying the forest, us all being together. Hey, wanna play fetch, Woofer?"

"Woofer play fetch. Where ball?"

"Aha, I have a surprise for you," laughed Phage, so pleased to finally be a proper part of such conversations. Her eyes sparkled, cheeks rosy with a flush of happiness.

"Have sausages?"

"No, not sausages. Jen, you want to go get it?"

Jen nodded, then happily ran ahead, jumped into the cart, and rummaged around. She hopped back down then raced back to us and revealed what she was hiding behind her back.

"Is new ball!" Woofer ran circles around us, overjoyed by the bright orange ball.

Everyone laughed. Everyone was happy. The day was perfect as Jen played fetch with Woofer while Phage and I held hands as we followed Bernard on the forest path.

For just a little while, all seemed right with the world.

And then, just like that, the forest ended and we found ourselves blinking as we stepped into Peth's world.

"Grandma!" Jen spied Peth over by the communal area and dashed off with Woofer barking at her heels.

"Guess the fun and games are over," I noted sourly.

"I can't wait to go home." Phage smiled, full of sympathy for what she knew awaited me. There was fear in her smile, too. Fear of what might happen to her family.

Would the man she loved kill her mother? Would her mother kill him? Would life ever be the same again?

The Necronote squirmed in my pocket.

Not long until we'd find out.

Certainly not long enough.

"An unexpected visit," noted Peth by way of greeting.

"Yes, sorry, Mother, it's all been rather rushed." Phage kissed Peth on both cheeks, a definite upgrade to meetings in past years where it had been awkward nods and sometimes even handshakes.

"Nice to see you all." Peth played with the pendants hanging low around her neck.

"We hope this is okay?" asked Phage.

"Yes, of course. But a call would have been nice. So I could make preparations." Peth's freaky eyes bored into mine. She knew something was up. She knew the date, not that I'd got a card or anything.

"Grandma, there was a man in the woods."

"What? Who was he?"

"You know, a stranger. Dad... Um, they... Anyway, it's done now, and at least his note's finished with. Can we go see Oz? How is he?"

"He is well. Why don't you run along and go say hi? I'll be there in a few minutes. Let me have a word with your parents first."

"Okay. See you later!" Jen ran off with Woofer, both excited and seemingly happy.

Peth stared at me even harder. Damn, why'd it always feel like she was reading my thoughts?

"Because your body language gives you away," she said, a trace of a smile passing across her face like a brief breeze.

"Guess it does," I admitted.

"The man wasn't your mark?"

"No. I hadn't even considered Jen would think he was. But that's a good thing, I guess."

"How did he get in there, Mother? We thought the woods were safe now. You told us they were."

"I shall certainly look into it. Now, why are you here? And please don't try to lie."

"I can't tell you why, Peth. And by saying that, I am telling you more than I should. You understand?"

Peth nodded, having undoubtedly understood the reason for our visit the moment she set eyes on us. "I understand. Come, we will talk more later. But please know, I don't blame you, Soph. I have often wondered over the years how it would happen, and this was always a possibility."

"Never," I told her. "I won't do that. Not to Phage, or Jen."

"Soph, my dear Soph, of course you will. If that is the price, then you must pay it. I understand, and certainly wouldn't blame you. But enough of this. Let's go and find Jen." Peth headed back towards her house.

Phage and I exchanged a glance. Neither of us knew what to make of Peth acting so nice. It was a very hard thing to get used to, but she'd certainly changed of late. She really was mellowing in her old age.

I wondered how she'd take the news we'd got from Mawr. Bet she wouldn't be smiling then.

We trailed after her.

"Oh, I'll just stand here, shall I? Yes, you go right ahead. I'll just wait here until I die. Don't mind me."

I rolled my eyes at Phage, then told her, "I'll sort out the grumpy unicorn. You go ahead."

With a peck on my cheek, Phage left me to it.

"Let's get you sorted out, Bernard."

"Only if it isn't too much trouble," he moaned. "Which it clearly is."

"Sorry, I've got a lot on my mind."

"I'm sorry too. I know you do. Life's hard for you humans, isn't it?" he asked softly.

I was taken aback by his understanding. "Sometimes it's a fucking nightmare," I sighed, then led him over to the stables. "An absolute fucking nightmare."

"Forfeit!

"Don't you bloody start."

It was going to be a long couple of days.

The rest of the day passed by in a blur of excitement for Jen at being back at Grandma's, and anxious waiting for Phage and I. Interspersed with scowls from the other witches, who never took kindly to a man in their midst.

They had too many secrets, too much history as a women-only group, and more than their fair share of horror stories when it came to men for them to ever accept me. Of course, there were exceptions, but the older the witch, the less pleasant the stares. Some deigned to grunt, a few youngsters even spoke kindly to me, but for the most part they kept their distance.

Phage had her own set of problems to contend with. She wanted to confront Peth about Mawr's revelations, but there wasn't any time for that with Jen seemingly needing to have constant attention. No doubt it was brought on by the events of the last few days—she'd been through more this week than the rest of her life—but it meant the adults were never alone.

After a communal dinner, Jen finally ran out of steam. She got taken to bed by Phage, and half an hour later the other witches had drifted off to their own homes or to sit around campfires, leaving just the three of us at the communal eating, meeting, and shouting obscenities area.

Before Phage could get into it, Peth spoke to us both.

"Clearly, we cannot talk about Soph's note, but it is obvious why you are here. I said it earlier, but I want to restate it now. If it comes to it, then I accept it and will allow the outcome. Soph, don't think for one moment I couldn't destroy you if I so wished, but I do not wish that. I understand this is a decision you have already come to, but you must change your mind. I won't have my daughter alone, or my grandchild without her father."

"What, father's are important, are they?" snapped Phage.

"He has raised her, so yes, it's important," said Peth, giving Phage a quizzical look.

"I can't do what you're asking," I said. "Jen would never forgive that."

"She will understand in time. I have decided."

"Sorry, but it's my decision to make," I told her.

"No, it isn't. And besides, how do you propose it to work? You let the time run out on your note? Then what? You will die. Who is to blame, then? It would be me. I could have stopped it. So, you do what you must, Necrosoph, and ensure you remain with your family. My family."

"Let's just wait and see what happens," I told her, knowing this would get us nowhere, but as surprised as Phage that Peth had offered herself as sacrifice so I'd be there for them.

It was clearly rankling, as Peth hadn't felt it necessary for Phage to have a man present her entire life whilst she was taught the ways of the Necroverse, raised solely by a gaggle of batty old witches with only one thing on their minds. Magic. Misery and magic, that was their focus.

"I can't bear this!" shouted Phage, finally snapping. "How can you both discuss this like it's a game of cards? We're talking about your lives. We're talking about an impossible choice here. How can you bear it?" Phage gulped her glass of wine. I hadn't touched mine; I wasn't in the mood one bit.

"My dear, we are grown-ups. What other way is there? Everyone's time comes. The notes endure."

"It's okay," I told Phage. "I understand. But honestly, I don't know what else to say? I wish we could discuss this openly, but we can't. We're probably pushing it already."

"And you," Phage pointed an accusing finger at her mother, "talking about fathers like they need to be present. Well, guess what? We just came from Mawr's. Yes, that's right, he told me. How could you?"

"I had every right," snapped Peth. "I did what I felt was best. He would have been no help. You were better off here, with me. With others like us."

"Like you wanted me to be, you mean. You never gave him the choice. You never gave me the choice."

"He knew, even if he didn't care to admit it."

"You told him I wasn't his."

"I did, but it was obvious he didn't believe me. So, now you know. Mawr is your father. That fool would have done you no good. Filled your head with foolish nonsense. All wizards are the same. All men. You needed guidance. I guided you. I know I made mistakes, and I am doing my best to earn your forgiveness, but I will never apologize for this choice I made."

"You never apologize for anything." Phage poured herself a generous glass of wine, downed it in one gulp, glared hard at Peth, then stormed off.

"I see she is still as hot-headed as ever," noted Peth.

"She only seems to get that way when around you."

"Indeed. Mothers and daughters. It has been the same since the beginning of time. Well, goodnight. Let's hope it isn't the last for any of us."

"Goodnight."

I watched Peth glide across the clearing, following in Phage's footsteps.

Peth's words rang in my ears. How many more nights would there be?

A Hostile Takeover

The problem with Necronotes, besides the obvious, is there's no time stamp. You don't bring up the app, get the location, and discover the day, the hour, or even who your mark is.

So I was still at an utter loss.

The communal area had at least one occupant from dusk till dawn, and often throughout the night, too. Witches kept irregular hours, always popping in and out of their beds when some esoteric claptrap took their fancy. I spied countless wafting across the enclave, shrouded in dreams or lost to thoughts of whispers, spells, and potions. Or babbling about ways to crack open portals to places no sane mind would venture.

So you'd often find a witch or three sat around drinking tea, coffee, or a bullshit flavored concoction at all hours of the day or night. They often ate there in groups large or small at bewildering times of the day, held meetings, bickered, or played games. They even got down to some serious naked action there once in a while, although thankfully that hadn't happened while Jen was with us.

How the goddamn bastard fuck was I supposed to know who I was meant to decide the fate of? It was beyond frustrating, and now here I was, after having already gone through more in the last week than I had in years, although I guess that thing with Eleron was pretty epic, and I was running out of time.

Phage was hiding in the house, unable to bear it, as she knew well and good what the deal was and had trusted me with making the right decision. How this must be hurting her.

Jen wasn't quite savvy enough to know the score, and believed the deed was done, but it wasn't. I had to decide. What time had my note come?

I realized I had until the following afternoon to complete this or I'd be finished. An evil eye would open, then gobble me up and drop me into the pits of Hell where I no doubt belonged.

Would I find peace then? Or a never-ending purgatory where I couldn't even begin to make reparations for my sins, even if it was eternal damnation?

For now, I was making the most of the rare peace. Hoping for answers, expecting none. My little girl was asleep, safely tucked up in bed, and that meant more than anything else ever could.

"I know the struggle you endure, Necrosoph," said Peth as she flounced onto the raised platform and wafted across the boards like a wraith.

"I'd be shocked if you didn't, Pethach."

"We lead a weary, impossible life. So much death."

"So much beauty, too."

"Would you change anything?" she asked, raising a perfect eyebrow, watching me intently with her freaky, goat-like eyes.

"That's a trick question. There are a million and one things I would change if I could, but they wouldn't mean anything if I did. All the important things? No, guess not."

"Not even the death of your son?"

"Don't you dare... No, not even that," I whispered, my anger dissipating.

"I didn't mean to offend. I was genuinely curious to see what kind of a man you really are."

"You know what I am," I growled.

"I do. And my daughter is lucky. Soph, you understand the ways of Necros. You know that if you changed that most heinous of accidents, you wouldn't have the life you have now. I guess that's my true question. Would you swap his life for the one you have now?"

"That's not something I could ever answer. If he lived, I wouldn't have met Phage and thus no Jen. But it did happen, and they do exist. Would I rather they weren't here? Of course not? Do I want my son back? More than almost anything. Would I make a choice as I watched my hat blow into the water moments before he reached for it? If I was there now, I would stop him from drowning. What father wouldn't? But right here, right now, with a dumb hypothetical question? There is no answer I can give that wouldn't leave me feeling like the worst kind of human being. So, no, I won't answer that."

Peth nodded and never once broke eye contact. She smoothed her hair as she stood, straightened her flowing white dress, arranged her pendants neatly, then nodded once more.

"As I thought. I knew you were a good man, much as I have fought it and hated to admit it. But I have always known. You are a rarity in a mire of imbeciles and traitors. A man with integrity who knows his own mind and isn't afraid of anyone or anything. You deserve my daughter, and your own life. I do not. I choose, Soph. Not you. I choose my death over yours. Over the heartache and misery my daughter and grandchild will endure for eternity if they lost you. Especially if they lost you because of me. I will not let you die because of me."

"Peth... I... No, this can't be. Think how they will feel, how they'll see me. No, I thank you from the bottom of my heart for the offer, for giving yourself like this, but I can't. It would be wrong, for both of them."

"What, then?" she snapped, eyes angry, neck flushing. "You would rather they see me live, but abandon me because they cannot stand to set eyes on their own blood who killed their husband and father? Soph, you must let me do this."

"No, you're both wrong," said Phage.

We turned to her. But it wasn't Phage.

"Jen?"

"It doesn't have to be either of you," she snapped, her voice not her own.

"What's happened to you? And were you listening?" In the gloom, all I could make out was her slender, youthful form. Her shoulders were tensed, her arms crossed, and I would bet money she was biting her lower lip. But she sounded so much like her mother it was uncanny.

"What have you done, child?"

"Me? I haven't done anything! Ask your witches. Your damn dead sisters." Jen stepped forward into the pool of light cast by the oil lamp and I gasped.

"Your eyes! What have you done to your eyes?" I turned to Peth and hissed, "You did this. What the fuck?"

"This is not my doing. And mind your tongue, or I'll rip it out."

"So much for happy families," sighed Jen. "A moment ago you would give your lives for each other, now this?"

"We would give our lives for you, not each other," said Peth quietly. "Come, child, what has happened?"

"You know exactly what's happened," said Jen as she moved closer and I got to see the full extent of what had been done to her.

"You've got the same eyes as Peth. What did you do? I thought it was a lengthy operation. Peth?" I turned to her, but she was taking no notice of me, just studying Jen like a prized specimen.

"So, it has begun," she sighed. "So soon, and so easy. Did you feel no pain, child?"

"Pain? I felt the pain. I felt the pain of a thousand sisters clamoring for attention in my head. I felt the hurt of a thousand lost souls. A hundred thousand. A million, maybe? I don't know how many. They told me things. They showed me things. They did things. Then gave me the sight."

"What's she talking about?" I asked Peth as I got up and moved to Jen.

"No, not yet! Keep away for now," growled Jen, still sounding the spit of Phage.

I stopped and asked her, "Why?"

"Because they're still in here, that's why. Cackling, and having a right old fun time. Seeing the world through my eyes, telling me so much, teaching me what I don't want to learn. Make them stop. Make them stop!"

Peth was beside me and reaching for Jen. She didn't protest. I don't know that she could. "Just relax. Let them fade like a breeze on a summer's day. Can you picture that, Granddaughter? A bright sun on a clear day? The sky is blue, but it isn't very hot. A perfect day like you were told happened before you were born."

"I see it."

"Now, go back to then, when you were a baby, and then before. When you were warm and cocooned in your mother's belly. No sight, no thought, just being."

Peth caught Jen as she crumpled.

I helped her get Jen onto the floor and put a cushion under her head. One thing the witches weren't short of was cushions. They bred faster than rabbits. She was breathing slowly but steadily and I couldn't see any other changes, but that didn't mean there weren't any.

"What the fuck was that all about?" I hissed. "And who did that to her eyes? Is she okay? What did you do?"

"Calm yourself. I merely put her to sleep with my words. Gentle whispers, nothing more. Akin to hypnosis. She is fine. Not hurt in any way. And as to her eyes, well, that is unexpected."

"Damn right it is. She's a teenager. She can't have those freaky eyes. She has to go to school. Change them back."

"Soph, you don't understand. The sisters did this. Her dead sisters. They must think very highly of her."

"I don't know what you're talking about. I thought you had surgery to make yours like that. So you could see sideways and forwards, increase your peripheral vision. It's an operation, isn't it?"

"You may have assumed that, but no, it is nothing of the sort. I have been given goat eyes by my sisters. Those long dead, forgotten by all but me and my kind. My lineage stretching back to the beginning of time. They are all there in one form or another. Some strong, others weak. They gave me the gift, and now, it seems, they have bestowed this honor upon Jen."

"Goddammit! She can't look like that. What, will she have a forked tongue like you too?"

"Now that was a mere trifle," Peth admitted. "A simple operation to give me more of a presence, to intimidate. A foolish, childish act I would regret if I allowed myself such an emotion."

"You're telling me dead witches changed my daughter's eyes? Why?"

"To give her the sight, of course."

"What sight?"

"Don't worry, it won't manifest at her age. It can't. But for whatever reason, the sisters wanted her primed and ready."

"Peth, I swear to god if you don't start making sense I'll change my mind and put an end to you this very minute."

"Foolish man. As if you could."

"You wanna try me?" I growled.

"With these eyes of mine, and now Jen's, things can be seen that otherwise cannot. I see more than you could ever know. Phage could have accepted the sisters offer too, but she declined. She refused for you. So she could appear normal. Jen may not have understood the offer, or maybe they merely did it without her accepting. We will have to ask her. When she matures, she will be able to see the things no other does. Whispers and secrets, shadows, magic use, so much more."

"Like second sight?"

"No. More of the Necroverse. The stuff hidden even to most Necros. The very essence of magic. Its energy. Its reality. They are a mark, a symbol as much as anything, although it does allow me to see more than with normal eyes. But mostly it is a symbol of one who is powerful, who can connect easily with her dead ancestors and draw upon their knowledge, sometimes their wisdom, and see the Necroverse in action."

"A curse then. A weight around her neck. Something to mark her out as different. To cause her trouble wherever she goes. She'll be set apart for life."

"That's the opinion of a man. Not one of our own."

"Oh, fuck you, Peth. Enough with the chauvinism. Men are just as important as women. You bloody sisters and your superiority complex. It's sickening. You're not special, you just like messing about with things you shouldn't."

"And that is the assumption of a narrow-minded man."

"One who wants nothing more than to protect your daughter and granddaughter," I reminded her. "Those you would give everything for."

Peth nodded her understanding. She bent to Jen and placed her hand on her heart, then turned her head and got close to her mouth and listened. She remained that way for almost a minute. It felt like a lifetime.

When Peth moved away, she was paler than usual and looked unwell.

"What is it? Is she okay?"

"She's fine. But I can hear them. Their whispers and chatter. The sisters of old are awakening within Jen. They will fade, but Jen has proven herself. We knew she was special. This is the proof. All sisters will know of her. Know her power."

"No. That is not going to happen. This life isn't for her," I insisted.

"And it is not for you to decide her fate. A father must let go of his child's hand eventually, and push her out into the world."

"I will never let go. And if I do, I will be there, always, to hold her hand again and help her in any way I can."

"As is right."

"But you didn't, did you, Peth?" It was a low blow, but she deserved it.

"No, I failed my daughter. Failed all my children. I believed I was preparing them for what was to come, but no, I was wrong. We've already had this conversation. Why do you despise me so?"

"I don't, and that's the whole point. I want you to be there for them both. I know you've been trying, and I appreciate it. So, please, cut the witch bullshit. You know I can't stand it."

"I apologize. But understand, this is my life, my whole existence. For hundreds and hundreds of years, this is all I have known. I am far removed from the modern world, have next to no part in it. I learned how to survive, how to live, how to teach children when I was very young and it's hard to know how to adjust."

"You aren't doing so bad for an old-timer," I told her, winking and smiling.

Fair play, she took it well and only scowled a little. "When she wakes up, you mustn't make her scared. Don't tease her, or keep talking about her eyes. It will be hard enough just learning how to see again."

"I would never make fun of her. And what, she won't be able to see?"

"Of course she will! But not how she used to. She will have increased peripheral vision, and it can take a while to grow accustomed to it. I know when it happened to me I kept bumping into things for a few days until my brain reconfigured. Then it was truly wonderful. A real gift. You should be proud."

"Oh, yes, I'm over the moon. How will she cope with this?"

"She wears contacts. Or better yet, she uses a simple whisper."

"No whispers," I told her. "She's too young. I don't want her doing spells at her age. Hell, Phage hardly ever does them even now."

"In your presence," snapped Peth, like there was plenty to be said on the topic, but now wasn't the time.

"No whispers," I insisted.

"She can learn a simple whisper to shroud her eyes. They will look how they always did, but perform like these new ones. If she's old enough to have this sight gifted her, she's old enough to learn how to hide them. In fact, I wouldn't be surprised if she already knows. Her first true whisper. How exciting." Peth smiled, genuine and warm, and clapped her heavily ringed hands together. Her bracelets jangled as she clapped again.

As if it was a wake-up call, Jen shot bolt upright, grasped her head, and groaned, "I had the strangest dream." She looked around her, then at me, then Peth, and shook her head. "Where am I? Why is everything so blurry? How can I see what's to the sides as well as in front?"

And then, as quick as she'd awoken, her eyes snapped shut, her body relaxed, and she fell back onto the cushion with a soft thump.

"Guess they're working then," I said glumly.

"Indeed."

Peth smiled at Jen. I tried not to punch her in the face. Luckily, I succeeded. It would have been a shame to break a rule such at that. No hitting women, even mothers-in-law.

We sat at the table and watched Jen's chest rise and fall. Not another word was spoken for an hour. The night drew on and Jen continued to sleep. It may have been an unnatural rest, but it was for the best. Come the morning, she would be better able to deal with what had happened.

With that thought, it struck me that maybe I wouldn't be here in the morning to look after my little girl. Would she be stuck with Peth and the other crazies, encouraging her to do all manner of mad things? No, Phage would ensure that never happened. She was strong, and willful, and could never let her mother take control.

But I wouldn't be here to stand by her side and pull faces at Peth.

So the night slowly faded, and the dawn chorus began. A cacophony of calls to signal the start of another day in paradise.

No sudden revelations, no deep insights, no frenzied attacks by Peth or one of her cronies. Just us, my sleeping princess, and the birds.

I didn't even see Peth leave, but she stood in front of me with two steaming mugs of coffee so she must have left to make them.

"Drink it. You look like you need it."

"Thanks." I cradled the mug in my hands and took a scalding sip. Hot, sweet, and tasty. "Wow, real coffee?"

"We don't drink that ubermarket crap."

"It's unbelievable, right?"

"The worst." Peth sipped her drink and watched Jen for a while, then she sat at the bench and locked her strange eyes, eyes my daughter now shared, on me.

"Your time is nearly up. What have you decided? I am ready to leave this world. Don't feel bad for doing what needs to be done. It is the way of things. The notes endure."

"They sure do. But there's time yet. A little. Not much, but let's see how this plays out."

"If you miss your deadline, you know what happens?"

"At least that way nobody's to blame. No blame, no guilt, no hate."

"But I'd know that you could have lived. So will Phage. That you could have taken my life and been with them. Do it, Soph. Do it now and be done with it." Peth placed her coffee down and pulled apart the lacy blouse to reveal her chest a little more. She pulled her pendants to one side then told me, "Just do it quick. A single thrust of your new blade and it will be over."

"I can't. I just can't. It feels wrong. There's something missing here, but I don't know what it is. I can't do it, Peth."

"Then let me. Give me your knife and let me do it."

"No, you know I can't do that."

"Then I'll take it." Before I had chance to react, Peth's whispers were in my head, clouding my vision and mind as she morphed the insignificant distance to my side. The popper snapped open on my sheath, and I felt the weight at my side change as she drew my knife.

Instantly, the moment she laid hands on Bone Slicer, her whispers were cut by its edge and Peth was slammed across the room and into one of the structural posts. There was a loud crack, then she slumped down onto her arse and stared, dumbfounded, at her hand. It was burned badly, shining silver and almost screaming. Or was that my elven blade?

The knife vibrated on the wooden planks, the runes glowing bright silver. "Back you go," I told him, and my knife sprang upright, balancing in its tip, then shot up and glided gently into the sheath. The fastener closed, locking it back into place.

"Didn't I say?" I asked, smiling. "Only I can handle it."

"No, you didn't," hissed Peth, wide-eyed, jealous as fuck, and in a fair amount of pain judging by the way she held her hand in her lap.

She closed her eyes and her lips moved almost imperceptibly as she began her whispers. I turned away, not even daring to lip read, as I felt the magic build.

"You can look now," she said a few minutes later.

I turned to find her standing, regal as ever, a scowl on her face. Her forehead was beaded with sweat.

"You okay?"

"I am healed. But that is a very powerful weapon. More powerful than I'd have believed."

"Sorry, I didn't think to say about that. Slipped my mind."

"I'm sure. What is that thing? It's... It's so strange. I could hear it, feel it. It hated me."

"It does that sometimes. It's almost like it's alive."

"Not almost. It is."

"How so?"

"I have no idea. It's elven, unknown to the witches. But incredibly powerful. Dangerous too, Soph, so take heed and take care."

"I intend to."

"I have the answer," screamed Jen as she shot to her feet and stared about wildly.

Everyone's Up

Peth and I turned to Jen, shocked by her outburst and the state of her.

"Jen, it's okay," I soothed as I moved to comfort her.

Peth put a hand to my shoulder, eyes full of concern. "Don't," she whispered. "She's not herself."

"She's my little girl. She needs me."

"She's not your little girl. She's something else right now. Speak slowly, carefully, and don't push her."

I nodded, then turned back to Jen. Her hair was soaked and stuck to her head, her new eyes danced madly, flickering in the light of dawn as a fiery sun shone into the compound. She turned her head left then right, cocked at a strange angle, listening, staring like the world was fresh and new.

"It's okay, you're safe," I told her.

Jen glared at me like I was dirt under her boot, less than nothing.

"Speak, my sisters. What answers do you have?" asked Peth.

No wonder she despised me. Currently, it was the sisters peering out, not Jen. How I hated them all. Hated this place. It was because of the witches' magic that Jen was this way. I had no doubt about that.

"The notes endure," chanted a thousand witches through my daughter's mouth. A broken, throaty rasp of countless crones clamoring for attention.

"The notes endure," repeated at least a dozen real life witch bitches standing behind us in various states of undress.

"What's happening?" asked Phage as she shoved through the others to get to my side.

"The bloody dead sisters have taken over Jen. They changed her eyes and now they're talking through her."

"What!? Mother, what's the meaning of this?"

"It's not my doing. She came to us and I put her to sleep, but now she's awake and the sisters have something to say."

"To say about what? And Soph, is it over? Your note?"

"No, it isn't. But my time's almost up."

"You must do it," spat Peth. "I told him he must. I will gladly sacrifice my life to keep your family whole."

"Enough!" ordered Phage. "How do we help Jen?"

"I need no help from you!" shouted Jen as she pointed a finger at Phage. "You are but a child. We have answers," echoed the voices of a thousand dead fools. "We know. We know. We know," they chorused as Jen's body spasmed and her arms twitched manically. She was possessed, that was the truth of it.

"What do you know?" asked the other excited witches. I turned at their words. They were all here now. The whole bloody enclave out to watch the show. So much for this being done on the quiet.

"She is not the one you seek." Jen pointed at Peth, then her arm dropped as her head snapped around. She looked past us to the other witches. "Come forth and let the Necronote endure."

Jen gasped, her eyes rolled up in her head, and she began to foam at the mouth. I reached to catch her and she collapsed into my arms. As I laid her down gently on the cushion once more, Phage came beside me, face a mask of concern.

"What's been happening? Why didn't you wake me?"

"She just came over while Peth and I were talking. Her eyes were funny, like your mother's. The sisters were inside her. Then Peth put her to sleep for a while."

"What is this all about?" asked one of the other elder witches.

I turned to the group and told them, "There's a lot I can't really say, you all know that. I don't want to get any of you into trouble."

"But I can say. I knew as soon as you arrived," said Peth. "Soph has a Necronote yet to be fulfilled, and we assumed it was for me. At least, that was our presumption as the morning dawned. But Jen knows different. The sisters know different." Peth turned to face the witches and ordered, "Come forth. The child has spoken. It is not I who must die, but one of you. Your time is nigh. Die well and be remembered. Die badly and forever be forgotten. Why are you chosen?"

A witch I'd seen around over the years, even back before Phage and I got together, shuffled forward timidly. I'd never liked her, although I'd forgotten her name. She was always sly and sneaky, up herself, looked down on me the same as the rest, but she was worse. Wouldn't talk, just glared at me, nothing but insults or mutterings under her breath whenever I was around.

Nothing unusual about that. Quite a few of them were like that. Diehard witches from the old times who wouldn't modernize or accept change. They hated men, especially ones who wouldn't bend the knee or kowtow to their nonsense.

"He comes for me."

"No, he comes for me," said another, much younger woman I liked. She was always friendly and polite, keen to chat.

"No, you're both wrong. It's me he has come for. I thought I was wrong, but now I know I wasn't. It's me." Elsie hung her head and stepped forward past the others until she was alone. She was visibly shaking and tears fell freely.

"Elsie, what do you mean?" I asked softly as I got to my feet. "You've always been kind to me. You bandaged me up after that fight I had. Remember?"

"I remember. You're nice. Strong, but gentle too. A nice man." Her hair was long now, dark as my heart, and it hung over her face, hiding her features as her head bent lower and lower and her shoulders sagged.

"Why would it be you? It can't be."

"Speak," insisted Peth.

"I... I think I broke the rules. I did something wrong and this is my punishment."

"What could you possibly have done?" I asked her. "You're so young. What, in your twenties still?"

"I'm twenty-six," she mumbled through her hair.

"Lift your head, child. Have you no dignity in what you are?" Peth stepped forward and took Elsie by the shoulders firmly then lifted her head and brushed her hair away, revealing a red face, bloodshot eyes, and streaks of tears.

Peth returned to Phage and I as we waited for Elsie to get herself together. The other witches remained still. What I wanted to know was why had the others assumed I was here for them once they knew my note led here? What secrets did they hold? Guess they all held some. Didn't we all?

"You can tell us," I told her. "It's okay. I'm not about to kill you."

"You will!" she sobbed. "You have to. It's the rules. It's me! You have to kill me," she wailed.

Peth morphed beside her, slapped the terrified girl across the face, then was back beside me in the blink of an eye.

Elsie gasped. Her hand moved to the red mark on her cheek, then she summoned courage from hitherto unknown reserves and raised her head. She stared right at Peth.

"I told. I was scared and worried, and hated what I'd done, so I told another what had happened. All of it. She let me, but she was just being kind. I've killed before, but this last time was so horrible. I couldn't bear it any longer. I had to tell someone what happened. So there. I broke the rules and now I have to die."

"It doesn't matter," I told her. "I understand. That shouldn't be a crime. That's normal. Natural. You hated it, you were afraid, disgusted, and you needed someone to talk to. It doesn't matter," I repeated.

"It was me. She spoke to me. And why not?" said a defiant older woman, probably as experienced as Peth, but without the desire to rule over others. "Poor girl was falling apart. And who can blame her? Why do we let them do this to us? So I took a stand. I let her unburden herself and I don't regret it." She was talking to Peth, nobody else, and remained defiant.

"You fools! Look what you have brought upon us. A man has come to destroy what we built. You bring this on yourselves. We must endure. The Necroverse must endure. This must be done. Now you will be marked. Your time will come too, and all because you felt sorry for this pitiful child?"

"Mother, that's enough," shouted Phage above the din of the others. Most agreeing with Peth, some not.

"This is my house and my rules," spat Peth.

"Have some compassion. She's afraid. You're all shouting, but a young woman is scared. Be gentle. Even if she dies, shouldn't she experience kindness before she goes?"

"She's not going anywhere. Only away from here if she wants to," I told Peth and all the rest.

"This is my home. I like it here. I want to be a great witch," said Elsie. "But now I can't."

"You can do what the hell you want, because I won't kill you. And look, we don't even know if it is you. Did anyone see Jen point directly to Elsie? No, they didn't. You all thought it was you because everyone has secrets to hide. You broke the rules. We all have. Don't you get it? This is a joke. A sick, twisted joke. Go back to your houses. This show is over." I turned my back on them and bent to check on Jen.

I knew they remained, but I didn't care. I would not kill what amounted to a child. Never.

"Everyone stays," warned Peth.

I felt her glare through the back of my skull, but I refused to engage. Jen was more important, but she just lay there, unconscious, the dead witches assaulting her mind. Without knowing why, my hand reached out and rested lightly on Jen's warm forehead.

My mind emptied as tight muscles relaxed and a deep lethargy took me over. Knots and strange spasms in my back I hadn't even noticed came to the fore as I connected deeply with my own body for what felt like the first time. Hyper-awareness of a kind never before experienced.

What was this? Every twitch, every involuntary spasm, tiny cramps at the base of my neck, an ache deep in my spine, a tingle in my right calf, it all became of prime importance as my hand warmed and the nerves danced. Not pain, but a deep connection. A merging of body and mind that had never been there before.

I was Soph, the complete man. Not just thoughts and a general background noise that was my body, but a deep, true merging of the two disparate parts of myself. I felt my bowels, my kidneys, my liver, all running how they should. Processing and dissolving. Heart pumping, veins throbbing, lungs expanding and contracting as I breathed in and out with fast, shallow breaths.

Sound dissolved as I focused first on myself then on my daughter. I felt her skin as though it were my own. A connection deeper than any I'd ever experienced. Words came as if they were spoken to me, but they weren't my thoughts or even Jen's. They were the words of the witches. Dead witches.

These ancient ghosts clamored excitedly for my attention, joyous to be heard by another for the first time in their long, sorry non-existence. Disgruntled too. For I was an impostor, not one of them. An intruder. And worst of all. A man.

They recoiled in horror once that became clear. I didn't care what they thought; they weren't even real. Just memories, vibrations that had somehow managed to cling to a faded semblance of existence. All I cared about was Jen. The ancient bitches argued and shouted, called me names and then tried to woo me with complements and praise, but I would have none of it.

They were hurting my little girl, overwhelming her, so I told them, and ordered them to leave her alone.

Laughter was all I received at first. A cacophony of mad cackles from long-deceased magic practitioners who believed themselves to be invincible. They didn't have a fucking clue. I was Jen's father and would never let them have her. Never.

"Leave," came a voice from deep within me. A voice not my own. One of countless other men of all ages and all types. Rich, poor, powerful, weak, Necro, and plain old boring men who'd never had a day's excitement in their whole lives. My ancestors. My lineage. My brothers. Expanding in reach the further back it went in time, until my brotherhood encompassed the entirety of all men. All fathers. All sons. All brothers.

My brothers.

The witches screamed as they recoiled at the sheer power of that single word imbued with the strength of countless men joining together to protect their own. The sisters were no match for this, for they were merely there for the magic. I was here for the love, and so were my ancestors.

Save their daughter.

Our little girl.

My princess.

With a whoosh of noise in my head, the witches were gone. Not banished for good, but quietened. Receding into the background. Fading from Jen's young, impressionable mind until she was stronger, older, maybe even wiser, and better able to handle their presence.

My skin grew cold. I tingled all over, then everything shut down and I fell backwards, the connection lost.

All was emptiness.

Waiting

Annoying voices woke me from a dreamless slumber. My back throbbed dully, my right foot was still asleep, and my head pounded like someone had gone to town with a big bag of nails and a new hammer they were keen to try out.

For some peculiar reason, my eyeballs ached, so I daren't move the lids for fear of them popping out and making a mess of my shirt.

"He heard his brothers. That's not possible."

"It isn't even allowed, is it?"

"He's a blasphemy."

"That's our thing."

"Did you hear him? He was rude to our dead. Our elder sisters. The nerve!"

"We should kill him, before he murders one of us."

"You fucking try. I'll rip your guts out and boil them in your stupid fucking cauldron!" That was definitely Phage.

"Enough!" Peth hissed, her words more than just words. There was magic behind them; the others had no choice but to obey.

"Daughter, nobody will harm him." I didn't need my eyes open to picture the glare Peth was giving the other witches. "Listen, my sisters. He is one of us. Yes, I know he's a man, but he is my family. The father of my granddaughter, a remarkably special girl, and the husband of my daughter. Soph has proven himself time and time again to be unlike any other man we have encountered. He is strong, more powerful than he knows. His abilities keep surprising us all, especially me, and even more so himself, and he has this very annoying habit of being in the right place at the right time. He knows things no other man knows, has a gift from the elves, even got something more special than any of you know from a man I hadn't heard from in years, and many other things have singled him out. But most importantly, he is the guardian of Jen, and she is undoubtedly important to everyone's future. So nobody touches him. Ever!"

"So we wait for him to wake up and kill one of us? Maybe even you?"

"I believed it was me he had come to kill, but now I'm not so sure. All of us have our secrets, and several of you will have a heavy price to pay for your treachery and deceit. The punishment is cruel for the rules you have undoubtedly broken, but you will not harm him."

"I don't like this."

"Neither do I."

"What if he kills us all?"

"He won't," said Phage. "He's a kind man who never wants to hurt anyone. You heard him. He won't hurt Mother, he won't hurt Elsie. He'll find a way and come through this. He always does." Phage's words sounded hollow. She wanted to believe what she was saying, but even she had her doubts about this. It wasn't surprising. What the fuck was I meant to do?

"My daughter is right. Now leave us. All of you," ordered Peth.

The witches grumbled, but receding footsteps told me they did as they were told. Soon, there was silence.

Who was I here to deal with? Did I even have to kill, or was this another sad test? And Jen? How was she? Time to open the old peepers and pain be damned.

"Soph, you can open your eyes now," said Phage softly. "We know you're listening."

I grinned sheepishly as I reluctantly let the light in, expecting a world of hurt or at the very least some eyeball misfortune, but the pain receded as I peered blearily around me and clambered to my feet. My foot remained numb, so I shook it out along with the rest of me, and stood facing mother and daughter who were now sitting at the table, observing me carefully.

"You heard?" asked Phage, smiling sweetly but looking like stress on sexy legs.

"Of course he did. He's no fool."

"I heard. And thanks for the support, Peth. I appreciate it."

She nodded. "I meant every word. But this has to be done. Finished with. How long do you have?"

"Until about half three. A few hours is my guess. Was I out long? Ugh, silly question." I checked my watch. I was basically out of time. No wonder my stomach was rumbling. I'd missed breakfast and lunch, and had been out cold for the better part of the day.

"How are you?" asked Phage kindly.

"I feel fine now. Had a headache and my eyes hurt for a while, but I'm good. Damn, that was weird." I rubbed at my temples and tried to process what had happened, but already it felt like a dream, fading fast.

"Everyone kept coming and going while you slept. They wanted to see what you'd do next. See if you'd do something else," Phage told me. "And some wanted to, er, kill you."

"So I heard. Been like that all day, has it?"

"Pretty much."

"How's Jen now?"

"She asleep inside. Oz is watching over her. Woofer too. Protecting her. Soph, you did it. You made the sisters leave her alone. You used your own magic to save her."

"Incredible," whispered Peth.

"Yeah, well, I guess I panicked. She's okay?"

"She's fine. We thought it best she rest. But don't worry, the sisters have left her, like you told them. More like ordered! I don't think that will happen again. Not for a while, at least."

"You probably scared them too much," said Peth with a hint of a smile. "How did you do it? It's unheard of, you know. Men don't have access to their lineage."

"They were just there," I shrugged. "I guess somewhere deep inside me they were waiting. I didn't know what to do, but they did. They just kind of came. It hurt like hell and it sure didn't feel nice, but if it worked."

"It did. She's just overwhelmed. Everything that's happened here, all the magic. The air's alive with it. It got to her, that's all."

"She's too young for this. It will damage her," I said.

"Jen is a strong, powerful young woman," said Peth. "These things can happen. She is rather young, but it happened to me, and to Phage, so don't be too concerned. It's worrying the first time, but it might be years before she hears from them again. Each time, it gets easier. You have more control, can tame their wildness."

"That's reassuring. I think." I sat opposite them at the table and stared off into space for a while, unsure what to do but sure I should be doing it.

I knew they were both watching me, waiting for something to happen. A word, a plan, something.

I had no plan. No ideas. I wasn't even sure I had any hope.

Time passed in that strange, slow way when you do nothing but wait for it to pass. This was the first time I'd ever sat around like this, counting down the minutes until my time was up. I'd come close to missing my deadline a few times, but only because I was tracking someone elusive or in the throes of a fight to the death. Never just sitting around with no clue who the mark was and no way of finding out.

"You both need to leave. Tell the others to stay away, too. If you aren't here, then it isn't you. This is the right place, so leave me alone and I know you'll be safe. And promise me one thing."

"What?" sobbed Phage, tears flowing freely.

"Do not let Jen come here until this is over with. Whatever happens, and I mean this, do not let her out of the house. Go and watch her, just so I know she's safe. Phage, promise me. She can't be traumatized any more. She's seen enough these last few days. More than enough."

"I promise. We both love you. Don't leave us."

"I'll do my best. And I love you too. More than life itself. Tell Jen I'll always watch over her, even if I'm dead. I'll find a way. Always."

We moved to the end of the table and hugged each other like this really was the last time we'd get the chance. I whispered that I loved her into her hair, then stepped back and nodded.

"Come, daughter. Soph will be fine." Peth led a shell-shocked Phage away from me.

A Death

The sun beat down relentlessly. Even in the shade, the heat was nigh on unbearable. I was antsy, and kept finding I was tapping my foot in stress. I was sweating badly, and very thirsty, yet I dared not move now.

Nothing to do but wait. See this through to the bitter end.

Birds sang cheerily from the cool of the surrounding woods. How I envied them their simple, uncomplicated lives.

Bees, the mighty bees that had returned to the country in their billions, rejuvenating the plant life, attracting other insects, and thus encouraging the bird populations to rise dramatically, had decided to use the communal area as a main thoroughfare.

A constant background drone of buzzing filled my ears as they performed the very important business of ensuring the survival of their species through the harsh winter months ahead. Be prepared. There was a lesson to learn there.

At least they knew their purpose, had a clearly defined job to do. More envy of the little guys.

Mixed with the drone of the bees was the general hum of the witches as they went about their daily tasks. Some tended the gardens with a litany of complaints about the weather, how much watering they needed to do, and the quality of the yields. Others were exercising, a form of meditation for some, a way to let off some steam for others. From tai-chi like movements perfected over millennia, to punch bags, and even hardcore weight training, they did it all, sweating through their training.

Women went to and fro. Some rushed, many ambled, all cast a quick glance at me as they passed—none smiled or even nodded. Guess they had their orders from Peth and knew better than to disobey. The matriarchy in full, terrifying effect.

I just waited. And sweated. My guts hurt. My thirst increased. My heart ached for Jen. There was nothing I could do to help her now. There might never be.

Slowly, I became aware of a change in atmosphere. The bees had gone quiet, so had the birds. And even the witches were hushed. I glanced up to find that they were all just standing and staring.

I followed their scornful gazes. Looks full of vitriol, pure hate, barely contained anger.

A tall, slender woman approached. Her skin was burned by the sun over years until she was roasted dark brown. With gnarled fingers, she brushed hair blacker than even Peth's away from her face. The gathering witches gasped as the woman sneered without slowing.

She walked casually, calmly, head held high. Her bare arms revealed livid scars that criss-crossed her exposed skin and wound their way under a tight, pale yellow vest. She ignored the looks, the murmurs, the rising bile that the amassing witches clearly felt.

Our eyes met. Hers were such a pale blue they could be mistaken for albino, but that wasn't it. It was her age, her experience, her knowledge that shone back at me. It was clear she was older than any person I had ever met, and certainly more powerful than any of the others. Magic practically oozed from her pores, and she shone faintly as she gathered her power like a cloak—protection from the whispers already gathering force as the witches focused their not inconsiderable powers.

This newcomer ignored them, merely shrugged slightly as if annoyed by a bug. Without fanfare or warning, her own whispers shot out, so strong I could see the wispy lines of words made power as silver strands finer than the finest thread. Without breaking stride, immense force sprang from a knotted, compact bundle of throbbing power at her abdomen and ensnared, then nullified, the whispers on the wind directed at her.

Every witch gasped as they recoiled at the assault.

The newcomer kept her gaze locked on mine and reached the steps up to this sacred meeting place. With an almost imperceptible nod of her head, she took the steps then moved silently into the shade and sat opposite me, crossed her legs gracefully, then clasped her long fingers together and rested her hands on the table.

She smiled sweetly at me. It was a nice smile. Kind. Warm. Inviting. Daring. As though the world itself was amusing to her. As if she understood on a deep level that life was but a joke.

I laughed, genuinely warmed by her outlook and ability to project it. "Finally, someone who gets it."

"I do indeed. And I see you do too. It's nothing but a joke. A wicked game we have no choice but to endure." Her voice was mellow, but there was no doubt she was a woman who knew her own mind, and understood exactly what she wanted out of life. And death.

"So it's you?" I asked her.

"Indeed. Were you afraid I wouldn't come?"

"No, not really. I'm more afraid that you did. It's going to get nasty, isn't it?"

"Oh yes. Very." She laughed again, the lines around her eyes crinkling as she tilted her head back and exposed her throat. Up close, it was clear she wasn't merely slim, she was verging on malnourished.

This woman was truly old. One of the ancient ones who'd surpassed the mundane, the everyday. I'd heard of them, everyone had, and Phage had spoken of several witches she'd been told used to live here who had finally become if not enlightened in the true sense, then certainly achieved a status no longer quite human. Passed through the usual trials, teachings, and endless practice to emerge as a being very different to those around her.

She most likely never ate or drank, survived on raw magic, the essence of the Necroverse. Roaming, or sealed away hermit-like for years, whatever took her fancy.

From what I could recall, there had been none like her for a very long time. And the last to leave had left disgraced because she dared challenge the wisdom of those who remained. But the witches were always having disagreements, internal struggles for dominance and authority, so it wasn't anything I'd paid much attention to. Just another story amongst many Phage had told me over the years.

"Why have you come back?" I asked.

"It certainly wasn't because I missed them," she said, waving a hand to indicate the groups of women watching us with hate-filled eyes. "So naive. So wasteful. So young."

"You moved on to bigger and better things, I take it?"

"Indeed. But that was a long time ago. Look at them. They despise me, yet I only recognize a few faces. Most have never even seen me, yet they still hate. We witches do so enjoy holding a grudge."

"What did you do? Why did you leave?"

"Does it matter?"

"I guess not. How'd you know to come?"

"Let's just say that once you get to be my age, and with my knowledge, you know these things. I saw. Do you understand?"

"Sure. You have the gifts of a seer. You're beyond that, though. Something wilder. Untamed. More Necro than human."

She chuckled, genuinely amused. "Something like that, yes. I have roamed, I have slept for decades at a time, I have sat and communed with beings impossible to describe or imagine. And now, finally, I have seen all I wish to see and know all I wish to know."

"But do you know why? That's the only question that matters, isn't it? Why the Necronotes?"

"No. There is no why. As my sisters like to say, the notes endure. There is no answer, Soph. Just a cosmic joke we will never be told the punchline to."

"You're wrong," I told her. She raised an eyebrow. "I know the answer to the joke."

"Then maybe you will share it with me before my time on this plane comes to an end?"

"It's because. That's the answer to everything. Why the Necronotes? Why this game of death? Why put us through it? Why to any and all of it? Because."

"Oh, how wonderful!" She clapped her hands together with glee then was still again, her eyes still sparkling with mirth.

"You want this?" I asked her.

"I do. But please, let me give you a gift."

"I don't want a gift. I've had enough gifts lately, and never asked for a single one."

"Even if it means being relieved of your burden for once? A reprieve from the anguish, the guilt, the hatred that grows inside? Come, we all want that."

"There have been so many. I'm already way beyond saving."

"You are never beyond saving. Not you, Necrosoph. I see you. I know you. I will let you keep your hands unbloodied today. Let's call it my parting gift to you. A final act of mercy in a world so very devoid of kindness amongst Necros. We must fight it at every turn, keep our humanity. Such as it is. Now, on to the next stage. I am keen to continue my journey." She bowed, then turned away from me. As she stood, her arms spread wide and, with a single whispered word, the threads holding the incensed witches at bay all snapped simultaneously.

They descended on her like a rabid mob. Had she merely released them from her hold, or had she coerced them? Forced them? Stirring their anger to new heights? I liked to think it was the latter, but sadly I think they just had this inside them all and here was the perfect opportunity to take out their fears on something too different even for them to understand.

I was shoved aside by a horde of screaming madwomen as they stormed the platform. Eyes were wild, long hair was flying, teeth were bared, screams were yelled, spittle flew, weapons were drawn, whispers thickened the air into a magical pea soup until I found it nigh on impossible to wade through the almost gelatinous substance.

Magic gripped my mind, froze my soul, chilled me to the bone with its force and sheer hatred for something that should never have been hated. Someone.

Why did their anger run so deep? What could this woman have possibly done?

The stranger remained upright as long as possible as the witches tore at her clothes until they were rags. New wounds covered ancient scars as they clawed at her arms with long fingernails or sliced with knives.

Pinned back against a post by the sheer volume of women clamoring for blood, and the whispers that kept me from even speaking, all I could do was watch.

They yanked her hair until her head was a mess of bloody bald patches, the floor littered with trampled clothes and fine, dark hair. Blood streamed down her body, pooling in the folds, soaking into the strands.

Over and over, the witches screamed abuse, a terrible blight on us all. A cheer went up as the group held one of their own aloft, naked now, her body smeared in her own blood. A hundred individual, smudged fingerprints. Proof of a crime never to be punished. They slammed the unresisting woman onto the massive table and scraped nails down her long legs in a perverse, provocative act.

Four women nodded to each other as if in silent conversation; each took a limb. They spreadeagled her, then pinned my mark's hands and feet to the table in unison, their short knives buried to the hilt. Everyone howled with demented delight.

Unable to turn my head away from this ghastly display, I watched as otherwise timid women sliced flesh from her thighs in long, thin strips they twirled around before flinging away. Ancient crones gnawed on the still-conscious, unprotesting ancient witch's toes like rabid dogs. The ferocity stunned me. The sheer animal nature they had inside. A barbarism nobody could ever justify.

Witches of all ages stabbed, gouged, bit, and spat. At least half of them bit chunks from their captive. Nearly all lapped at the blood, licking the bloodied flesh with relish, lost to rapture.

How could one woman cut another's nipples? I had no answer. Why would they desecrate another human being in this way? Cackling madwomen sliced between ribs like they were preparing for a barbecue, while others took joy in snapping finger bones one after the other.

I saw Elsie, sweet, young Elsie prize open a wound with her black painted nails and thrust a fist inside the woman's abdomen.

I shuddered at a scene only too familiar. Was this me? Was this what we were all like deep down? Surely not? I had gone too far, but hadn't tortured, reveled in such madness. Had I?

Elsie hollered with pride and joy as she pulled out entrails and held the string up for the others to see. Again, way too similar an act for me to deny the connection.

Buoyed by the bloodlust, utterly lost to the madness, the others redoubled their efforts. They bit off her ears, then flung them aside. They punctured her eyes with their knives, then smashed her teeth with the hilt of blood-soaked weapons, and still they wouldn't stop.

Countless women clamored for their own personal pound of flesh. Taking chunks with their knives from her legs and arms, then throwing the meat aside where even the dogs that patrolled the compound refused to investigate.

My head was spinning. I felt sick, disgusted by their lack of compassion, the depraved acts the witches could commit as a group. They were lost to a communal madness of their own making and seemingly unable to stop or offer any form of reprieve for this mystery witch.

"Enough!" I shouted, the whispers holding me weak now, my presence forgotten. I barged through the crowd, not caring what damage I did with Bone Slicer already drawn and calling out with his own whispers, forcing the others from us, allowing me to make it to the table.

I held my foreign weapon up high, clenched tight in both hands to make a fist, then plunged it through the neck of the dying woman. With a final gasp, and then a gurgle of blood, her body went limp. Her ordeal was over.

Bone Slicer was stuck fast in the table, so I yanked him out and held him up to inspect him. Clean as a freshly forged blade polished by its creator, it glinted in the sunlight. The runes throbbed, glowing pale and powerful, then I slowly lowered my arms and slid him back into the holster. The click of the popper was the only noise in the compound.

I shook my head as I walked away, stumbling like a shell-shocked soldier over to a fire pit where several witches had been preparing one of their damn potions in a ridiculously oversized cauldron.

I don't know why, or even if it was my idea or his, but I removed Bone Slicer once more and plunged him into the potion. The murky liquid hissed and bubbled so violently I had to turn my head to protect my eyes and face. The smell that arose was noxious beyond belief.

Call it intuition, call it coercion, call it my brothers talking to me from beyond the grave, but whatever the reason, I pulled out the pack of Tyr's powdered droppings and sprinkled the contents onto the thick membrane of the pungent soup then stirred it again with my knife.

The morass bubbled, frothed, and spat in anger, but I continued to stir and stir, lost to the swirls. Things began to appear in the potion. Faces, words, whispers, spells. A source of power I was yet to understand.

Silver promises surfaced then sank, tendrils of otherworldly power and insight promising who knew what.

I carried on mixing, deep and hard, lost to it now like I'd been lost to the bloodlust so many times. I was the potion, the potion was me. We were one and the same.

This was my escape from the madness that preceded it. I had no eyes for the foulness here, no ears for the sounds of their screams, no awareness at all of what they were now doing. All I had was this cauldron and its contents, claimed as my own.

Steam and spitting liquid blistered my fingers and even my face; I didn't care. Didn't even feel it.

All that remained was the blade, the potion, and my arms stirring rhythmically. My escape, my meditation, my release from the horrors I encountered wherever I went in this world.

I just wanted to go home.

At some point, I noticed another hand over mine. Familiar. Warm. Steady. Kind. My stirring slowed. I turned and looked into the beautiful face of Phage.

"It's okay, you can stop now." Phage's hand remained as I slowed, then ceased, my movements. She smiled, full of sympathy, then removed her hand so I could pull my blade from the foulness.

Bone Slicer hissed as though satisfied; I noted the runes glowing red with unbridled glee.

With a sigh, I secured him in place once more, then stood with my arms slack by my sides, not knowing what to do, what to say, where to go, or if I even wanted to anyway.

Unable to stop myself, I glanced over to the scene of such barbarism. A white shroud covered the dead witch. The others had left, not another soul in sight apart from Phage by my side and Peth standing over the corpse. Her hands were in front of her as if in prayer, mourning for the dead woman her living sisters had torn apart.

"I could kill them all. Each and every one of them," I growled.

"I know. So could I. But it isn't that simple. They weren't themselves."

"Is it ever that simple?" I asked her.

"No. It isn't. Never. Come on, I made tea."

"Tea? Ha!" For some reason, I began to laugh, and I couldn't stop. If you're happy, have tea. If you're sad, have tea. If a group of demented witch bitches with untold power tear a defenseless old woman to bits, and enjoy doing it, while you watch, have a nice cup of tea.

But then, what else could you do?

Witchy Bitchy

"Seriously, we're going to drink our fucking tea and pretend there isn't a disemboweled woman laying there?" I looked at Peth with utter contempt. I could feel no other way.

"What would you have me do?"

"Move the bloody body! Oh, wait. No, you can't, because her insides would fall out. What's left of them. Did you pick up all her fingers? Find the bits of ear? All the lumps of flesh your women ripped from her while she was still alive?"

"I had no part to play in any of that," protested Peth. "You know I promised to leave you to your Necronote. I did not know she would come. I believed you were doing your duty and would never interfere."

"Liar. And that's utter bullshit! You know who came, you know who she is, and you knew exactly what was happening here. I'm sure you watched."

"She did, Soph." Phage put a hand to her mother's shoulder to stop her from talking over her. "She watched, but it wasn't Mother's fault. She was powerless to stop it."

"Powerless!? I'm seriously meant to believe that? That she couldn't intervene?"

"It's true. That woman, she was the one who did this. It wasn't the others. You were there, so you must know."

"I know she gave herself freely. I know she controlled the witches and stopped them making a move, then she released them from her whispers and they went utterly fucking apeshit on her. They tore her apart! They ripped her ears off with their bloody teeth. Elsie tore her guts out and held them up like a prize. She was smiling. Happy. Where the fuck are they? You lot are twisted. There's something utterly wrong with you all. "

"Soph, you don't understand. Mother couldn't intervene. She wasn't able to."

I gulped my tea, just to be doing something. It was hot and bitter, exactly how I didn't like it. Fucking bitches couldn't even make a nice cup of tea when a man needed it most.

"I am shamed by their acts. I am even more shamed by my own. I am so sorry. Beyond sorry. We have brought terrible darkness upon our group. I fear we will never recover from such a depraved act. But this was your note, Necrosoph, so you are not free from blame. You could have done what was needed. I heard, I saw, I watched. I was as good as there. She did what she had to do and took matters into her own hands to save you from what was by rights your duty. Yes, the others despised her for deeds past, but they would never have acted in such a way."

"Don't you dare try to lay this at my feet. That's inexcusable."

Peth was ready to reply in anger, but she held herself in check then quietly said, "You are correct. I am so consumed by grief and despair, and the shame, my own inability to act, to save her, knowing I could not, that I am not myself at all. Apologies."

And then she cried. She didn't try to hide it, turn away, let her head hang low. She owned her tears as she held her head up high and they streamed down her face as though the woman was her own flesh and blood.

Slowly, and I felt dumb for having taken so long to put the pieces together, the truth dawned on me.

"She was your mother, wasn't she? Phage, was that your grandmother?"

"That's what Mother says. I missed out on any grandparents. Or a father." Phage couldn't help sounding bitter about that, even though she wasn't trying to be cruel. "But yes, she was my blood. Jen's blood too. She never even got to see her. Now she's gone."

"She's been gone a long time already," said Peth as she wiped her eyes on a lace fucking handkerchief of all things, then stashed it in the folds of her blouse.

"I'm sorry for your loss," I told her. "What happened? Why did she leave here? Why the vitriol from the others? And damn, Peth, how could you let that happen?"

"I'm not sure I can explain it. And please don't take offense, but especially to a man. It's a sister thing, a witch thing. A Necro issue, but so much more besides."

"Just try, Mother. I'd like to know too. I never knew her, and you refused to speak of her. All I heard were snippets from the others, and it was never kind."

"Mia, that was her name, was incredibly old. I mean one of the very oldest amongst all Necros. I was born into a very different time when there was hardly a thing in the world. Life was basic, very different, and incredibly hard. There weren't machines, nary a road, so people stayed put. But Mia was wild even as a child, and she went back even further to a time when the world was unrecognizable. She traveled the country, then settled here. As she grew older, so she became more involved in the arts. In magic. Consumed, I guess."

"Just how old are you, Peth?" I asked.

"Old. Years, decades, and centuries passed. Over time, others came. You must understand that this was an era when magic was everywhere. When it was taken for granted, believed in. Witches held a special place in everyone's hearts. They helped, they healed, even offered advice. It was all gladly offered and gladly received. Magic filled the world. The witches of old were always connected deeply to the Necroverse. Mia was the matriarch. She was a tough but firm ruler."

"Sounds familiar," I said.

Peth tutted then resumed. "She had children. Many. Most disappointed and were left to their own devices. None remained for long. Then she had me. I was her little darling. For many years we were extremely close, even though she was formidable and strict. It was all I knew, and that was how things were back in those days. More women came, life became more organized, but she began to change."

"How so?" asked Phage.

"The dark arts took hold, and I don't mean like you worry they do with us. With me. I mean a whole other level that I could never explain. She delved deeper, uncovered many truths we still live by to this day. But then, one fateful day, she took it too far. She sacrificed every single witch in the compound, and there must have been over a hundred by then. She killed each and every one in the name of an unknown entity she had become enthralled by."

"You mean possessed?" I asked.

"Yes, I suppose so. Mother wrecked everything she had taken centuries to build. All those lives lost, all that knowledge gone. She destroyed her entire world. Do you understand? She murdered her own. Not because of the notes, not because of love, but for power. She got it all right, and the creature she offered the energy of the murdered witches to did what all such otherworldly creatures do. It took what it wanted then abandoned her."

"How could she do it?"

"She was dominated by greed and most likely not of sound mind. How could she be? She used her whispers to kill, and take their power, then gave it away for her own selfish needs. The only one she spared was me. For years we were alone here. She grew utterly insane, forever trying to find the creature again and reconnect. But it was gone. She grew cold, distant, and very cruel. My life was miserable, but I couldn't abandon her. Not even then. She finally just wandered off one day and I never saw her again until now." Peth sank back into her chair, pale and stiff, bottling up the true emotions because she couldn't face how tight they would grip her if she let it all surface.

"Oh, Mother. I'm so sorry."

"So am I. Truly. I didn't know. None of us did."

"The others here knew some of it. That she had murdered so many. But only a very few knew she was my mother, and I wanted to spare you that, Phage. I swear most here never knew. Only that she had betrayed her own. As the years passed, new women ended up here, and I cautiously began to rediscover what it was like to live with others. It was hard. I was remote, still am, but I tried, and I put her out of my mind. I somehow found the will to rebuild what had been lost, vowing it would be different this time. Understand, this was so very long ago that the memories have faded. I cannot recall most events from that time, but the feelings, and the knowledge of what she'd done and how she treated me, remained."

"You did it though. You built this from nothing," Phage told her.

"I did. So no, I didn't intervene, and now it's too late. I wish I'd helped her. She didn't deserve to die that way. But she did this. She forced the others to kill her that way because she couldn't live with the shame and believed it was what she deserved. But once again she's destroyed lives. How are they meant to ever forget what they did? This will ruin them, especially the young ones like Elsie. She's a babe. Mother had no right to inflict that upon her or any of us."

"They're tough old crows. They'll be fine," I said, maybe not that helpfully, but I was way out of my depth here.

"Thank you. You may be right, but I fear not."

"Most of us have witnessed far worse, been involved in worse," soothed Phage. "They'll recover."

"I hope so. Excuse me, I need some time alone. I'll check on Jen, but she should still be sleeping. Let's leave her be until the morning, then we can go back to as normal as any of us ever can."

"Agreed. Let the dust settle, and let Jen sleep off the stress of the sisters visiting her head." I nodded to Peth as she turned and walked across the compound like a zombie.

"She's going to take this hard," noted Phage.

"Bloody hell," I said, watching Peth stagger, then regain her composure and continue her trance-like walk.

"I never knew any of that. Why didn't she tell me?"

"Ashamed? Too much hurt. Most of the memories are already lost. And most likely, she just couldn't bear to think of her life back then."

"Maybe. Are you okay, Soph? You witnessed all that, too. You were part of it. You didn't want that. You tried to stop them. The only one who did."

"I'm fine. I'm made of tough stuff, you know that."

"And I know you put on an act most of the time. Really, how are you?"

"About as sad as I've ever been. Disappointed, utterly grossed out, terrified by what people can be made to do. But I already knew we can be made to do just about anything. Take a group of people and it just gets more horrific. At least they had an excuse. What I did to that man, what Jen saw me do? What was my excuse? I'm worse than any of these women."

"That was different."

"I'm not so sure."

"You didn't torture. You didn't enjoy it."

"No, but that still doesn't make it right."

Phage nodded that she understood. Both of us had committed atrocities that could never be atoned for. "What was she like? My grandmother?"

"Truthfully? She seemed like a very nice lady. Kind, calm, happy. A free spirit. She was full of light, Phage. Like an angel. So far beyond the rest of us I don't even believe she was strictly human any more. She was lovely."

"Nothing like Mother described?"

"No, nothing. My guess is that she's spent the time since she left here trying to make up for all she did wrong. Hell, could that be a thousand years trying to find peace? A way to forgive yourself, to make amends? I wonder why she came now?"

"Because she knew her name was on the Necronote. She knew she had come to the end. Maybe because she'd finally found peace and accepted it was her time."

"She certainly acted that way. Like she wanted it. And she said the strangest thing. She said she was glad to move on to the next stage. She knew. She genuinely knew what came next."

"Maybe there's hope for us all, then."

"Maybe."

Vial Poo

"Why were you over here?" asked Phage as we stared into the murky, dark depths of the oversized cauldron.

I shrugged. "No idea. It felt like the right thing to do, I guess. Not that I was doing much thinking. Everything was messed up. My body wanted to do this, so I went along with it as I didn't have the energy to protest. It felt cathartic."

"How so?" Phage stirred the contents with a long-handled spoon. We watched as the viscous liquid bubbled at the disturbance, releasing gases that made us recoil. I could taste the magic on my tongue. It was that potent.

"You know when you get really stressed, or you're hyped on bloodlust after a kill?" Phage nodded that she understood. I knew she did. We all did. "There's usually something that brings you back down, soothes your mind. Let's your head put things into order. For me it's smoking, and damn, I'm going to do that in a moment. No, right now." I fumbled out Old Faithful and packed then lit the pipe and puffed away anxiously, letting the almost forgotten power of the harsh weed work its true magic.

"I like to talk to Bernard." Phage smiled weakly.

"That would put anyone into a coma. I get it. There's always something, right? A way to use your body that's comforting, to have a familiar companion, or a set series of actions so you can zone out and let the mundane take over. It's why having Tyr around these last few years has been such a nice thing. Something to occupy me. I can train him, talk to him, laugh at his antics when a wyrmling. He's been good for me."

"You'll miss him when he's off with Jen."

"I will. Hell, I miss him already. He's so different now. But I think he'll still hang out with me when he can. At least I hope so."

"Tyr loves you. If he can, he will."

"That's what it felt like," I said, puffing away. "I was drawn to the cauldron. So I went with it. My head was a mess, I was stressed out, and I just despaired. Do you know what I mean?"

Phage nodded. "I do. Just so fucking despairing of everything. Of what others do. Of what we do. Of what everyone's forced to do. The unending unfairness of it all."

"Exactly! There was a temporary escape route, so I took it with open arms. I don't know what was in the cauldron, but it called to me and I forgot about all this other crap for a while and stared into the liquid. It was warm, inviting in a gross way, and so I stayed. I stirred it with my knife. The runes came alive. They did something to the potion, I'm sure of it. Then I added in all the powder I had and it reacted somehow. Again, I didn't know what I was doing, or why, but it felt right."

"Like sometimes I suddenly decide to go for a walk or make a meal I haven't made for ages. Sometimes your unconscious tells you what's best for you?" suggested Phage.

"That's it exactly! For some reason, everything I did felt right, like it was what I needed. I'm pretty sure it was also the influence of my dead brothers, and damn, I hate calling them that. Fathers, grandfathers, and back it goes. More like dead bastards in my head, but let's go with brothers."

"Mother hates that you did that." Phage's eyes twinkled; we both knew Peth would never accept men being as powerful as her oh-so-precious sisters.

"Me too. Not that they were directing me, but their presence was part of it, for sure. Then I was in a trance. I just did what was right without knowing. I added the powder, stirred, and was lost to it. Ha, sounds so stupid! Me, making a potion. And besides, there was no goal in mind. I have no idea what was in this to begin with, and I doubt it's still any good. Just me messing about. A distraction."

"You don't believe that."

"How'd you mean?"

"Soph, you don't believe the thick, stinking mess in the bottom of this ridiculous cauldron is nothing but horrid brown goop. This is me you're talking to. I know you too well. So, come on, what do you think it is?"

"I honestly have no idea."

"But I do." Peth nodded proudly at us both. She'd showered, changed, and sorted out her emotions. Shoved them down and out of sight. But the telltale signs of anxiety, weariness, and potential stress overload were visible no matter how well she tried to disguise them with poise.

"And are you going to share that information with a lowly man?" I asked, keeping my tone light.

"I think we can all finally agree that you are as competent as any witch."

Phage and I exchanged a shocked glance, then stared at Peth, jaws slack.

"What did you just say?" I asked.

"Don't push your luck," Peth snapped.

"Okay, it was worth a shot," I grinned.

"Soph, your brothers may have influenced your decision to lose yourself in the mysteries of potions. For many of us, it is a meditative experience as well as a test of our power. Yes, there are silly little potions that you hardly need pay attention to, whilst others take complete focus and you daren't make a single mistake or lose your focus for a second. This," she indicated the cauldron, "was to be something rather special, and not a potion many could accomplish."

"What was it?" asked Phage, never one to mess with this kind of thing.

"It doesn't matter. It is ruined."

"Oh." I was genuinely disappointed. For a moment, I'd believed I'd actually done something unique.

"The original potion is no more. You have made something better. I can read it, smell the magic. It has immense potential. It has healing power, the ability to increase cognition, understanding, heighten senses, awareness, and unlock hidden gifts yet to emerge. This has the power of the dragon, am I correct?"

"It's got a lot of shit in it," I admitted.

"A true taste of immortality," mused Peth. "But there is more. It has elven spirit. Elven magic. True power direct from the Necroverse."

"I have to admit, I don't understand what you're saying. What will it actually do?" I asked.

"I have no idea. But I do know it will be quite unexpected and very strong. Use it at your peril. Both of you. Be careful, choose wisely, and expect the unexpected."

"I'm not going to bloody drink it," I told her, aghast. "It might do anything. What if it turned me into a half elf, half dragon freak?"

"Don't be so silly. How could it?"

"How the bloody hell would I know? You witches get up to all sorts."

"I think it's exciting," said Phage with that familiar sparkle of excitement in her eyes.

"Really?"

"Yes, of course. It's unique. It's meant just for us, and you made it. Your very first potion."

"But I didn't make it. It was already here. Come on, Peth, what was it for?"

"To help recover from injury. Think of it as healing whispers in liquid form. But now it has dragon power, elven strength, and something else too."

"And what's that?"

Peth turned to me and raised an arched eyebrow in surprise. "Why, it has the knowledge of your lineage. All the way back to the very beginning."

"Oh. Um, great."

"And this is why men shouldn't make potions." Peth laughed, amused by her own words.

"No argument from me."

"Come, let us ensure it doesn't go to waste. Do not squander it or use it unnecessarily. And be careful."

"We will, Mother," promised Phage, altogether too happy about the whole thing.

"I'm never going to touch it."

From the folds of her silk blouse and loose matching trousers, Peth produced three shining silver chains with a long, slender glass vial pendant. Each had a thick silver clasp that attached them to the chains.

"Mother, really? You'd do this for us?"

"I would. I may not be able to give you much, but I can give you these. I never told you, but they are from your grandmother. I know you always admired them. Now they go to your family. It's only right."

"They were hers?" asked Phage.

"Yes. She made them herself and kept them safe. When she left, they remained with me. Many times she had told me that I'd know the day they were to be handed on, and only when I knew exactly what they were for would I decide to part with them. They have never been filled, never been worn, never been used by another soul. I was told the glass is unbreakable, the silver mined by dwarves in days long lost to history. Now they are yours."

Peth unscrewed the decorative stoppers from each vial, then dunked and stoppered each in turn. After she wiped them clean with a silk handkerchief, Peth placed one around Phage's neck, then one around mine, and told us, "When Jen awakes, I will explain everything to her in a way she can understand. Then you will have to field the many questions I am sure she will still have. Is that suitable?"

"Mother!" Phage flung her arms around Peth and squeezed her tight in a show of affection that was hard for her to give because it was never returned.

But things were different now, had been for some time, and Peth hugged her daughter back without any awkwardness or rush to escape the embrace.

"Thank you, Peth. That's a very nice gift. Are you sure about this?"

"I am as sure as I have ever been about anything. I didn't know it until now, but these were made for you. For the three of you." With a nod, she was gone.

Somehow, her step seemed lighter.

"This will hit her hard. She's going to fall apart," said Phage as she watched Peth.

"She's made of strong stuff, but yes, it will be tough for her."

"This is too much. After all this time, and I only learn of my family when it's too late."

"It's not too late for Mawr. He's still alive. He likes you. He loves you. And you saw him with Jen. He adored her. That's promising."

"It is. He's a nice man. But I don't know him. Not like you do. And I don't appreciate being used like a pawn."

"Me neither. They're all the bloody same. Playing their games. I don't know how, but when he took me in he bloody well knew and that's why he wiped my memory of him all those years ago. So Peth wouldn't suspect anything when I came to visit and we met."

"I just want to go home. For it to be just us. No more death and no more being made a fool of. I want to be where things make sense. Where we know we can trust each other."

"We could go now," I suggested.

"Jen needs her rest. But I promise one thing."

"What's that?"

"We aren't coming back any time soon. Mother can come and visit, but I can't stand to be here any more."

"It's your decision to make. But Phage, I don't think it's the right move."

"Why not?"

I pointed at the scattered groups of women either walking in a daze around the grounds, or those like Elsie, sat alone crying her heart out as she tried to come to terms with what had happened.

"Some of them need you. You were a part of their lives. I know the youngsters like Elsie didn't arrive until long after you left, but still. She needs someone like you to help her through this. Someone who has distance."

"Maybe you're right. Okay," she said, determination in her voice, "we'll stay tonight. I'll see what I can do to help, but then it's our family first. It has to be that way, or I'll lose my mind. Do you think that's bad of me?"

"I don't think you have a bad bone in your body. You're perfect. My perfect lady. The pendant suits you," I told her.

"And so does yours. You look very... mysterious. Like a real wizard! Jen will be pleased."

"Hell, that's the last thing I want." I lifted the vial and peered into its dark depths. Little flashes of purple hinted at the power contained within. I hoped I never had to find out what that power was. I tucked the chain and pendant under my shirt and with it came a sense of finality.

My energy waned, my head was empty, and I wanted nothing but to sleep.

"Come on, let's get you to the bedroom."

"Really?" I asked, feeling better already.

"Men," tutted Phage. "I mean you look exhausted. You need to sleep."

"Oh, okay." I was rather disappointed, but we had a lifetime together so maybe just bed and rest was the best idea.

I didn't wake up until the following morning.

Birds were singing, strong sunlight streamed in through the thin curtains, and I could hear Jen shouting with delight at something Bernard was doing outside.

All sounded well with the world.

But it wasn't. It was broken. Everything was broken.

Home to Peace

"But why can't I just have a quick sniff?" whined Jen from the rear of the cart. Wily beyond her years, she shuffled forward and squeezed between us on the front bench and kissed us both on the cheek. "Love you guys."

"We love you too," I laughed, "but you made a promise to Grandma and she isn't the kind of lady that you break a vow to."

"She'll eat you for her supper if you do," agreed Phage with a wink.

"Don't be silly. She's a big softy really. You should see her when she reads to me at bedtime. She gets all teary when she's doing it. She won't mind."

We swapped incredulous looks as we tried to picture Peth sitting beside Jen all tucked up in bed, reading a story then welling up. It didn't compute.

"You don't believe me, do you? It doesn't matter. I know what she's really like. Hey, so, can I crack it open and take a snifter?"

"A snifter? What are you, a dock worker?"

"Dad, it means a tiny taste."

"I know what it means. I was the first man to ever take a snifter."

"You might be old, but even you aren't that old," giggled Jen, then she poked me in the ribs and hugged me from behind.

"Must be strong, must be strong," I repeated as my resolve began to fail already.

"No potions until you are of age," warned Phage once more.

"But I won't be twenty-one for eight years. That's ages!"

"We know!" we both shouted happily.

Jen continued to moan and pester us, Bernard whined about the fact half the main roads were now young, immature forests, and he was hot, cold, hungry, tired, bored, too excited, needed a pee, wanted to go home even though we were doing just that, and he thought he should have a vial, too. Throughout it all, Phage and I sat close to each other and smiled when we caught the other's gaze.

Nothing better in the world than going home with your family. Especially when you aren't suffering multiple stab wounds. Which was novel.

Eventually, Jen settled down in the rear and fell asleep. Either that, or she was doing a fine impression of a snoring mountain goat.

"She's still exhausted," whispered Phage.

"She probably will be for days. I know I could sleep."

"Take a nap."

"Maybe when we're home. It's nice sitting with you. Just our family."

"It is, isn't it?" Phage got as close as possible then said very quietly, "Her eyes are still the same. What should we do?"

"Like Peth said, either get her contacts or you'll have to show her how to create a whisper to mask them. She said it would most likely fade in a day or two anyway."

"I don't think it will. She's marked, same as Mother."

"Why didn't you tell me she hadn't had an operation to make them look like that?"

"I didn't want to worry you. Stress that our daughter might look the same. I hoped it would never happen. It hasn't happened to me. Yet. The sisters tried, but I refused. Jen didn't have that luxury. I didn't want to be like Mother."

"You're nothing like Peth."

"In some ways, I think I am. Same stubborn streak. I'm always right."

"You are," I agreed, smiling.

"Seriously though, we are alike in many ways. But I don't have her desire for magic. I want different things out of life. I want you. And Jen. That's enough."

"Same here. I wonder what Peth would have been like if her mother had been different."

"We'll never know. Neither will she. But Mother's changing, so it goes to show it's never too late."

"She's surprised us all," I agreed. "Nobody more than herself."

"Come on, Bernard, get a move on, please, or it'll be dark by the time we get home," said Phage.

"I'm doing my best. I keep having to dodge little trees and these stupid guards around them."

"Then go into the other lane. It's not like there's any traffic."

"I liked it better when she couldn't understand me," sighed Bernard.

"I heard that!" Phage called.

"I know. You've got ears."

Bernard continued his miserable march. Phage and I smiled at each other and for once enjoyed the trip home after a successful Necronote.

Drones buzzed high above, watching.

Always watching.

Good for the Soul

I swung the hammer and smashed the nail through the side of the stud work and deep into the noggin that gave extra rigidity to the replaced section of wall for the Necropub.

Again, then two more for the other side. Each blow was smooth and satisfying. I grunted with each whack, not from the effort, but from the mental imagery of the hammer smashing the skull of those fucking obscene witches.

The moment we'd returned, I'd got to work. I had no choice.

The frustration and energy inside me knew no bounds, so it was either this or go do something I'd regret and would most likely bring nothing but sorrow to our family.

I stripped back the entire front section of the Necropub, saved what cladding I could, repaired the door with a new drip stop, and was now just finishing the stud work. Rot hadn't been as rampant as I'd anticipated, so the restoration was almost complete.

Satisfied, I stood back to inspect my workmanship. Maybe a fraction wonky, but that gave it character. Plus, I was in no mood for precision. Just whacking.

Soaked through, naked from the waist up, the blood was pumping strongly through my veins as I flexed my muscles, feeling alive and grounded. I peered through the framework to the dead interior. The grime was impossible to eradicate. It was as though without the Brewer the place was sulking and releasing dirt like it was shedding skin. Buildings might not have feelings as such, but they had an essence. Now the essence of this place was gone.

"Where are you, my old friend?" I wondered. There was no reply, just the groaning of the roof from the blistering heat.

Regardless, I needed this. Had to get the energy out somehow. I didn't want to think, I didn't want to do anything but curl up in a dark room. Maybe tenure down in the Brewer's cellar and lock myself in for a thousand years. But that would solve nothing, either. Death and despair would find me wherever I holed up.

I took a swig of water, then grabbed the old waney edge oak cladding and began nailing it back into place. I mixed it up with new boards that had been sitting in one of the barns for years so it wouldn't look so odd, and in a few years when it weathered you'd never know the difference.

Phage and Jen, even Woofer, came and tried to talk to me, but I couldn't stop, just slammed in nails and kept on going. Early afternoon, I found a pile of sandwiches on top of the cladding waiting to be fixed in place, so I chewed and swallowed without tasting much and just kept at it.

Late afternoon and I was almost done. I rubbed my body with a towel to dry myself off a little, pushed my sodden hair from my eyes, then carefully fixed the sign back above the door where it belonged.

A smile, the first of the day, came to me as I recalled making it then showing it to the Brewer before fixing it in place for the first time. He'd been so proud. Me too. This was not just a man cave, somewhere to escape to, although it was certainly those things. It held significance, was important. Just like Sanctuary for Jen, Tyr, and Rocky, this had been a sanctuary too. My *mantuary* in times of stress, but also, and more importantly, for the Brewer.

Yes, he was about as odd as they came, dangerous too, but what kind of honorable man would I be if I didn't look out for my own? Would you scorn your child if they were different? Disfigured? Challenged in any way? Of course not. And it was the same for friends. Family.

I sighed as I admired my handiwork. My work here was done.

Now all I had to do was find my friend. And find him I would. In a world growing madder by the minute, suddenly his peculiarities and afflictions didn't feel quite as big as they'd once seemed. After all, it's the ones that look normal that you clearly have to worry about.

"It looks great, Dad. Nice job," said Jen.

"Damn, you made me jump." I turned back to the Necropub and said, "Not bad, eh?"

"He'll love it when he comes back."

"I hope so."

Jen hesitated, then gave me an awkward cuddle, her body tense, unsure if I'd shun her or not.

I pulled her in closer and held her tight, the stress lessening as I enjoyed the connection with my own flesh and blood.

"Sorry I haven't been talking or doing anything with you. I had to do this, you understand?"

"Of course I do. It's hard for you, I get it. You have a lot on your plate."

"Yes, but it should never come at the expense of you or your mother."

"Speaking of adorable ladies," smiled Phage as she came around the corner of the Necropub. "Can I get in on this cuddle action too?"

"Of course you can," I told her, smiling.

We grouped together and there was no need for words. Just us, together still, and even in one piece this year.

"Play ball with Woofer?"

"Sure. Go fetch. Good boy."

Woofer ran off, tail wagging, and we laughed as he returned not with a ball but with a large round stone.

"Soph, the Necropub looks great. And so do you." Phage winked at me; Jen groaned.

"Hmm, I think I could do with a shower."

"Too right. You're all stinky and sweaty and now I'm covered in old man smell," complained Jen, but she was smiling and so was I.

"Just let me look at you for a while longer." Phage looked me up and down, then said, "I approve." She winked. I winked back. All was right with the world once more.

"Sorry about all this. Leaving you two to sort everything out when we got back. I had to. Don't be annoyed with me."

"We get it. Completely. And us girls managed just fine without your manly muscles. Everything's sorted out and stored, bar a few things in the kitchen. Back to normal."

"Back to normal. Sounds good to me," I told her.

"Throw hard ball for Woofer?" Woofer nudged the rock with his nose in case we didn't know which ball he was talking about.

"Woofer, it's so nice to be able to hear you all the time," said Phage sweetly.

"You won't be saying that in a month," I told her.

"Don't be mean. But we can't throw rocks for you. You could break your teeth."

"Where'd you get it, boy?" asked Jen as she bent and picked it up.

"Up by big rock."

"What big rock?" I asked him. "We don't have any big rocks."

"Big rock in garden that was gone then is back. Looks like funny man."

"You mean Wonjin, the troll?" I asked.

"What troll? Is man made of rock? Is not rock for peeing on?"

"Don't pee on Wonjin!" we all shouted.

Woofer licked his nose, then returned to staring at the rock in Jen's hand.

"It's very heavy," she told us as she threw it into the air a little. "Like it's made of lead or something. So smooth too. And it's warm. Really warm."

We peered at the rock that just about fit into Jen's palm. It was very smooth, like a pebble from the beach, but there was something off about it.

With a shrug, I said, "Come on, let's go see Wonjin. That's awesome he's back. I missed the big guy."

"Me too," said Phage. "The garden felt empty without him.

"He must have completed his note," said Jen, skipping off with Woofer to get there first.

I went to follow, but Phage put her hand to my shoulder and blocked my way. "Are you sure you're okay? I know that hit you hard, and I can't believe what they all did. But you were weird afterwards, making that potion. All the stuff with Jen and your own ancestors. That's a lot to take in. Mother will never get over it. A man, not even a wizard, making potions and controlling the witches."

"I'm fine now. I just had to do this, make things complete, you know? If he comes back, the place is ready for him. And all that? I don't know what to say. It was beyond strange, and I don't know what really happened. Part was the knife, the elven magic, but part of it was definitely my brothers inside my head. I don't like that, Phage, and I won't let them return. That's not me, you know that. I hate all that crap."

"I know. You're just a big, dumb hunk of firm meat." Phage pinched my bum and licked her lips.

I laughed. "You always know how to cheer me up."

Arm in arm, we braved the heat and went to get some good news for a change.

Welcome Home

"There he is," I noted as we strolled up the garden.

"Can't exactly miss him. He wasn't there when we came to see you, so he's literally been here for minutes. I'm glad he's back."

"Me too. Bet he's got some adventures to tell. Or maybe not," I grumbled, my mood souring.

"Hey, this is a happy time, remember?"

"Sorry. He's back, that's the main thing."

Woofer was sitting, tail swishing the lawn as he stared up at Wonjin. Jen was tossing her stone from one hand to another whilst talking animatedly to the returned wanderer. It was a very one-sided conversation. The big guy was silent. Immobile. Like he'd never gone.

"Hey Wonjin. Great to see you. We missed you," I told him.

"You've been gone a long time," noted Phage. "Although, I guess not so long for you. What was it? One troll year is a day for us?"

"No, that's not right," instructed Jen. "He said a hundred years for trolls is one year for humans." Jen pondered that then added, "Um... Er..."

"You're both wrong. A hundred human years is one troll year. They get a note every century. So a year for us is three point six five days for him. I think."

"Is correct," came a voice like a talking box of gravel being shoved through a rock crushing machine.

His words echoed off the fences and bounced back twice as deep and sonorous. Woofer's ears pricked up as he searched for the source of the noise. Poor guy might be immortal now and a true creature of the Necroverse, but it hadn't made him any smarter.

"It's the big lumpy thing in front of you," I bent and whispered to him. "His name's Wonjin. You've met him before."

"Woofer remember. Um, what name?"

"Wonjin is the name," said our friendly resident troll.

"How'd you get on?" I asked.

"Wonjin is alive. Other troll dead. So sad." He shrugged.

"It is."

"But also good news. Met mate troll from long ago. Thought had lost her. Found again. Made baby troll. So one troll gone, another will come. Is very rare and precious thing. Never new trolls."

"That's awesome," said Jen as she threw the ball high then caught it behind her back, showing off.

"Is very exciting." Wonjin's lips kind of, almost, maybe possibly moved a fraction. He really was overjoyed.

"And how long before the baby troll is born?" asked Phage.

"Not work like mammals. Male and female troll make baby. *Make.* Take part of each and smash together, then rub and rub—"

"Er, yes, thank you," I interrupted.

"—and rub and rub until much friction. Then is ball. Baby troll come from ball. The Jen be careful with baby troll?"

The rock was in mid-air when his words permeated her mind and she froze. The baby troll-to-be plummeted, so I snatched out and caught the smooth ball of rock.

"Er, yes, we will be careful. Do you want it back? Of course you do. Here." I handed the rock to Jen and she offered it to Wonjin. He bent his back, reached out, and gently took his offspring, if that was the right word, in his hand. The rock looked like a tiny pebble laying on his palm. It jumped like a magic bean, then settled into the creases and began to glow.

"Wow!" gasped Jen.

"Male troll keep egg warm. Always this way. Keep hot and wait for new troll to come. Then mother come and help care for new life."

"Guess you've got quite a wait then," I said.

"No, not long. Six months, maybe less."

"That's such a shame. It would have been awesome to see him or her soon. But that's like, fifty years for us, right?" frowned Jen.

"No, Wonjin talk in human years. Just days for trolls. New life come, but is still mostly rock. Brain form slowly, take long time, hundreds of human years, but baby become real thing in days for Wonjin. Tired now, fast talk make head hurt. Must be slow now, act like real troll." His hand closed around the glowing egg, or whatever it was, his arms folded to protect his child, and his eyes closed. Wonjin stood immobile once more, a bodyguard you would never mess with.

"I can't believe you were throwing his child around like it was a rock," I laughed.

"Hey, I didn't know. Woofer found it." Jen pointed an accusing finger at our innocent pooch.

"Woofer found egg," agreed the grinning Lab.

"Where?" I asked.

"At feet of big rock."

"I think maybe our friend wanted you to have the egg for a little while. His homecoming gift," I told Jen.

"Aw, that's so sweet. Ugh, it's so hot. And I'm beat. Can I go and watch TV?"

"Afraid not, kiddo. It's Wednesday."

"What, already? Can I? Please, just this once?"

"You know the rules. Dark Wednesday means no tech. Go play a board game. Read a book. Do a jigsaw. Maybe get your paints out, or play with Woofer. Do some gardening. Go see Tyr, have a ride. Or Kayin."

"God, you are so lame. There is never anything to do around here." Jen stormed off, leaving us standing there, mouths open, gobsmacked.

Up by the house she turned, laughing, and shouted, "Gotcha! Who's for a game of cards?"

We chased after our mischievous daughter. Against all the odds, I believed we'd actually be alright.

For another year. But then it hit me. Phage's Necronote was a matter of months away. I might be able to take it easy, but she couldn't.

Ah well, at least we had today.

"Where's me bleedin' gold?" growled a very angry, very red, very sweaty dwarf. He was shaking uncontrollably and had developed a nervous tic at his eye. He was also wielding his battle axe.

So much for our quiet family time.

And I still hadn't had my shower.

"What gold?" I sighed, knowing from past experience this wouldn't go well, or end any time soon.

"You know what gold," he sneered, hefting his mighty weapon from hand to hand like it weighed nothing, not the forty pounds it did.

"We haven't got your gold. I've been outside fixing up the Necropub, Jen and Phage have been unpacking. Besides, have you seen any of us down there?"

Shey Redgold frowned as he rubbed his beard, then he growled, "Well, someone took it. I know it was one of you. Dirty rotters, stealing my gold. You know it's mine. All of it!"

"Shey Redgold, you watch your manners," warned Phage. "You will not accuse us of thievery in our own home."

"My home too," he countered, looking smug.

"Yes, your home too. And that means we should get along, not make false accusations.

"It was you, when you came down the other day. Or was it last month? All of you came. Made a right mess. It's taken until now to tidy everythin' up and make the stacks zing again. Bleedin' nightmare it's been."

"Don't give me that," I told him. "You live for that stuff. All you ever do is count it, stack it, stare at it smugly."

"I'm a dwarf!" he hollered, like that explained everything.

"A bloody annoying one," I muttered under my breath.

"I heard that!" he screamed, incensed.

"No, you didn't, because I whispered."

"Why you..." Shey Redgold advanced towards me.

"You better take a long, hard look at how you're acting," I warned. "Do not ever, and I mean ever, threaten me or any of us. After all the crap we have to deal with, home is our... well, it's our home. Just don't."

Shey Redgold backed off and lowered his weapon. "Sorry, you know I'd never hurt any of you. Unless you stole me gold," he added quietly.

"We wouldn't. Would we?" I turned to the others.

"Of course not," said Phage.

"No way," said Jen. "And I promise you, I haven't taken anything."

"Then where's my coin?" he demanded.

"All this over one coin?" asked Jen.

Shey Redgold gasped. I shook my head at the ignorance of youth. Phage patted the top of Jen's head like she was a dumb animal.

"Is she simple in the head? Has she had an accident? Did someone perform one of those brain operations?"

"A lobotomy?" I inquired.

"Maybe, if it's the one that makes you extra stupid."

"I was only asking. No need to be mean," said Jen.

"Dwarves see every ounce of gold as just as special as the next. Think of it like favorite teddy bears, or priceless antiques. It may as well be all of it," I explained.

"All of it! What? Has it all gone? Is someone down there now?" Shey Redgold panicked, eyes spinning in his head, then he dashed back into the house, clattering as he went.

"I swear I didn't take it," said Jen.

"We know. We believe you," Phage told her.

"We do," I agreed. "But we won't get a minute's peace until we sort this mess out. Ugh, this is the last thing I need. Why does everyone think it's a good idea to mess with me this week every year?"

"Dad, you're as bad as Shey Redgold."

"Huh?"

"Don't you get it?"

"Get what?"

"It's not about you. It's always like this. And you always ask the same question when things get a bit bonkers."

"Is it? Do I?" I asked.

"Yes," said Jen.

"It is. And you do," agreed Phage. "It's just that when you're stressed you remember it. But our life's always like this. Give it a few months, then write down what happens. I bet you it's just as mad."

"No way. It couldn't be."

Both women gave me their special pity look. They'd had plenty of practice, so nailed it. Maybe they were right.

"Come on, let's get inside before he rips the house apart."

"Shey Redgold, stop that right this instant!" ordered Phage.

The resident dwarf froze; Phage was not a woman to be messed with and he knew it.

"That's my chair!" I screeched, rushing into the living room before he ruined it completely.

"It might be here. I have to find it." Shey Redgold shoved fat fingers down the side of the cushion and searched frantically, standing all over the various pieces of my chair he'd already dismantled.

"Stop messing with it. Shoo." I bum-bumped him aside, then put everything back where it was meant to go. Nervously, I eased into my chair to test it. "Now it's all wrong. It'll take ages to make it feel right again." I gave the moping miniature misfit a solid glare, then kicked back to begin the settling-in process.

It felt nice to relax. I hadn't realized how worn out I'd made myself with the work. The cool of the house was glorious too, and I began to shiver, then realized I was still topless.

Feeling strange not wearing my shirt inside, I reluctantly heaved out of my chair and rushed outside to retrieve it, leaving the others to bicker amongst themselves.

When I returned, suitably attired, it was to find Jen and Phage forcibly holding back the mad basement dweller as he reached for the sofa and yelled about needing to slice it up to check for his coin.

Jen's grip loosened, and he shucked Phage off then dashed to the sofa, axe already slashing down.

I raced forward, then froze as a terrifying wail came from the sofa. It wasn't meant to do that. Normally it was quiet.

We stared in horror at the sight of Mr. Wonderful, who'd clearly been curled up fast asleep, pointedly ignoring the commotion.

"You chopped his tail off," I told him.

"I know. I'm sorry. Sorry little pussycat."

Mr. Wonderful turned his head slowly and took in the sight of his stump pumping blood all over the sofa, and the twitching white length of tail that bounced a little on the cushion then was still.

Knowing our cat, I backed away carefully along with Jen and Phage, while the dimwitted gold freak reached out and picked up the tail then offered it back to Mr. Wonderful with a mumbled, "Sorry."

Mr. Wonderful dialed the full power of his glare up to eleven and vibed Shey Redgold for all he was worth.

"You chopped off my tail," he hissed, tiny pink tongue poking out.

"It was an accident. Here. Take it."

Evil personified stared at the tail, then back at the diminutive dunce with a savage grin. He stood, stretched out his sleek body, bones cricking, then with an audible *snick* his tiny cat claws extended.

We backed away another step as Mr. Wonderful launched at Shey Redgold's head and wailed in that special way only cats can do. Like a baby whose milk supply has been cut off mid-feed.

But it was as nothing compared to the terror yell that emanated from Shey Redgold's mouth before all sound was muffled. The white menace blocked his airways and tried to shit up his nose whilst simultaneously attempting to remove the ears from his enemy's face.

"I'll get a tea towel to mop up the blood," I said helpfully, thinking it a reasonable excuse to vacate the premises for a while.

"Coward," laughed Phage.

"Lightweight," accused Jen.

"Smart," I told them both. I grabbed several clean tea towels from the kitchen, then returned and began to wipe off the blood from the sofa while the other two had their fun.

Mr. Wonderful was a blizzard of white fur and claws, slicing and dicing, blood flying everywhere as he went to town on any naked flesh he could find on Shey Redgold's head. For his part, the axe-wielder did a fine job of screaming and gasping, shouting and pleading, until, finally, once he was prone on the floor and a final swipe of the inside of a nostril had satisfied Mr. Wonderful, the cat jumped off the bawling lump, sauntered over to his tail, and backed up to it.

The curled, lifeless tail twitched, then slid to the exposed raw stump and, with a fizz of energy direct from the Necroverse, it sucked back into place. Nerves and blood supply reconnected, and Mr. Wonderful swished his tail to check it was functional once more.

"You mean you could have just reattached it?" gasped the flailing dwarf as he tried to right himself.

"So what? Doesn't mean you can chop it off. It's my tail." Mr. Wonderful give everyone in the room an expert glare, then wandered off, mumbling, "That dwarf is mine now. I own his axe. I own his stupid beard. I own that sofa. That rug is still mine..." On he droned until we heard the catflap bang and the room became silent.

Woofer, smart dog that he was in times of crisis, snuck back into the room and peered down at the still beached rotund chopper off of tails and asked, "Is it safe?"

"It's safe," I told him.

"Silly dwarf," noted Woofer.

"Yes, very," agreed Phage. "Now, can we please relax a little and think about this logically? Shey Redgold, you get up this minute. You're bleeding everywhere. Go and get yourself cleaned up, then we'll try to figure this out."

We watched him roll around a while longer, just for some amusement, then I took pity on him and hauled his considerable weight to his feet. He muttered through his beard as he stomped off back to the basement where he could somehow clean himself up even though there was no water supply.

Over the years, I'd asked many times how he did what all of us do, such as peeing, defecating, and washing, but he was always evasive. Either there were some nasty mounds under the gold stash, or he had other means of sorting himself out.

We heard the door slam, but moments later there was an almighty crash from the kitchen.

"He's seriously starting to annoy me now," I told the others as we dashed to rescue our crockery.

"Do not smash that bowl," ordered Phage as she stormed up to the house-wrecker, the bowl poised above his head.

"It might be in there," he whined.

"It isn't. It's a bowl. Give it to me and sit down there, and stop ruining our house."

"My house too." He lowered the bowl and handed it reluctantly to Phage.

"Yes, so don't make such a mess. Sit!"

Shey Redgold sat.

"Okay," I sighed, as Jen and I joined them at the table and we all took a chair, "let's figure this out. When was the last time anyone went into the basement?"

"We visited before we left," said Jen. "We were all down there to give Shey Redgold a piece of cake. Remember?"

"Yes. So," I asked Shey Redgold, "have you been out of the basement since then?"

"Only today, once I couldn't find my gold."

"Then that means you miscounted. We didn't take anything out of there when we left, so you must have got your numbers wrong. I mean, how can you know for sure you got your sums right?"

From under his bushy eyebrows and mess of hair and beard, he managed to look shocked, verging on apoplectic. "I'm a dwarf. We don't get our numbers wrong, you know that. We're always right. I'm always right. It's not just the countin', or the weight of things, or even the size, it's the feelin'."

"The feeling?" asked Jen, intrigued despite herself.

"Yes. I've felt wrong for days now. Becoming ill, feelin' strange inside. My head is messed up and I'm all nervous and strange thoughts keep coming. I knew somethin' was missin'. It's my hoard and nobody else is allowed to have it! It's mine."

We exchanged worried looks. This was serious. Comical, but serious nonetheless. He would genuinely go a little mad in the head if this wasn't resolved to his satisfaction.

Dwarves amassed their gold, then it was theirs for life. Only theirs. It was a part of them, as necessary as limbs and eyes and all the other important bits. Lose some, or have it stolen, and it genuinely was like losing a piece of yourself. Many a dwarf, most in fact, had gone stark raving mad from losing even insignificant amounts of their hoard.

We had to find it.

"Okay, let's retrace our steps then, just so we can be sure nobody accidentally pocketed a coin. Everyone go put on what you were wearing. I'm good, because I always wear the same thing. You too," I told the worried dwarf gnawing his nails down to the quick.

"Already am. Always wear this. It's my clothes."

I nodded to him. Jen and Phage went off to change while we sat in silence and waited. The quiet was extremely welcome.

When they returned, I told everyone, "Okay, Shey Redgold, you go into the basement and we'll come down exactly how we did that day. While we're there, everyone will check pockets and whatnot and we can finally put this to rest. But we didn't take it. Maybe it was a mouse."

"There are no mice in my basement," he insisted, licking his lips. I shuddered a little, but absolutely did not ask.

He shuffled off, and I turned to Jen and Phage. "We just need to retrace our footsteps so we can prove to him it wasn't us. We'll never hear the end of it otherwise. So, what did we take?"

"The plate with cake. That was it, wasn't it?" asked Jen.

"I think so. Phage, was that all?"

"Yes, the plate with the cake. It's still in the fridge. There was some left. Probably spoiled by now, but it might be okay."

"I didn't mean for us to eat it. Ugh, no way." Jen stifled a giggle, but I wagged a finger in warning. "Um, I meant because it's old."

Phage held up a palm and said, "Spare me. I know it was horrible. But Shey Redgold liked it."

"He did," I agreed diplomatically.

Phage retrieved the "cake" from the fridge. It sat moping, sagging on the plate, the cover still on it. She handed it to Jen. I gave her the same smaller plate as before.

"Right, so that's us set. Let's do exactly what we did."

We walked to the door under the stairs, checking the floor as we went, just in case.

"I unlocked the door, you two had your shoes off, I put on my basement boots, then we went down. Oh, you went and put clean shoes on."

I pulled out my keys while they grabbed their shoes, pretended to unlock the already open door, put them back, then checked my basement boots for coins and put them on. I turned on the light, got the usual complaint from the myopic dwarf, then we descended and moved through the sea of bling to where Shey Redgold awaited us in the same spot.

"Okay, now Phage lifts the lid off the cake, you get given a slice on a smaller plate, and you eat it."

We repeated the task, and he even ate the cake.

"Now you give the plate back and that's it. Wait! It gets dropped. Drop the plate, Jen."

The plate was dutifully returned, then dropped and retrieved, and we watched Jen stack it under the larger one with the remains of the cake still on it.

My eyes went wide as I said, "Can it be that simple?"

"What?" everyone asked, hope in their eyes.

"Check under the big plate. I think I've solved the mystery."

Jen pulled the smaller plate from under the larger, then held on to the crime against deserts everywhere so she could tip the plate sideways. There, stuck to the underside by crumbs and impossibly sticky icing, was a dull glint.

"Me gold!" shrieked Shey Redgold. He lunged forward, scraped off the coin and cake, then licked and licked the coin until it shone brightly.

He smiled and his shoulders sagged with relief as he held the coin up. "You're home now. Don't worry, it's okay. I won't ever let you out of my sight again."

"Happy?" I asked, smiling.

"Very," he said.

"No more cake for you," I told him.

"Hey, it wasn't my fault."

"No, but if you weren't holding the damn coin in your grubby hands when you handed the plate back, we wouldn't have had a problem."

With a tut each, and a shake of the head, we trudged back up the stairs. I removed my boots, turned off the light, and locked the door. I leaned back against it with a sigh.

Jen looked at Phage, I looked at Jen, then we burst out laughing.

"See, I told you it was always mad around here," laughed Phage.

"Maybe you're right," I admitted. "Right, I need to sit in my chair. Just to make it comfortable again."

"Shower first," said Jen, pinching her nose.

"Maybe I am a bit whiffy."

I dutifully trudged upstairs to get myself cleaned up.

I got halfway up when I froze. A scream of terror from the living room saw me vaulting down the stairs in a single leap. I swung around the newel post and raced towards the shouts of Jen.

Five bloody seconds of peace, that's all I had. Five goddamn seconds!

Naughty Mice

"What's wrong?" I shouted as I careened off the kitchen table, knocked over a chair, and wielded Bone Slicer, ready to fuck up the intruder in new and inventive ways. If I could think of anything new or inventive. Some simple slashing and stabbing might have to suffice.

"A... a woman!" Jen pointed a shaking finger at, well, at nothing.

"Where? In the garden?"

"No, there. She was right there. Where's she gone? What's happening?"

The door to the garden slammed open and Phage raced in, a small rusty trowel held high, face flushed.

"What is it?" she gasped.

"There was a woman, honest. Now she's gone." Jen glanced around the room then shifted to my side, my left, leaving my knife-hand room. She was learning.

"What you going to do with that? Dig them a hole?" I asked Phage, pointing with Bone Slicer at the trowel.

"I was about to do the gardening. Who was here?" she asked Jen.

"I... I don't know. A woman. She was here, then she wasn't. Look!" Jen pointed to the pile of our things on the countertop, waiting to be washed or stored away.

I turned, and for a brief moment I caught sight of a woman sitting cross-legged on the counter. Then she was gone in a shimmer of sparkling, tasty light that put Bernard's rainbows to shame.

"Did you see that?" I asked Phage and Jen, shocked.

"I did," said Jen, her strange new eyes excited now she'd calmed a little and had backup.

"I didn't see anything. Who was it? Where was she?"

"There," we both replied, pointing at the sparkling bum imprint.

Phage glanced at the counter, then shrugged. "Very funny. Can I go back to my gardening now?"

"Phage, I'm telling you there was a woman there. Take a proper look. You know what I mean."

"Fine, but this is silly. You could have at least thought of something more believable." Phage studied where we pointed, but this time she really focused, letting her senses expand and her innate abilities shine through. She might not be into the witch ways like her mother, but she was trained by Peth and had many abilities that she chose not to use in our daily life.

The air changed, became thicker, as if fading into the background as she focused all her attention on the spot we'd indicated. Jen and I both shivered as our world faded and a circular area came into sharp focus. A shimmering silver shape emerged through the mists of magic.

The indistinct outline of a woman could be clearly seen. A ghost memory of an aura or a presence no longer present. Then it too faded, and the air rushed in to fill the voids. We could breathe freely again.

"That's so strange. She was there. But not now."

We moved closer to the counter, cautious but curious.

Phage ran her hand across the surface, then shoved aside several packs and random piles of clothes. Her hand froze. She turned to me and said, "It's open."

"What is?"

"The box."

"What box, Mum?"

"This one." Phage lifted up an old-fashioned matchbox. It was empty.

"Malka?" I whispered.

"It must be," gasped Phage.

"Why are you whispering about a matchbox?" asked Jen, confused.

"It had a... a little mouse in it," I told her.

"You keep a mouse in a matchbox? Why? That's cruel. Dad, you should know better. You too, Mum."

"You don't understand. It wasn't just a mouse. It was... er..."

"It was me," sang the voice of an angel.

We almost jumped out of our skins as we tried to find the source of the siren call, but there was nobody there.

"What is happening?" screamed Jen, utterly freaked out. "What's this about mice? And who is this woman?"

"We should have told her," I told Phage.

"We decided not to," said Phage, trying to find Malka.

"Look, the mouse!" Jen shrieked, then reached out and tried to catch the dormouse scurrying across the counter. "Get it. There it is!" She tried again, but Malka darted behind the clothes.

Phage grabbed things, trying to make space, so I did the same. The little Queen scampered from one pile to the next, then hid behind the kettle.

"That's my chair. I own that table," droned Mr. Wonderful. "I own these people. That dog whining at the door is mine, but he's too stupid to have his own little door like me. I own that mouse. Mouse!" Mr Wonderful leaped onto the counter in one fluid motion.

"No, leave it!" I ordered.

Mr. Wonderful glared at me, then said, as if to explain it all, "It's a mouse." His head snapped back around and he swiped out with a fluffy paw faster than you'd believe possible. He scooped up Malka, then bent to decapitate her.

"No!" Phage shouted, in a voice never heard in our house before. A voice full of whispers, of menace. One you couldn't disobey.

Mr. Wonderful paused, jaws open. His tiny, sharp white teeth dripped with saliva. He glared at Phage, then snapped down on the neck of the mouse, clearly immune to the powers of the witch.

And he was thrown across the room, slapped against the wall, then slid to the floor where he lay in a mangled heap.

"Mr. Wonderful!" Jen ran over and scooped him up in her arms as the entire room turned all kinds of frosty. Almost all light vanished, replaced with the gloom of dusk. Dark, cruel whispers circled in a frenzy. Spears of anger and death poised, ready to strike.

"Who dares to attack Malka? I will have their heads."

A woman eased herself off the counter and stood, the air alive around her. Teasing her raven, short-cropped locks. Whipping at her simple green gown. A show for us all.

"It was just the cat," I told her, finding it hard to find my voice. Her presence, her spirit and energy, was almost overpowering. I felt weak, almost helpless. Like a child with everything to learn.

"It was an accident," Phage told her breathlessly. "Just our cat doing what cats do. He was hunting."

"Ah, a hunter. And so little. I understand." She waved a hand benevolently in Mr. Wonderful's direction. His limp form cracked and spasmed, then shot from Jen's hands and into Malka's. She stroked Mr. Wonderful's fur and the idiot cat shuddered then gasped as life returned.

"I own that matchbox. That kettle's mine. I own... I don't own the Queen, but she doesn't own me," he added hurriedly.

"Hush, little cat. I forgive you. But you must never attack again. Understand?"

"I understand," said Mr. Wonderful meekly.

"Now, begone." Malka placed him on the ground and he wandered off, none the worse for wear and seemingly fine with there being someone in the house he didn't instantly lay claim to. It was a first, and I think I was just as shocked by that as Malka's appearance.

"Now, where were we?" she asked, smiling beautifully at us.

The air relaxed, the light grew bright once more, and things were back to normal. Apart from the bloody faery in the kitchen.

"You were freaking out my kid and acting all grumpy," I told her.

"Soph!"

"Dad!"

"What?"

"He's right. I apologize for the rather exciting appearance. But I am here now."

There was an awkward silence as the three of us exchanged confused glances, then I had to ask, "Why? Nobody called you, did they?"

"Of course they did. I would only come in times of need, and I suppose it's past due anyway. But, oh, how restful my dreams have been. No cares, no worries, just sleeping. Becoming the tiny dormouse so I could sleep away the years and let my powers rejuvenate. I am well-rested now, so what ails you?" she asked Phage.

"I... Oh... Well..."

"Speak child. You called for Malka, Queen of all the fae, and I have come. You woke me from my slumber."

"You never bloody came when I was about to be killed," I grumbled.

"Dear Soph. Poor, dear, kind Soph, I knew you had your faithful companion to save you. I was not needed then. Now I am." She turned to Phage again, and asked, "Well?"

"Play ball with Woofer?" asked our sneaky pooch as he crawled from under the table, almost on his tummy, then looked up at Malka with sad puppy eyes.

"Oh, hello. Woofer, isn't it?" Malka reached down and stroked his head. "You've had lots of adventures lately, haven't you?"

"Woofer immortal now," he said proudly. "Had lots of sausages." He thought for a moment, then asked, "Have faery sausages?"

Malka patted her gown theatrically, raising a perfect dark eyebrow and frowning cutely, then shrugged and told him, "Sorry. I'm all out of faery sausages. Maybe next time?"

Woofer wagged excitedly, then asked, "Is deal?"

"Yes, is deal," she agreed, chortling with delight.

Satisfied, Woofer returned to his safe place.

"What was I saying?" mused Malka. "Ah yes, you called me?"

"I didn't actually call you as such. I was just thinking earlier that it would have been nice if you'd come to help us when we needed you. To stop some of the bad things happening. It's been hard. There was a death, a sad death, and I wished you could have stopped it. But I didn't ask."

"That is exactly a call. You wanted me here to help you. I could not assist with that. It was her choice and it was for the best. But now I'm here, although I came not for you, not strictly, but for her." Malka pointed at Jen.

"Me? And, er, who are you? A faery? You said the Queen."

"Yes, I am the Faery Queen."

"She's been asleep for a thousand years, apparently," I told Jen, like she wasn't finding this weird enough already.

"Oh, right, that's fine then. Just the most important faery ever is in our kitchen and you two never told me you were looking after her."

"The time never seemed right," I mumbled.

"And now does?"

"Um, not really," I admitted.

"You came for our daughter?" asked Phage. "Why?"

"Because it is time for her. She has the eyes. The gift. The sight."

"Time for her to what?" I asked, getting a strange feeling in my belly.

"To begin."

My guts crunched into a tight, hard ball, my head screamed, and Malka clicked her fingers.

They were gone.

"Fuck, fuck, fuck. Where are they?" I shouted in a panic.

"I don't know," wailed Phage. "She's taken her."

"But where? What the hell is going on here?"

Phage began to shake with fear and stress. My hands were jittery, and I wanted to rip the world apart. This fucking faery had taken our daughter. My daughter. I'd tear the fucking faery realm to bits to get her back, and nothing would stop me.

The air was sucked out of the room, darkness descended, then there was a pop as it all rushed back in. Our kitchen brimmed with magic so pure it made my heart stop. With a crack like thunder, the light of day returned, and there before us, hand in hand, stood Jen and Malka.

"Oh, wow, that was incredible," gushed Jen.

Malka smiled benevolently at our daughter, then she released her hand, clicked her fingers, and all that remained was a tiny dormouse on the counter. I watched, dumbfounded, as the tiny creature scampered over to the matchbox, scuttled inside, lay down, and began to snore loudly.

The lid slid closed, cutting off the sound.

"Are you okay?" asked Phage as she rushed to Jen and hugged her. "We were so scared. You vanished."

"I know, and I was terrified for days, but Malka promised me we'd only be gone for a few seconds for you guys." Jen's eyes were sparkling with energy, her face was shining with magic, and she seemed different somehow.

"Exactly how long have you been gone?" I asked her, dreading the answer.

Jen shrugged. "Months, I think. It was hard to tell. We traveled a lot, met loads of people, and, er, well, it was kinda weird. Like I was having a really long dream. But wow, it was amazing."

"Fucking faeries. I warned you about them," I told Phage.

"She's back, and safe. That's the main thing."

"Yes, but what did she do to our little girl while they were away?" I wondered out loud.

"Can I go watch TV?" asked Jen, seemingly over her excitement in an instant.

"What? No, of course not. You tell us you've been off with a faery for months, and now you want to watch TV? And besides, it's Dark Wednesday."

"Ugh, that!"

"You seriously want to watch the TV after what you just told us?" I asked, gobsmacked.

"Yeah, I'm beat. What's for dinner?"

And somehow, just like that, life was back to normal. Normal for us, weird as fuck for anyone else. And I hated to admit it, but I wouldn't have it any other way.

Then I heard a scream from the basement and changed my mind.

The End

Blood Ties is the next in the series. You know what they say about blood. It's thicker than unicorns!

Be sure to stay updated about when new Necronotes arrive through Soph's letterbox! Visit www.alkline.co.uk.

Our Little Chat

Just as I finished the first draft of this latest novel, it struck me how many of the problems facing Soph and his family are eerily close to our own. Not the faeries, or the unicorns, or even the dwarves, but there are plenty of worrying examples.

Here in the UK, we have just emerged from the worst of the Covid crisis to find ourselves at the peak of another. People are finding it hard to afford their homes, to eat, and to stay warm.

Our electricity bill has almost tripled, which is crippling. We heat our home with oil as we aren't on mains gas, and the price of that has tripled too. It's a tremendous expense. Food prices have soared, petrol is insanely costly, making it eye-watering to fill up the car.

Interest rates have risen sharply too, and are forecast to rise further, leaving those with mortgages in a truly horrendous situation.

Wars started by madmen are destroying millions of lives in a literal sense, and the repercussions are rippling around the globe, affecting billions more.

The cost of keeping my family fed and warm may be worrying, but it's as nothing compared to the sheer horror whole countries are facing when their cities are bombed and their populace displaced. It's hard to imagine that one day you're out eating in a restaurant, the next your city is under siege and the TV is showing you how to make a Molotov cocktail.

What the last few years have shown me, shown everyone, is that even if we believe our lives, our jobs, our health, all of it is moving along happily, things can change in a heartbeat.

Pandemics, energy crisis, wars, and who knows what else can strike out of nowhere and turn everything upside down.

The world Soph lives in really isn't so far-fetched. In fact, I'd go so far as to say it isn't far-fetched at all.

We may not have a yearly Necronote to contend with, but everyone has their own note hanging over their heads. A monthly paycheck that won't come close to covering costs. A credit card bill. A mortgage payment. An immense cash dump to fill up a tank of oil to keep the family warm, or a call from the electricity supplier saying the monthly bill is doubling. Each of these are our own personal Necronotes, something that can cause sleepless nights, stress us out, and make us wonder just what the fuck is happening, and what's wrong with the world. Did we make all this mess ourselves?

And yet, there is always hope, always beauty to be found in the everyday world. A smile of a loved one, the skip of a child, a relaxed stroll in the woods.

Sorry if this sounds pessimistic, I didn't mean it to, as there is considerable good in the world, so much to rejoice over.

But, I do wonder what's next. I try to imagine what the next twenty years will bring, and realize that it truly could be Dark Wednesdays, ubermarkets, roads ripped up, cars almost a thing of the past. Energy needs to be free, but it never will be. There's always a cost. Always.

So what do we do? Cherish our loved ones, support our neighbors when we can, look after ourselves, and read the next book in this series so I can continue to keep the lights running.

Buy Blood Ties, and keep the faith.

Stay jiggy,

Al

Don't forget to stay updated about new notes by signing up at www.alkline.co.uk.

Printed in Great Britain
by Amazon